MW00533817

How Does That Make You Feel, Magda Eklund?

How Does That Make You Feel, Magda Eklund?

A NOVEL

Anna Montague

An *Imprint of* HarperCollinsPublishers

HarperCollins books may be purchased for educational, business, or sales promotional use. For information, please email the Special Markets Department at SPsales@harpercollins.com.

Ecco® and HarperCollins® are trademarks of HarperCollins Publishers.

FIRST EDITION

Library of Congress Cataloging-in-Publication Data
Names: Montague, Anna, author.
Title: How does that make you feel, Magda Eklund?: a novel / Anna
    Montague.
Description: First edition. | New York, NY: Ecco, 2024. | Identifiers: LCCN
    2023056286 (print) | LCCN 2023056287 (ebook) | ISBN 9780063353640
    (hardcover) | ISBN 9780063353671 (ebook)
Subjects: LCGFT: Novels.
Classification: LCC PS3613.O5473 H69 2024 (print) | LCC PS3613.O5473
    (ebook) | DDC 813/.6—dc23/eng/20240112
LC record available at https://lccn.loc.gov/2023056286
LC ebook record available at https://lccn.loc.gov/2023056287

ISBN 978-0-06-335364-0

24 25 26 27 28 LBC 5 4 3 2 1

To Isabel: this book was always for—and thanks to—you.

I think friendships are the result of certain needs that can be completely hidden from both people, sometimes hidden forever.

—PATRICIA HIGHSMITH, The Price of Salt

Contents

Home, 2011

1.

—

"I REALLY THOUGHT YOU DIED THIS TIME." GWEN SIGHED. "I know I shouldn't freak out, but every week I just think, *Well, this is it, you know? It's going to happen, and I'm going to be the one to find her.*"

She stood in the threshold, shifting from foot to foot, until Magda gestured toward the couch. "Please."

Gwen shrugged past her. "Sorry. I know that's insensitive, and, like, age is just a number."

"It is," Magda said, easing into her own chair. She reached for her notepad, added, "Let's talk about how that makes you feel."

Magda already knew the answer, though; the creeping wave of existential dread had not slowed for Gwen since her mother's death a few years prior. Following that initial grieving period, Gwen's resultant issue was a fixation with mortality that sank tenterhooks into her daily life, rendering most endeavors doomed from the outset. "Like, if we're all going to die anyway, I mean."

In recent weeks, Gwen had begun arriving at their sessions early— by five, ten, fifteen minutes—her presence alert and agitated. "The psychological Cerberus" was what Magda's colleagues called her, having seen Gwen, on various occasions, pacing the waiting area. Magda could usually sense Gwen just beyond the wooden doors, the dog-eared paperback of *Fear and Trembling* upon her lap, running again through the scenario: *Okay, I find her, then what?*

At the moment, Gwen was saying how she didn't disagree with what Magda had said in their previous session, exactly, about how the fear might be actively diminishing her quality of life. "Like with Steve," she said. "I get that it's not good for our marriage, the being together all the time. And him feeling like he's *managing* me, you know, always talking me off a ledge. But I keep feeling like, I don't know, the bad things can't happen if I'm there. If I'm focused enough. Like how . . ." She motioned vaguely toward Magda. "You know."

Magda set down her pen, steepled her fingers. "What if we try, in this moment, to turn away from the fear. Let's shift our focus to the present. What do you observe is happening, right now?"

"I mean, you're alive."

A glance at the clock, then: forty-seven minutes to go.

Magda was examining the lines on her face when the buzzer rang to announce her next patient. She saw Bill every Tuesday, and had, without fail, for many years. In January, he had begun to caution Magda that this year—their thirteenth—was suspicious, and that if something were to go wrong with their working relationship, they were perhaps on the brink of that moment. He had said as much during years seven and eleven as well. "It's the prime numbers that are suspect," he said grimly, rubbing at his chin. "But thirteen *especially* so."

Hirsute and tall, Bill crouched reflexively upon approaching a door. He wore the rote uniform of bankers: fitted suits, loafers, never without pomade. He had a loud and confident way of speaking about things that held little or no value to him; he could bloviate about market-rate housing in Manhattan for indefinite periods, but could not talk easily about—or to—his wife. If he tried, his movements became agitated—worrying at his beard, a fastening and unfastening of his watch, a slow rotation of the wedding band encircling his thick finger.

After more than a decade of Magda's gentle prompting, and of granular strategizing, Bill still couldn't admit to his wife that he was only attracted to men. Nor could he come clean about the affair he'd been conducting with a bookkeeper from the office, a man named Ernesto. During their last session, he told Magda that the thing he dreaded was not the inevitable divorce, but that his wife would think he didn't care for her. "That, and the reputation. You remember what happened to Chet Lundberg."

Magda had nodded. The banker whose affair with the building mailman was made public after an ill-timed tryst in the stairwell. Bill brought him up at least twice a month, shudderingly, to say that the man now lived in Iowa. He worked in *insurance*.

Bill had interrupted himself, saying, "I know, I know, I wouldn't need to move to Iowa."

That day, as he sat down, Magda said, "Let's start with one good thing."

"A good thing," Bill repeated. He opened his mouth, closed it again.

"Or," she said. "Is there another place you'd like to begin today?"

The grooves in Bill's forehead deepened as he squinted over at her. He cleared his throat.

"I don't even know where to start. I just have a bad feeling about this summer, that's all."

AFTER WAVING BILL OUT, MAGDA PRESSED HER EAR TO THE OFFICE door. It was as she hoped: quiet, but for the consistent rumbling of the sound machine. There were no signs of her colleagues Boomer and Theo, who, in recent weeks, had become insistent that she have some sort of party. "Seventy is a *big* year, Magda Eklund," they kept saying, as if she weren't aware.

They badgered her about it in the shared kitchenette, in the elevator, and in a series of increasingly ridiculous voicemails espousing the benefits of celebrating one's longevity. She was listening to one such message as she activated the security system, keying in the code, which Boomer had chosen years ago: 37383. Magda and Theo had immediately protested. The conversion to the alphabet was too predictable; of *course* they would be robbed.

"It hasn't happened yet, but it will," Theo liked to remind Boomer. "I mean, it's a bit obvious—*Freud*?" He'd jab a finger toward the fish tank, where a fat orange goldfish swam in lazy circles. "That's his name, too, in case you forgot."

It was one of their oldest arguments, and Freud the latest and longest-surviving of their eight goldfish, all of whom had borne the same name. Though in their decades of practice they'd yet to change the code, Theo needled Boomer about it in the same genial way he did with other issues. Most recently they'd been debating whether the gay marriage act would be legalized in New York. As with their ongoing conversation about the goldfish, the arguments were mild and, often, unsolvable—made more dramatic, it seemed, simply because Magda was looking on. Though Boomer and Theo agreed that marriage was a miserable endeavor, they believed anyone who *wanted* to should be able to. "I just don't see why they would, is the thing," Theo would add.

"Gay or not, they should be able to make the same foolish choices," Boomer concurred.

"I don't see it happening here, unless there are some closeted Republicans. How much did Edith Windsor pay in estate taxes—half a million? Unless it's a tax break, I don't see it going their way."

Boomer's jaw hung slack. "Theo talking taxes? Who *are* you?"

Theo laughed. "Another New Yorker now, just like you."

Magda and Theo had found their way to New York from pockets of the Midwest, while Boomer was a pedigreed Manhattanite. Like much of their cohort, his background was immaculate, with parents who were a socialite and a lawyer, respectively. For his wealth alone, Magda would have written Boomer off, except for seeing his relationship with Theo. They proved to be each other's inverse: Boomer with his patrician features, pressed khakis, and moss-colored cardigans, and Theo, big-nosed and cheerful, his pants always a few inches too short. It was his cheerfulness that disarmed others, made him seem familiar enough that, within weeks of school, nobody could quite remember his last name; there was one, surely, but memory fogged. He was someone who, even if he had been to a restaurant once before, would return to find the waitresses addressing him by name, with coffee—just the way he liked it—already on the way to his table.

Magda and Theo had been placed on the same rotation during residency, and he had, on various occasions, insisted on walking a catatonic patient to the corner just before six p.m., when the ice cream truck jangled down the block. One of their classmates, Marty, complained about how he made the rest of them look lazy, for leaving when their shift ended at five, to which another classmate—desperately in love with her—quipped, "He's just from Minnesota; the guy doesn't even know *how* to say no." At this, Marty rolled her eyes, and the young man flushed, looked away. That wasn't it, Magda knew; Theo didn't stay late in order to get ahead. He did so because the patient had once said, during a rare expansive bent, that rainbow sprinkles helped.

"With what?" Theo had asked, to which the patient intoned: "Well, everything."

Only with Theo would one hear the bellow of Boomer's laughter, catch his surprisingly quick wit. Boomer was more self-contained and had, in Magda's memory, always been that way. Handsome, with neat, regular features and a low voice that tended toward quiet. He came from the sort of money that rendered his professional success inconsequential, and Magda had initially mistaken that humility for laziness. She had later been astounded in reading his scholarly papers, both at the quality of Boomer's writing and his ambition, both evidence of a wildly capable mind.

The three of them had fallen out of touch after school. The early years, for her, were spent in a sprawling basement office shared with a developmental psychologist and her legion of surly adolescents and their forcefully cheerful parents. Magda had never had much inclination toward adolescents, even when she was one, but the parents she found interesting. Something about the aggressiveness of their reassurances that their child was fine, it was a phase, he absolutely would *not* light another classroom on fire. The psychologist plastered inspirational posters around their waiting area, shellacking a landscape of the Rockies with TOUGH TIMES ARE TEMPORARY to Magda's door. The arrangement was short-lived; after Magda peeled it off, tearing the poster in the process, the psychologist began accusing Magda of various slights, including pilfering the miniature bottles of white wine from their communal refrigerator. "I know you did it," she would say, breath sour.

Home was a dismal walk-up apartment where Magda spent most of her time. Back then, after the initial free consultation, patients often canceled second appointments. She spent their sessions on the fire escape, tipping through thick psychiatric journals and trying not to think about the money, or lack thereof. To think of any future milestone was to panic: *What next?* she kept thinking. *What next?*

Then she was twenty-nine, most nights having two cigarettes instead of dinner. And, one day, there he was: Boomer, waving from the other end of the subway platform. He made his way toward her, and she surveyed him. Warmly dressed, his cheeks fat; her own were pinched, with one hand inside of her coat, holding up the waistband of her skirt. As the train pulled up, he had asked whether she knew of anyone looking to share an office space, someone who wouldn't mind taking over a few referrals.

Theo and Magda still worked there regularly, and she with the longest hours, but they continued to split the rent three ways. It was unfathomably cheap, a deal that had arisen through a unique set of financial opportunities; Boomer's father had wanted to take on an additional investment property but, upon acquiring it, realized that he had no use for the place. The building was in a desirable part of midtown, but on a street then lined with men who reeked of whiskey and urine. All that the three of them would have to cover, Boomer explained, were the maintenance fees. Magda, who didn't understand, had it explained to her by Theo: "He bought it with cash." At her bemused expression: "He paid for it all, up front."

Boomer had also covered the cost of furnishing. "Just our luck," he had said, motioning toward the sweaty men hefting furniture from the elevator. An aunt had recently died, and the estate needed to offload her furniture— poufy Chesterfields and a red leather couch so lush that for months Magda and Theo merely orbited around it, never quite daring to touch the fabric. It was this aunt's apartment that Magda inherited—"I put you down as her daughter," Boomer said. "The landlord didn't even check"—and in whose trash can Magda found the invoice for the movers. Thousands of dollars, of which Boomer had asked them to pay exactly nothing.

Magda was usually the first one into the office, flicking fish food into Freud's tank and plugging in the sound machine. She brewed the coffee in their kitchenette, often while sneaking a cigarette out the bathroom window, which she inevitably blamed on the bullish realtors downstairs with whom they shared an air shaft. Theo, who was agreeable on most fronts, detested smoking, and threatened at various times to go down there and speak to them himself because he did *not* need to get cancer like his uncle Geoff had in Minneapolis, who had *died* just because some people didn't care about their own health. Boomer, when he was around, would listen to Theo's rant and become increasingly riled up himself, but on the occasion that Theo was elsewhere and he himself caught Magda smoking, he would pull a few drags before chastising her. They had been trying to quit since medical school, he reminded her, though really it was something he had said often enough to her that it simply seemed to become a mutual decision.

For weeks, Magda had successfully avoided any real conversation about her birthday, but after Bill left, the fatigue rolled heavy through her bones. Until Boomer appeared in the doorway, eyebrows raised, Magda had believed herself to be alone. In that moment, hunched over the kitchen table with a cigarette, she knew that there would be a party; she was helpless to prevent it.

"You can't tell Theo," she said.

He plucked the cigarette from her fingers and inhaled. Coughed into his fist before revealing the addendum, clearly rehearsed. "A small dinner," he said. "If we have it in June, it'll be a whole month early. It won't even feel like a birthday party. It won't be anything like the party Sara would have thrown. But it would be meaningful to us—to Theo and I—if we could celebrate."

He went to the sink, stubbing the cigarette into one of Theo's mugs. In sitting down again, he ran a hand through his hair. The gray was becoming more pronounced at the roots, then whiter and blond toward the tips. "And you know we've been worried, ever since, about the late hours, the weight loss. Obviously, we're not blaming you," he added hurriedly. "It's not *easy*. You're going through something awful. We're just worried, is all."

She drew another cigarette from the pack, and Boomer shook his head twice before accepting. With the exhale, he remarked on how good it felt, and how they could never, ever mention this habit to their general practitioner.

"We're trying to quit, anyway," he added. "People have done it."

"We are trying," Magda agreed, before taking another drag.

Boomer's habit could be waved away to Dr. Stein as the occasional breach; it didn't happen often enough, she felt, to even impact his health. On her part, she did try to smoke less before visits to Dr. Stein, and afterward, tried not to think of the neon pamphlets in his office featuring tarred lungs and menacing text: DROP THE CAMELS OR DROP DEAD! She focused instead on how, upon reviewing her list of medications, Dr. Stein would nod encouragingly. "Fewer pills than most women your age," he had said once, surveying the purse full of multivitamins, calcium, Ripsledin, chalky discs of Tyrc, Proxyditin, and Linthugo.

Not that the containers had been opened, but still—still! Impressive, he said. Dr. Stein had come with sterling reviews, and while he warranted those, he made Magda feel desperately old. The man was charged with youthful vigor, not just for medical advancements, but for the voracity of his own being. Next to the framed license in his office were photographs of him hiking, biking, even a shot of him finishing the Boston Marathon, fisted hands arced skyward.

"Have you been?" he asked her once, noticing her eyes fixed on the photo.

"No," she had said, too quickly. "Never."

Usually, Magda didn't mind him, though she could do without the lectures on exercise and drinking. Worse were the comments about depression, folded in with questions about her routines—how often she drank water, whether she was meeting new friends, or making time for the old ones. "How is old Harold, anyway?" he asked, and to her blank expression, "Harold Boomer?" He would ask whether she was getting enough sleep, how she felt she was *coping*, ever since . . . well, Harold had mentioned.

It wasn't that Dr. Stein dismissed her, so much as he didn't acutely understand the difficulty of aging. He was sympathetic, sure, in his assurances that the issues she presented—aches, migraines, the feeling that her brain had been wrung dry and then ladled with molasses—all of those were normal changes. But he spoke with the remove of someone who didn't actually expect to grow old himself, who believed he could somehow subvert the natural way of being. In any case, it seemed impossible to Magda that at a certain point she was meant to become apathetic, shrug away from her body like some novelty item for which she couldn't quite remember the use.

He liked, as she was leaving, to ask the question: "What's Magda doing for Magda?" He would point at her then, clap a hand to her shoulder. "Think about that one, yeah?"

The thing was, Magda was fine. *Alive*, as she so often pointed out to Gwen. Over the past year, while her peers were retiring and absconding to Florida, she had taken on still more patients, spurring a swell of desk files that spit forth from the drawer. Papers poked out no matter how rigorously or often she rearranged. It reminded her of the myths her father had told about the River Styx, the souls of the dead idling below Charon's ferry. In her case, it was not souls but other people's problems floating to the surface of her own life. There: a divorce, flanked by chronic anxiety, complex PTSD, commitment issues, OCD, and there, and there . . .

She had her routines with food as well. Coffee and a banana tided her over until dinner, which she bought on the way home each night. The Italian place on the corner was a perennial favorite, but there were also microwavable meals from that organic grocery store, and there was Two Wok on the opposite corner. A few blocks south was a Mexican restaurant, Sara's favorite. That was the place Magda frequented least often, as the weeknight waiter tended to be overly familiar, always asking after her friend. "Fine." Magda would smile, picking up the plastic bags. "She's busy."

To avoid questions, she tended not to order from that place on weekdays except by necessity, and when she did, she ordered their usual two main dishes, one of which she would scrape into the trash or leave on the doormat of Mr. Tyson, just down the hall.

"Really, we should quit," Boomer said when they finished the cigarette. This one, too, he placed in Theo's mug, before running the faucet atop it.

"I'll clean it in the morning," she said. "I have an early day. We'll talk more about the party, okay? I'm not saying yes yet."

Boomer nodded knowingly, and slipped into his own office. He poked his head back out to say, "You know you don't need to activate the lock until the end of the day, right?" She blushed and waved a hand in goodbye, opening the front door to the low murmur of his voice. She knew, as she gathered her bags and stepped into the hallway, that he was calling Theo. A verdict, delivered.

Dismal, that's what it was. To celebrate birthdays—to look forward to them, really—felt like a privilege enjoyed only by the young. When Magda had turned twenty-one, irrefutably becoming an adult, she had felt it then, this tight, furtive hope of what her life would become. That night, emerging from the dim bar to bright lights spilling over the sidewalk, fireworks crackling overhead, she had felt certain that everything lay ahead, just out of reach. If she stretched one arm forward, there was her future: all of it close and yet utterly unknown.

But seventy?

No, Magda thought as the elevator inched toward the lobby. No, she wasn't especially excited about that.

3.

BETTER, PERHAPS, THAT BOOMER AND THEO WERE DOING THE planning, because Sara's parties tended to go disastrously wrong. Rarely was Magda privy to the logistics of her dearest friend's planning, but inevitably, a problem would arise at the eleventh hour—say, a miscalculation of guests, or an attendee's forgotten but severe food allergy. "Forgotten?" Boomer once chortled. "As if everyone hasn't at some point or another wanted to poison Marty."

"One shrimp," muttered Theo. "That's all it would take."

In their late thirties, Sara had recognized the futility of her efforts. A compromise, she proposed: she would not throw Magda a party each year, but once every five years. The fine print was that Magda could not complain that night, or ever after. Were she to do so, Sara proposed a litany of retributions: Sara would be allowed to dye Magda's hair magenta, they would go skydiving, Magda would go on a date every night of the week with different men of Sara's choosing. Magda had agreed to the parties only because the infrequency seemed like her best option, short of Sara forgetting.

For her fortieth birthday, Magda insisted on looking at the guest list. She managed to strike fifteen names, such that it became an intimate dinner party, but five of them woke late in the night to curdled stomachs. Magda dragged her landline into the bathroom and spent the rest of the weekend examining the veined grouting between tiles, as Sara—one of the few not to get sick—assured Magda that the next party would be different, that she would chart the course without failure. Nothing, she promised, nothing would go wrong.

Five years later, when Magda arrived at the restaurant, there were dozens of people—many of whom she did not recognize—hoisting coupes and yelling their congratulations. There was Sara's husband, Fred, in one corner, chatting with Boomer and Theo. When Fred glanced away, Theo rolled his eyes at Magda, stabbed an imaginary knife deep into his ribs. In the opposite corner stood Marty and her husband, other friends from medical school. Sara, though, was nowhere to be seen.

Magda made her rounds, allowed herself to be swept into conversations about weather, politics, the veritable state of the union. *Sara has to be somewhere*, she thought, even as champagne tickled her throat, as she gripped the hard lip of the glass between her teeth. Something had gone wrong, something had gone horribly wrong. Boomer sauntered over, his voice soft when he said, "Don't worry, she'll be here."

Magda imagined a subway car derailed, red sparks grinding from the axles. A deranged client at the gallery, blade in hand, the wailing of an ambulance, Magda's answering machine alight with messages she wouldn't see until it was far too late. "Right," she told Boomer. "Of course."

Two glasses later, in came Sara. Magda saw her as Theo told the punch line of a joke, and she laughed the loudest out of everyone.

Sara was by her side, then, threading an arm through hers. "Finally, you found me," Magda whispered. "What *happened*?"

"It's a long story," said Sara, and Theo cut in, "Well, where have you been?"

"Really," Sara demurred. "Long story."

She was still out of breath, her curls gone frizzy at the crown, flat on one side.

Magda cocked her head. "You fell asleep on the subway again, didn't you?"

There was a beat of quiet before Sara burst out laughing, said yes, she had woken up somewhere deep in the Village, a drunk man rifling through her bag. "Of course you guessed it; I should've known I couldn't outsmart a psychiatrist."

"Some, maybe. Have you met Boomer?" Theo asked.

All of them laughed again.

Sara, beaming, raised her glass: "To Magda, who hates surprises."

So it went on.

For her sixty-fifth, Magda didn't want to do anything. The idea of being in the city—anywhere besides her home, really—set her stomach roiling. Only a few years had elapsed since the towers were hit, and Magda staunchly refused to travel by plane. She'd yet to step foot inside an airport, and had continued to beg off all air travel, even to visit her sister, Hedda.

Casual, was what Magda told Sara; low-risk, was what she meant. The first of her friends from medical school had died that spring, keeled over while jogging in Central Park. An aneurysm—gone within minutes. The man had been the healthiest among them, as Boomer put it. For that birthday, Sara had come over with a bottle of champagne and those finicky, trussed-up cupcakes that neither of them much liked, but which seemed appropriately festive. Sara kept saying how she was breaking her diet, how good it felt to eschew societal norms, how desperately she hated menopause, how she had to get back on that diet tomorrow. They each drank two flutes of champagne and fell asleep on her couch.

The next morning, pangs of anxiety lifting, Magda allowed Sara to convince her that a bonus party would be necessary. Perhaps for sixty-eight. It was only fair, Sara argued, because the previous night couldn't count as a *real* party. "Fine," allowed Magda, sixty-eight seeming far enough away that Sara might forget.

"I have big plans for seventy," Sara told her a couple of months later. They were at a café, Magda nearly finished with her latte. "But we'll do something for sixty-eight as well."

Magda, returning the cup to her saucer, said, "We could go to the fish market, get raw tilapia directly from the source."

Sara batted at her arm. "We could do that, sure, or we could break routine. You could actually, I don't know, let me make a plan."

"Technically speaking, the routine is you making plans," Magda said.

Sara sighed. "Semantics. Can we go scarf shopping? I'm in need."

They were shuffling around a department store display when Sara brought it up again. "You can't script everything, you know."

She wrapped a dotted ascot around Magda's neck and wrinkled her nose. "No, not that color. And anyway, it's not always up to you. A contract is a contract. It is my *right* to celebrate you—legally, I mean. It's what I'm owed."

"Fine," Magda said. "But this time you can't surprise me by not showing up."

Sara, already rummaging through another rack, looked over. There was a crumb from her breakfast croissant hanging over the bow of her lips, flecks of mascara clotted under her eye.

"Mags, I will only ever surprise you by showing up, okay? For the rest of your life, whenever you least expect it, I'll be there."

Despite herself, Magda smiled. She licked her thumb and pressed it to Sara's face, wiping free the makeup. "Okay, sixty-eight is a party. Seventy is just us, no big thing with other people. And you get to haunt me forever, how's that?"

Fine, Sara had agreed. No other people. And then Sara had died, and all that was left was everyone else.

4.

THE "EVERYONE ELSE" INCLUDED SARA'S WIDOWER. BEFORE, Magda would have made—*did* make—excuses to avoid Fred. Only in the after did they form an uneasy truce.

Not even a week had passed since Sara's death when Fred first called unexpectedly: "Listen, I was thinking—do you want the couch? I'm going to sell it, unless you want it." And she, who had recently bought one, said yes.

It had gone that way for the next few months, him calling with updates and offers—"It's a big apartment," he chortled. "I keep *finding* things." Magda had said yes, she would take this, and that, no, she didn't mind, lingering in their—*his*—foyer for progressively longer with each pickup. She had once brought coffee, and sat in dutiful silence with Sara's dog, Eugene, as Fred shuffled about collecting dishware. The dog's panting proved louder than the silence as Magda waited for Fred to say something—to offer her Eugene, maybe. Buttoning her coat in the elevator at the end of their awkward visit, Magda had thought, *That won't happen again.* But only a few days later did Fred call and say, actually, there was some more cookware he was going to donate—unless?

Magda arrived with a coffee cake and empty bags, along with a pile of letters Sara had written her. She had found them in her desk just that morning. *Fate*, Magda thought, her heart tripping over itself at the discovery of Sara's loose scrawl, her scratchy writing. Fred had merely looked at the pile and shuddered, lightly, before going to pour the coffee. Again, they spent an hour in near silence, at the end of which Magda left abruptly, embarrassed at herself for presuming such closeness between them. To think that after forty years they were suddenly friends, and might read Sara's letters together? She was reminded of the sulky lull that had materialized right after Sara died, when she had suggested to Fred that they might scatter the ashes. He had rebuked her, swiftly, by simply leaving the room.

After the furniture and cookware came the clothes, and then the toiletries. Sara was something of a collector. She'd stowed mail-in samples and hotel products under the bathroom sink; to open those drawers released an overpowering blend of rose, eucalyptus, spearmint, musk, honeysuckle. On that trip, Magda left with two massive bags worth of lotions and cosmetics, heavily scented and long expired. By the end of the ride, both she and the cabdriver had watery, reddened eyes.

Later, once the big and bulky items had been cleared, Magda and Fred moved their meetings to a diner, neither acknowledging the bag under the table until it was time to hand it off. Inside: books. Catalogs from the various galleries where Sara had worked, or whose pages she'd skimmed for inspiration. Bric-a-brac. A pouting ceramic monkey from a trip to California, blown glass from Murano, a number of velvet boxes. "For an installation, I think," Fred said, rattling one before setting it back down, gently, atop the others. All of it, Magda brought home, filling the spare bedroom with evidence of Sara.

Saying no to Fred had felt like too risky of a decision. Were she to, say, reject those sweaters, one could show up on a person ambling along Lexington. Say no to the couch, and it could appear in the window display of the neighborhood Goodwill, and then Magda wouldn't be able to help herself—she would buy it, because she couldn't be sure that couch wasn't *the* one. Better to know that the items were contained, that she would not have to leave her apartment anticipating ghosts.

The truce notwithstanding, Magda approached her conversations with Fred with a particular unease, waiting for the next offer to come in. Nearly a whole year kinked by grief, and the flow of items had ebbed, but not Magda's fear. It was the last thing, he promised each time, and she thought: *Of course.* This time, they were at the end of it.

Yet each time she thought that, Fred called again.

Which he had been doing, regularly, for the past week. Three times so far, the message light pulsing on her answering machine. The night Boomer had mentioned the birthday, Magda picked up the phone without checking the caller ID.

Fred only said hello before hedging, "Look, can I ask you a favor?"

A simmering anger rose in her chest, then—something else. She should have guessed; she shouldn't have answered.

"You know what," Magda said, eyeing the takeout on the counter. "I'm on my way out, but there's this dinner coming up—I'll send you the details. We'll talk then."

Magda's grief was not recognized in the same way as Fred's, couldn't be. She was not the one with whom Sara had shared a home. They did not, each month, sit at the dining room table and itemize bills. They did not deliberate between liquor cabinets and couches, or squabble over chores, one nodding off during a stalemate as the other sat sulking in the living room. When it came time for the holidays, they did not debrief on relatives: who they were getting on with, who was drinking too much these days, whose house smelled worrisomely of mold, whether it was better to leave a few days before Christmas or on Christmas Eve itself, the prices were ridiculous, but wasn't that always the case?

And yet.

It was Magda who had helped Sara furnish the apartment, Magda who went to all of her exhibitions, Magda who, in support, briefly renounced meat and primary colors and cardio, who had not once but seven times canceled a session in order to counsel Sara through an emergency, Magda who knew the detailed catalog of every slight ever made against Sara, every person against whom she held a grudge, Magda with whom Sara had exchanged letters for nearly forty years. And it was Magda, also, who had concluded that Sara would want cremation rather than a burial, who had planned the whole funeral, and after a certain point all people said to her was, "It gets better with time."

Things that did not, in fact, become better with time:

Going to the movies alone.

Going to dinner alone.

Going on vacation alone.

Having something that needed urgently to be imparted to the other person, only to remember.

Remembering.

"Okay," Magda told Boomer. "Not a party, just a dinner."

5.
___

THE RESTAURANT WAS AN UNASSUMING MEDITERRANEAN PLACE, and the waiter who greeted Magda was young, his skin ravaged by acne. He was overly attentive to her, reaching out dumbly for her elbow, as if, without his assistance, she wouldn't make it to the table where Theo was already seated. He had arrived early, he told her, because Boomer was bound to be late, and he didn't want to leave Magda alone with Fred.

Boomer was on time, though, trailed by his girlfriend. Behind them, Marty, wearing a fitted black coat. She wrapped Magda in a hug and whispered, "Younger every year, huh?" at Boomer's back before extending a hand toward Theo, who shook it bemusedly. She and Theo had briefly dated during medical school, him calling it off in order to pursue a surgical resident. Marty's antipathy toward him softened after she became engaged—to a *surgeon*, had she mentioned?—and yet ever since she acted, each time they saw each other, as if they were in staunch competition for the better, more laureled life. Seated, Boomer overzealously poured the too-sweet house wine, spilling onto his girlfriend's coat before Marty had even managed to take hers off. Marty looked between them, and Magda angled her own eyes away, determined not to give Marty any more ammunition.

Marty had recently published a study on micro-expressions, and the ways in which psychiatrists could interpret them to better care for their patients. All of them had read it, of course, and Boomer's dismissal of Marty's logic—"pseudoscience, at *best*"—inevitably got back to her. Marty wasn't inclined to mention it directly to Boomer, but she wasn't above talking about upcoming publications, either. Passing him the pita, she shrugged. "What's new? Well, Harvard's been chasing, but we'll see. You know how these things go."

At that, Boomer rolled his eyes. His girlfriend elbowed him, deep, in the stomach. Marty had always known how to twist the knife, Magda thought; just by looking at someone, she seemed to perceive the deepest and most prevalent of their insecurities. She wanted, badly, to hide her own. Magda thought of the lines etched into her own face: *I really thought you died this time.* All those unanswered messages from her sister, Hedda, sweetly saying she'd try again. The number of times in the past year that Magda had called Sara's gallery in the pink-streaked hour after dawn, waiting for her friend's stale voicemail greeting to click on. *It's me, Sara.*

God, she wanted a cigarette.

Marty looked over then, smiling, and Magda took another sip of her wine. It seemed that Fred had skipped the party, and she was glad for that, and not surprised he'd forgotten to call. The toasts following the main course weren't too embarrassing: Boomer described her as a brilliant, keen mind; Theo chimed in about how lucky they were to have her as a colleague, sure, but more importantly as a *friend.* Even Marty offered platitudes about their time in school together. "The smartest in our class," she had said, looking toward Theo.

At the end of the night, in saying goodbye, there was some bustling at the curb. Theo nudged Magda, who looked up to see Fred, breathless and waving. "Hi," he panted. "I'm sorry we're late, it was one of those—"

"We?" Theo asked, his brow furrowed.

Fred waved distractedly toward the street, from which Magda then noticed a woman approaching. Petite, gray-haired, drawing closer and— impossibly, it seemed—reaching for Fred's hand. "This is Gloria," Fred said.

When Magda fainted, it was against Boomer's chest. The last thing she heard was Marty exclaiming, "Oh dear, oh *no*," and when she came to, Theo's eyes were squinted as he told the busboy it was fine and not at all his fault, no, not a stroke. Fred stood beside Boomer, worrying at the collar of Gloria's coat, and when Magda looked at him, his eyes widened. Theo motioned them toward the curb, whistling for a cab. Magda heard the door slam, and then someone was pressing a glass of ice water against her mouth, reminding her how to breathe.

6.

THE PHYSICIST ERWIN SCHRÖDINGER BECAME FAMOUS FOR HIS hypothetical experiment in which a cat, a flask of poison, and a minuscule amount of radioactive substance were placed in a sealed box. In the scenario, the atoms in the radioactive material were not known to have decayed; the box, after all, was closed. But if even *one* atom were to decay, the flask would shatter, the poison released upon the cat.

The idea was that two potential resolutions could not hold indefinitely. At some point, reality must eventually resolve into one state or another. Only with the box closed could both possibilities exist, could the cat ostensibly be both alive and dead. Upon opening the box, any lingering ambiguity would be obliterated: it had to be one or the other.

In medical school, Magda had found that line of thinking ridiculous. The cat ought to be presumed dead, she felt. The inherent risk, the sheer probability of death!

Up until receiving Fred's voicemail the previous year—really, up until the moment he'd choked out "She's gone," Magda had found the whole debate pointless, and bordering on superstition. So what if the box hadn't been opened yet? Surely, the cat would never survive.

7.

THE NIGHT SARA DIED, THEY WERE MEANT TO MEET FOR A MOVIE. Sara had chosen a pulpy thriller, the 8:00 p.m. showing at Lincoln Center. It was a nice gesture, Magda usually the one to make a few suggestions, before deferring to Sara's only—and totally random—choice. But it felt, lately, that the choices themselves had been dwindling: Sara increasingly prone to lateness, returning calls after nearly a week without apologizing or even offering up solid excuses. Work was hectic; she was *tired*; but she seemed to forget that so, too, was Magda. Tiredness hadn't stopped Sara from vacationing with Fred, had it, or from attending a gallery opening downtown when they were supposed to have dinner, leaving Magda opposite an empty wineglass and the house salad Sara had said she wanted to share.

At the time, Magda didn't really mind. She didn't want to see Sara: that was the truth.

After a tense few months, they'd impulsively taken a trip to Boston, which had failed to bring them closer. Since then, the easy rapport of their friendship had given way to something more polite, distanced, with Sara often distracted and forgetful. When they were together, Magda could ignore the nauseating panic of this dissonance; there was Sara, right there with her, and the warmth of Sara's presence canceled out Magda's annoyance. Then they parted ways, Magda increasingly optimistic, only for Sara to disappear again, to cancel yet another plan; the cycle began anew. What Magda suspected: Fred, poisoning the well, and Sara, allowing him to.

That night, she had left Sara a message, suggesting that they might meet another time, perhaps the following week; she wasn't feeling up to it. She offered a flat apology and hung up, and hours later, as she was filling the kettle, the phone began to trill. *You can call Sara back*, Magda reminded herself. *You don't always have to do whatever she wants.*

Not until the next morning, when she listened to Fred's message, did the floor shatter.

For weeks, she would find herself immobile, lodged under the covers of her bed and unable to do anything but breathe that stale air, note the beads of sweat pooling on her chest. An unsustainable grief, melted by the remembering of simple things: doctors' appointments and upcoming sessions, lives other than her own. The sadness needed only subside for a moment before she remembered that there was purpose to her day; she needed to get up, and to iron her blouse, because otherwise the patients would be left waiting, or, if she arrived unkempt and unprepared, they would be left wondering.

Even so.

Each day, Magda would peel back the bedsheets, tug her hair into an unruly bun, and have her first cigarette. Exhaling by the window, she would flip through the paper. That new Mediterranean place on Fifty-Eighth, that's what Sara would have chosen. Or no, perhaps they would have ambled downtown to a promising sculptor's exhibition, somewhere deep in the Village. Every morning, Magda read about the day she would have had, if Sara were still there to share it with her. Bundling the paper, she would then stub her cigarette on the windowsill and make her way to the hall closet, rummaging around for a minute before she left.

Any minute, she thought, Sara would appear on the front steps. In the park. At her office, lofting a paper sack of bagels overhead, during that brief midmorning window when Magda took her lunch and Sara didn't yet have to be at the gallery.

Sara would have her gloves on, already coffee-stained, and Magda would take her cup from Sara's hand, using the other to readjust a wayward curl that tugged over her friend's forehead. She would say, *There's an exhibition we might want to—* and Sara would interrupt by clapping her hands together. *Oh, I was so hoping you'd say that.*

Any minute, Magda would think. *Any minute and my life is going to come rushing back to me.*

What if she had picked up and said, yes, they could go to the movie, but only if they talked—*actually* talked—first? Or what if she had been a better friend, said nothing, and they had gone to the movie, Magda briefly leaving Sara in order to get their popcorn, the soda with its two straws? But what if Magda had been the one to come back and find her motionless, prone in the seat? Or what if the unknown variable, the killer, had been triggered by something in Sara's own apartment? Magda's voicemail, even—if hers was the last voice Sara heard. But what if Magda was the one who could have saved her? Had she gone to the movie, would Sara have lived? Could the cat ever be both alive and dead?

8.

DR. STEIN SAID HE COULDN'T BE SURE WHAT, EXACTLY, HAD caused the fainting spell, though he had his suspicions. Shock could induce collapse, and certainly in someone of her age. "Particularly someone who, say, was dehydrated. Someone who had been drinking," he added, raising an eyebrow.

"Really," Magda told him, "I *hardly* drink."

He suggested that Magda cut out alcohol for a few weeks, closely monitor her blood pressure, and really focus on hydrating. From the cabinet behind his desk he pulled a glossy silver thermos. "Something bright like this would remind you to drink water," he said. "But for now, take the day off. Try to eliminate stressors, lower your intake of sodium and sugar. And if you faint again, come back immediately."

Fred began to call her office.

One message said that he hadn't thought it would upset her, inviting Gloria to the dinner. He hadn't meant—

He was sorry if bringing his girlfriend had caused her grief; had he known that would be the case, he would have let her know in advance. He should—

She couldn't actually blame him for moving on, could she? Sara was *dead*; it wasn't like there was another due course of action. Was he meant to wallow indefinitely? Was that actually what Magda wanted, or . . . ?

Look, if she wasn't going to call him back, what exactly could he do? Not to blame Magda, but—

Theo and Boomer were delighted to have found something new to argue about. Fred was boring, they agreed, but not malicious. He wasn't the sort of person to intentionally do harm to another, but, Theo posited, he wasn't intelligent enough to intentionally *prevent* harm, either. He certainly couldn't intuit what would be harmful—on that they agreed.

"Idiotic," Boomer said. "Bringing a new girlfriend, with no warning?"

Theo had shaken his head. "And within a year of Sara, to *Magda*'s party."

Idly, Boomer asked, "Could we sue him for that, do you think?"

"Gross negligence, sure."

"When he was getting into the cab, he said he was sorry—did you catch that? But he also said . . ."

And at this, he paused.

"What?" Magda asked, to which Boomer winced.

Theo glanced between them, looking down as he added, "Fred said that, ah—he said that he loved her."

When Fred next called, Magda answered without saying anything, and the two of them sat in their respective quiet, breathing into their phones. With a jolt, she remembered how, at the funeral, he had briefly dipped his face against her shoulder and wept. She had petted his head as she might have done to Eugene, and whispered something about how they would be fine, in time. He, in return, had squeezed her hand. In that moment, she had felt a surge of tenderness toward him, a mutual sympathy for the grief-stricken years ahead.

"Already?" she asked.

He sighed. "It's not like—it's more complicated than that. We could meet? I can explain."

Magda thought again of the funeral, after which she and Fred were meant to venture together to the crematorium. He had dawdled on the front steps after saying goodbye to the guests, to the pallbearers. "I can't do it" was what he told her then, and Magda was left to follow the hearse alone and, later, deliver Sara's urn to his apartment. He was out to dinner, the doorman explained; she could leave the package behind.

"Serge," Magda had said. "It's his wife."

Were Magda to see Fred again, she might shove him. Shout at him. Breakfast, she agreed. She could upend a mug of coffee against his suit.

9.

ERNESTO HAD YET TO MAKE CONTACT WITH BILL, WHO HAD GONE to the office earlier to find his lover's desk occupied by a mousy-haired woman. Ernesto, it seemed, was gone. Thus the affair concluded after months of covert trysts.

The rumors abounded: the bookkeeper had been fired after getting caught, pants down, in a closet with the CEO; the leaving had been his own decision; he had returned to Miami; he was on an extended vacation from which he might or might not return. "The men are exasperating," Bill said. "As if any of them knew him at all, as if *any* of them cared where he had gone, and why." After leaving the fifth message, he began to feel desperate, because it could very well be the case that Ernesto was lost to him, and what would that mean? Should he cancel the divorce proceedings and just have a baby after all?

"Bill," Magda said. "You've been very clear about not wanting children. Don't you think that staying would be unfair to your wife?"

Fiddling with his coffee cup, he shrugged: *Even so.* He pulled a hand through his hair. "This is where you'll hate me," he sighed. "I don't know if I want to get divorced. I don't know what to do without *her,* either. I should have expected all of this, right, given that he and I met on a leap year? Unlucky even from the outset."

"Bill," she started, and he raised a hand.

"I'm not *saying* it ended because of that," he told her. "I'm just saying it's a factor, maybe, and could be telling me I should stay with Sharon. That all of this, I mean, was a mistake."

"But you don't love her," Magda said, and he bent his head toward the ground.

"Not like that, no, but I do need her."

The conversation was still in Magda's mind as she threaded her way along the congested sidewalk, a walk she could have done blindfolded. A rote motion, pulling from an expired cigarette before she noticed that her fingers were hot, swollen. A thickness in her throat. She thought, as she had for the past few days, about how it might feel for her fist to connect with Fred's face. Whether she was capable of that.

Fred, visible in the café window, was peering at his phone. He looked older, she thought. Tired. Coming up behind him, she bent to touch his shoulder, and he startled. She swallowed an apology, merely said, "Session ran long."

Fred whittled away the minutes before placing their orders with small talk—bemoaning the humidity, surely evidence for another wretched city summer—and then he steepled his fingers, clearing his throat.

"It was a mistake, bringing Gloria without telling you," Fred said. "I can see that now. But it's not like—I didn't meet her until well after Sara died, not until spring. Or late winter."

"Six months," Magda jabbed. "That's ages."

"Look," he said. "It's not—well, that doesn't matter. The point is, it's become serious. And she's going to move in. And I need to ask you a favor."

Magda couldn't bring herself to speak, and so he continued. "The favor. It's, uh, I need you to watch the urn. Just while Gloria settles in."

At that, a rush of blood in her ears. Magda thought surely she had misheard, that there had been some kind of mistake. But Fred was saying that Gloria had never been married before, and since they had decided she would move into his apartment, even he found himself uncomfortable with Sara keeping her spot on the fireplace. That sense of constant observation kept him from feeling he could truly move forward with someone new, and did Magda have space? Temporarily, he meant. He couldn't put Sara in *storage*, or, even worse, tuck her behind rain boots in the hall closet. It wouldn't be forever. Just until he could figure out what to do.

Magda hadn't said anything, but Fred told her that he was sorry, and that he wouldn't have asked if it wasn't urgent. "And I brought the last of her papers," he said. "Those you can keep, of course. Gloria's redoing the office and she said, well, that would be overwhelming for her, you can understand."

"What if I say no?" she finally asked.

He picked up his fork, set it back down again. "I really don't know," he admitted, making a small sound between grunt and groan. He looked down, grimaced, and then was tugging at something by his feet.

A canvas bag emerged from beneath the table, and a silver urn glinted up at Magda, who looked away, her mouth gone dry. She unwound her fists when Fred extended Sara toward her; she took the bag.

Magda waited in the elevator, not realizing until another person stepped in that she hadn't pressed a button. "Twelve, please," she said, wrapped a hand taut around Sara, sliding the bag behind her shoulder, where it could not be seen.

Upstairs, she opened the main door to find Theo eating a sandwich in the waiting room. He began speaking to her, crumbs flung loosely from his mouth, and she placed the bag on the red leather couch before walking wordlessly to the kitchenette, where she poured a cup of coffee, ribbons of milk swirling in as she made her way back. Theo asked, "Is everything all right?" and without looking directly into the bag, Magda placed Sara on the table between them.

"You're doing *what?*" Boomer harangued, his voice staticky through the phone.

"Absurd," Theo agreed. He tapped a finger on his desk. "Him asking you to babysit her ashes."

"But it's interesting," Boomer added.

"Oh, completely," Theo said. "I wouldn't say emotional transference, per se, but . . ."

Boomer, who sounded like he was rubbing his head, concurred. "There *is* something to be gleaned from this. A discomfort at the thought she might disapprove of him for moving on."

The men went back and forth with their suspicions—a schism, some schizophrenic break, Fred could no longer sense right from wrong. "Early onset Alzheimer's, that could be it."

"Nothing's early at our age," Boomer said. "But I wonder if he still considers himself a married man. That could be the underlying issue: loyalty."

Theo, mouth open, was cut off by Magda.

"It's not permanent," she said, and she went into the kitchenette, tipped more coffee into her own mug before doing the same for Theo.

If they were skeptical, they didn't say. Psychiatrists, after all, were taught to home in on the problem, push upon the most sensitive regions of a patient's brain. Close enough to make an impact, but never deep enough to draw blood, carve a new wound. So Boomer hedged his way into a new conversation: the trust fund student had taken a nosedive. One of Theo's clients seemed to be suffering an echopraxic break. Was there sugar in the cabinets? No? They'd have to pick up more.

Even as the men talked about symptoms, and considered new possibilities, Theo kept his eyes on Magda, whose hands were trembling again.

"Was there anything else in the bag?" Boomer asked, and Theo gingerly lifted Sara from its depths and picked up a deep purple notebook. Taped to its cover was a loose note card, dinged at the edges:

Dear M, my ancient friend. At last you're 70! All my love. Yours, S

There was no text on the cover, or on the inscription page, nothing until Magda flipped to the first lined sheet and there it was: *Our road trip.*

In the bathroom, the bile floated mildly in the toilet. Magda sat with her head pressed against the tile of the wall, the porcelain cool on her forehead. She could hear, faintly, the men talking at each other, debating whether or not to call Dr. Stein, or to break down the door.

"I'm fine," Magda called out. After flushing, she stood before the mirror. A globule of yellow vomit hung in the corner of her mouth, and she wiped it away before joining them in the hallway. "A road trip: that was her plan for this year. I'm fine."

Theo shifted in his chair, and, on the other side of the phone, Boomer, too, went quiet. It was agreed—tacitly, wordlessly—that the conversation would be tabled for the night.

10.

BOOMER CALLED LATER THAT EVENING, ONCE MAGDA HAD SET Sara on her bedside table, then in the linen closet, and, ultimately, upon the kitchen counter next to the cereal. "I'm having trouble with a patient," he said, dryly. "Female, seventy, a bit batty, saddled with her dear friend's ashes. Course of treatment?"

"Find new friends, I suppose."

"To be sure," Boomer chuckled. Clattering in the background: a clunk, then muffled sounds of cursing. His most recent girlfriend was a graduate student at Columbia—"in *sociology*," Theo said dismissively—and had only recently begun learning to cook.

"You'll need some new dishware," she said.

Lowering his voice, he said, "*Three* plates this week. Look, I've got to handle this, but you're all right?"

"Fine," she said. "I'm more worried about your dinner than I am about myself."

Another clunk. "Look," he said.

"Go." She smiled, though he couldn't see her. "I'm fine, really, I am."

An hour later, the phone rang again: Theo, having just returned from a date. He wanted to talk about the *situation*, he did, but first he needed to recount the sheer horror of allowing his sister to arrange his dates, which he would not permit ever again. "She works for a plastic surgeon," he said. "We talked for an hour about angioplasty, *vaginoplasty*, all of the plastys, really. She asked me if I wanted to guess what on her body was real. It was extremely disquieting," he concluded.

"The diagnosis?" she asked.

"Deeply insecure," he returned. "The breasts were real, though."

She started, "So—"

"No," he said. "God, no. Of course I'm not shallow enough to see her again because of that. And I called, anyway, to ask about you."

"Me?" Magda asked. "Oh, I'm fine."

Magda found she couldn't sleep with Sara in her living room. Placed upon the mantel, moonlight slanting off the side, she couldn't sleep with Sara right there, either—she couldn't drift off while being observed. Placing her on the floor proved too much of a risk; Magda would likely upset the urn by accident. The bathroom felt disrespectful. To leave Sara on the kitchen counter, though, seemed wrong—when Sara had stayed at her apartment, they had slept side by side, like sardines.

Finally, with Sara tucked under her other pillow, Magda could nearly forget how strange all of it really was. She was thinking of the lines across her own face, the act of breathing suddenly a tremendous task. As she fretted over getting older, it only ever continued to happen. The thing she yearned for—Sara lifting the pillowcase from atop her, and yelling *surprise*—that was the thing that did not transpire.

11

MAGDA GINGERLY PLACED THE NOTEBOOK UPON HER KITCHEN counter, nudged it open. Tucked inside was the sheath of letters Fred had mentioned: her own. She hadn't expected to see those again, had not considered that Sara would have also held on to their correspondence. To see her own writing only reminded her of the letters Sara had written her, which she had only once since Sara's death been able to muster the strength to look at. It was too much to see Sara's handwriting, which rang through with the clarity of her friend's voice—practically audible, if she focused hard enough. But that was the problem, that Sara's voice had already lost some of its tenor, enough so that Magda heard her and wondered: *Like that?*

Is that what Sara sounded like? Shouldn't I still remember?

Over the years, it had become habit to exchange letters whenever they were apart. The beginnings shorthand: *Dear M, Dear S.* The duration of trips—those, too, could be short. Sara, who traveled often, would even send mail from a weekend getaway, missives that she'd often ferry up to Magda's apartment. "Junk mail," she'd say, tossing envelopes and postcards into the trash. "Can't believe I wrote that." Magda waited until Sara went to the bathroom to fish those out, tuck them into the silverware drawer.

When Sara went away, Magda felt inclined not only to assiduously document her time, but to go out more than she might usually—see new exhibitions at museums and galleries, and describe them in great detail. Even after that awful artist Janet Yengelman made Sara's life a misery, Magda still made an effort to attend each of her shows, and scanned papers for the reviews which panned them. Those she would clip and mail to Sara, highlighting the most interesting words—*reductive, trite, uninspired*—her own commentary scrunched along the margins. *She may be your most profitable artist*, Magda wrote, *but she truly is a nightmare.*

Behind Magda's letters were stored a few sheets of the creamy monogrammed stationery Fred had given Sara for their first anniversary; two pieces of gauzy periwinkle paper and matching envelopes; a banded stack of birthday cards; folded yellow pages torn jaggedly from legal pads. Sara's lists: groceries, reminders, men to whom she might introduce Magda.

"Just *look*," she once said at dinner. "I've sketched the top candidates—that's Henning, see?—along with important information. Career, height, estimated weight, marital status." Sara winked.

Magda, skimming the pages, said, "Martin's engaged. We went to the party, remember?"

"Sure, but it's not the most serious of his engagements. This one will probably end by spring." To Magda's surprise: "Oh, come on now. *He* said that to *me*. I would have guessed summer, but you know how I am. A hopeless romantic."

"They look nice," Magda said. "They do. But."

"Well, that's not true—I'm a horrible artist. But they are nice men, Mags." Sara swiped at her own bangs. "We can take Martin off the table, fine, but the rest of them . . . they're *nice* men. Smart. Benson is a lawyer at Fred's firm; he's an absolute gas. And Steve—he's fourth from the top, I believe—he's an artist now, but before that he was a doctor. Optometrist or ophthalmologist, one of those. Now he makes sculptures out of *teeth*. Okay," Sara allowed, seeing Magda's expression. "So not Steve, that's fine, I can see that that one was a mistake."

The restaurant felt too crowded, ablaze with noise. Magda clenched her jaw.

"I do think Benson could be a good match for you, I do," Sara went on. With a more serious expression, she added, "It's been *years*. Not that men are strictly necessary, but don't you get lonely?"

Magda shook her head. "I have you," she said.

"Of course you have me, but . . ."

"And," Magda interjected, "I'm too busy to be lonely." She speared a wedge of potato.

"Why don't you just hold on to it," Sara said, motioning at the page.

She had, in the end, pocketed it, crumpling the page and tossing it away as soon as Sara was out of sight.

Magda found an early iteration of that list: *Henning*, in Sara's chicken scratch. In blue ink below that, *M?*

Another list: *milk, red apples (the softer kind), water, sugar, flour, yellow sponges, dish gloves, soap, crackers (square, not circular), cardamom, gruyere (not kind M hates), cream*

Another: *Yengelman. restocking for show: dish soap, hand soap, shampoo, hair dye, bleach (extra-strong!), fabric softener (medium-strength, low-scent), laxatives, cold medicine, applesauce, whiskey, blood (animal, if possible), orange juice*

Magda smoked another cigarette and reread the lists in the kitchen. The grocery and exhibition lists she returned to the folder with her own letters, and the list of men went into the trash before Magda ambled back, reluctantly, to fish it out. She had met Martin, not long after the ill-fated dinner, when sunning in Central Park with Sara. He was jogging, he and his wife in matching purple Lycra shorts.

"They'll be together forever," she told Sara, watching them pad away.

Sara cocked her head. "Give it until August."

Two years later, Sara mailed her the divorce announcement. Scrawled across the top: *We were both wrong. Any interest? FYI he's bald now.*

At dinner the next night, Magda had said no.

"How did I guess," Sara said dryly, motioning at the waiter for more wine. "You wouldn't hate him, if that's what you're worried about. That's all I'm saying, that you wouldn't hate him, or worse yet, you might even *like* him. Besides the lack of hair, I mean."

Magda shook her head, turned back to the menu. She looked up as Sara looked down, a loose curl falling over Sara's eyes.

"One day," Sara said, "you will be preposterously happy, and it's going to make you miserable."

Back to the journal, thumbing through it carefully. Magda drained her glass of water, and then smoked two cigarettes in a row. A heavier, candied smoke was piping in from the air shaft; Mr. Tyson, his daughter away for the evening, would have begun smoking just after dinner, at first in his living room, before throwing open the windows, retreating to his own room. Since the daughter had moved in, he had been sequestered to the second bedroom, the one facing the air shaft, kitty-corner from Magda's own kitchen window.

She waved at him, lighting her third cigarette, and he tipped an imaginary hat to her. Over the yawn of the air-conditioning units bellowed a door, and just after, Mr. Tyson dropped the cigar, ducking back in. The window clicked shut. The daughter would catch him, of course—she always did—but still he would deny it or insist that this *was* the last time. The cherry of the cigar was still visible, as Magda ashed her own on the windowsill.

She picked up the journal, touched the nub of her pointer finger to the words scrawled on the front. She briefly expected them to be debossed, for her finger to re-create the words as Sara had written them. That didn't happen, the *t* of *trip* smearing from the pressure, the dampness of her own finger. Magda flipped through the pages again, the stale smell lifting.

Nothing, still nothing. Not until she went through the pages in reverse, finally separating the first page from where it stuck to the endpapers.

A list: *Ohio, Tennessee, Louisiana, Texas, New Mexico.*

Below that, in black ink: *Provence?* The word crossed out, in blue.

A few loose pieces of paper: a yellowed announcement of the newly opened Georgia O'Keeffe Museum in Santa Fe, from the early 2000's. A pencil sketch of a two-story house, flanked by a sprawling oak. Below the list, a smaller, smudged rendering of two women. Tall, the both of them, and almost exactly the same height, affixed at the hand. A series of loose, faded drawings: twinkle lights puddled on the ground, an oblong, heavyset dog, a bottle of wine, half-drunk.

It had been a familiar sight: Sara, the side of her palm streaked gray with pencil, an eraser pressed to her lips. Magda had marveled at her friend's ability to coax images from her mind, render them permanent. It seemed another way in which their friendship pushed against the constraints of reality, became this bright, halogen thing running parallel to their actual lives, unvarnished by obligations and material concerns; Sara wrote or sketched what she wanted the world to be, and then, suddenly, Magda could see it.

Sara had, any number of times, said how incredible it would be: the two of them on the open road. Magda's hesitance did not deter her. It wasn't that Magda had wanted to *go*, exactly, so much as she had wanted time spent with just the two of them. She knew that, in actuality, the journey would be pockmarked by logistics: her own need for control, Sara's wobbly desire to deviate from plans in favor of more interesting prospects. Sara's inability to ignore items that were beautiful, strange; she would buy it all, weighing down the car until its trunk dragged upon the ground. Then there was the memory of their last trip to Boston, which, even years later, smarted like a fresh cut.

Sara being who she was, she had not surrendered; she had simply made a plan.

Ohio was where Magda had grown up. For years, Sara had suggested that they visit. She wanted, badly, to meet Hedda. "You're so close in age," she'd say. "God, I can't imagine having a sister. I'm *wild* with jealousy." On that page, Magda found a thin sketch of three women standing with linked arms, a small dog lofted in one's arms.

Next came Tennessee, which Magda knew Sara had hated unilaterally. There were no accompanying drawings, and even the word *Tennessee* seemed faint, uncertain. Sara had only ever made vague mention of Nashville, offhandedly calling it a place she would have liked, if given a proper chance. If given a do-over, really.

Deeper and farther south, into Louisiana, where Sara had been raised. Many sketches dotted this page: little houses, an oak tree, wildflowers. Two women in a car, a winding bridge atop water.

Then Texas—a place Sara had gone only the once. On that page a single bomb, detonated between the lines.

And finally, New Mexico, the only place Magda and Sara had both always wanted to see. For Magda, it represented the promise of desert, sand swirling around their ankles. For Sara, it was the siren call of the Georgia O'Keeffe Museum. Sunflowers, skulls, all those iterations of sky blooming above soft clouds; all of these sketches rendered in ink.

Provence had been noted as well, the word struck through deeply enough that the page had ripped. Sara knew better, at least, than to wheedle Magda onto a plane.

The phone rang, Boomer's voice hushed and uncertain. "I know, I'm calling too much. I'm sorry to bother you again, but I'm worried."

Magda sighed, surveying the alley from her kitchen window.

"No," Magda said. "You shouldn't worry. It was, well—her plan was a road trip. Places that mattered to us, places we wanted the other to see. It's a moot point, really; it's not as if I have a car."

"Take my second," he said quickly. "It's no bother."

"I don't know what she wanted, really," Magda said. "The plan, it was incomplete. It's just a list; I don't know what she expected to happen."

Boomer tutted, his voice soft when he said, "There's only one way to find out."

Magda traced a finger along the drawing of the two women in the car; one's head was tipped back in laughter, the other glancing in her direction.

"So you think I should go."

"No, I think you need to. Carpe diem and all," Boomer said, before adding, "And tonight, *carpe vinum.*"

12.

FIRST, MAGDA IMAGINED A FIRE, SET OFF BY ONE OF MR. TY-son's cigars, sweeping down the hallway and into her home.

Then a clever burglary, the sort in which only one valuable object was stolen, and the police unwilling to believe her claim that the thieves had made off with ashes. They'd look at her skeptically: "Wouldn't they have wanted the valuables, ma'am? The money? The jewels?"

Then a flood: the Hudson River rising up and up and over to engulf the whole of her home. Remnants of the Upper West Side floating toward Brooklyn, the urn lost somewhere along the way. Dinged against someone's favorite sculpture, punctured, Sara rising free and her container sinking down, down, down. The police would find it years later, lolling against the moldy overgrowth of the ottoman.

Magda could not, she realized, leave Sara at home—it was far too dangerous of a prospect.

13.

THEO, OPENING THE CABINET IN THE KITCHENETTE, GRIMACED. "You didn't."

He reached around for his mug: HAWAII FOREVER, in a flashy blue script. "Boomer would have you committed," he said, setting Sara next to the milk.

"I wasn't sure where else to put her," Magda admitted.

"Not here," he said. "There's got to be a better place."

They opted against the waiting room for the sheer possibility of chaos, the absence of surveillance. A client might open the urn, sneeze upon or spill its contents. A patient in the midst of a breakdown could tip Sara into Freud's aquatic home. It seemed too depressing, anyhow, to enter the room pondering some solitary individual crisis only to be immediately confronted by one of mortality instead. Besides, neither Theo nor Magda would be able to focus, knowing that Sara was just past the door.

Magda's own office would be too distracting, she feared, and Theo couldn't be counted on to control his own limbs.

"So it has to be Boomer's, then," she said. That option made the most sense, as he, of the three of them, had the most interest in interior design, which was to say he had collections. His office was flush with books and high-backed chairs. One display cabinet and its menagerie of frosted glass creations: turtles, a horse rearing back on its haunches, a mischievous, long-eared rabbit. "He'd go crazy if he found out, but probably he won't even notice," Theo predicted, placing Sara on a bookshelf stacked high with files and framed silverware. "You can reach this, can't you?"

Indeed, Boomer didn't come in that day or the next, during which Magda delivered and removed Sara no fewer than seven times. She brought Sara to lunch, and home for the evening, again to the office, away when she had to step out for errands. Even then, the needling feeling of something wrong, something amiss, struck Magda, and she had to peep into the bag, make sure that things were in order.

Not until that third evening did Magda realize the foil to her plan: Boomer preferred evening sessions. After the bashful couple had left—fertility issues, she guessed, or recent infidelity—Magda hedged past the door, pointed toward the shelf.

From his desk, still scribbling post-session notes: "Don't say this was Theo's idea."

It was decided that Sara could stay in his office temporarily—it was, Magda admitted, the safest place she knew. Just until she returned Sara to Fred, and went away on her trip.

At home, Magda swept, mopped. She rearranged the kitchen cabinets, filling two trash bags with the expired goods: canned soups, tea, condiments. She had a habit of pushing whatever she wasn't using toward the back of the cabinet, and then had to reach so far in she was afraid she might sprain her shoulder, throw out her back. The packages she pulled out were for dry noodles and protein powders, promising strong bones and overall improved health. Farther back were the supplements. Intellectual prowess, virility, all of the pills years past expiration. Thinking back, the last time Magda had thoroughly sanitized the place would have been at least a year prior, when she was coming off of a flu—and while that normally would have been miserable, she was relieved, almost, to find the pain centralized somewhere besides her chest.

After ferrying the bags outside, she smoked two cigarettes in a row before the tobacco made her woozy. She put on the kettle, and it had just begun to thrum when Theo called. He commented on her breathlessness, said it sounded like she had just run a marathon.

"Just cleaning," she said. "No analysis."

"I don't know what I'd be doing if I were in your place," he said. "Probably flee the country, leave no forwarding address."

She put the phone momentarily on the counter, and as she rummaged for tea bags, she could hear Theo saying something about Paris, how he would escape to the Seine.

Already in the suitcase was a mound of clothing, her laminated maps, and three of the psychiatric journals she had been meaning to parse through. Though she had considered it, she decided against bringing her patient files; for one, it wasn't strictly legal. The second and more compelling reason was that Boomer or Theo might, in an emergency, be in need of them. Life was going well enough for her patients at the moment, but she knew how things could tip, suddenly, into chaos. After some consideration, she ventured into the second bedroom and plucked a pile of Sara's letters from their corner; maybe, with some distance between them and home, she could read them. Maybe she would hear Sara again.

14.

BOOMER PLAYED TENNIS IN THE MORNINGS, WAS RARELY IN BEfore two, but even so Magda knocked on his door before entering. Old habits. The silver had caught a ray of light, and she took Sara lightly into her hands before settling into Boomer's chair.

It was a somber room, made more so by the thick maroon curtains flanking the windows. Bookshelves lined two walls, filled with leatherbound tomes gathering dust. Even the light that trickled in was underwhelming, reddened by the brick of the air shaft. Still, it wasn't like she could keep Sara in the room while seeing patients; it made more sense for Sara to stay in the office of a person who had experienced disorienting loss. Theo's divorce had run him ragged, yes, but it was Boomer who stopped sleeping after Sophia, Boomer who lost ten pounds in the span of two weeks, Boomer who began dating, in earnest, women twenty years his junior.

"It's a reminder of being alive," Theo theorized at the time. "Just a phase, you'll see." But that had proven to be false. The women stayed young, and Boomer continued to age.

It was similar to how Bill would speak of Ernesto in the early days: experimentation, nothing serious. It wasn't until five months in that Bill gave the bookkeeper a name, and then it became apparent that whatever existed between them was real and irrefutable. In the same way, Boomer took up salsa dancing and created profiles on various dating sites, swiping through profiles with Theo over lunch. Not this one, no, they had said, but perhaps the next. She could be the one.

Looking down at Sara, it seemed obvious: she couldn't be left alone.

That night, at dinner, Magda set down her fork. "I've decided to go," she told Boomer and Theo, to which Boomer nodded.

Glancing over at Theo, he said, "You're taking a vacation. That's good."

"And you're . . ." Theo trailed off. "You're bringing her with you?"

"It's what she would have wanted, isn't it?"

Theo scratched at his neck, looked toward Boomer. At the same time, they nodded.

15.

August 2002

Dear M,

France! Can you smell it?

Specifically, the tiny patch of the world where you can find me: this villa, banked by lavender fields.

I filled this envelope with buds, and it's my hope that the letter reaches you still smelling of florals—and, even better—zests the rest of Manhattan's mail.

How I love it here. Just the other day, I met a local painter, this tall woman with wild hair. We got to talking in the market and she invited me to her studio, just outside of Eygalières. I biked along behind her, and by the end of the ride there was this thin sheen of dirt across my face. I looked down, and the hem of my skirt was absolutely filthy, practically black. We got to talking, and then came wine, then dinner, and still more wine, and the next thing I knew it was after midnight. Oh, Fred was livid when I stumbled back. Hasn't spoken to me in a day.

I should say: I mostly love it here.

Even earlier on in the trip, when things were fine, I felt this static between us. Something I couldn't break through. We went to a movie, and throughout, we laughed at different lines. So I started laughing at lines I thought he might laugh at, and when he didn't, I got so annoyed. At myself, for pretending those bits were funny, but at him, also, for not laughing at the same things I did, not extending that same courtesy to think, what would Sara laugh at? And then I thought, what would Magda say?

Here's what I think: you would have pulled your glasses down over the bridge of your nose, and said we don't need to laugh at the same things, it's more important that we went somewhere together. That's what you would have said, right? That if you love a person, sometimes concessions need to be made. Or that concessions are just temporary measures until a difficult time has run its course.

You might also have said that he had a point, in being worried. In any event, it was too late to call, so I guess I can't know what you would have said. I'll be mortified, too, sending this off for you to read weeks later, when I'm presumably fine again. But I know you understand, and perhaps you'll laugh at this later on. So like Sara, that's what you'll say. Still, I wish you were here! Letter-writing requires you to be in two places at once, and I'd rather spend the month showing you street markets and lavender fields, laughing at the same parts of the movie. Would you consider flying next summer, please? Or a road trip? I still want to go to Ohio, you know.

It's otherwise a beautiful trip, and it's so like me—I know this, you don't have to say—allowing some petty dispute to become something bigger. Or is it not a dispute if one person is unaware? I just wish he and I found beauty in the same things, is all. In any case, I've enclosed a Euro, to ensure doctor-patient confidentiality.

Yours,

S

II.

The Road

16.

MAGDA DROVE WITH ONE HAND ON THE WHEEL, THE OTHER LAID flat against Sara. It took only a few blocks before the impracticality of the setup became clear, a series of abrupt stops threatening to catapult Sara from the passenger seat, launch her straight into the windshield.

She had forgotten how difficult it was, driving in Manhattan—and out of the city, especially. Vans weaving past, drivers laying heavy on their horns. The bikers who zipped by so quickly that the car seemed to shudder, a shock of vibrations coursing through her. Taxi drivers without their hazards on, stalled and blowing smoke lazily out their windows. Entering the Lincoln Tunnel: shouts, horns blasting a tune of hurry, *hurry*. Not until she emerged into the harsh sunlight of New Jersey did Magda find a quiet bank of road where she could pull over. The car rattled to a stop, and she wiped her damp palms upon her skirt.

In the back seat were her bags—a scuffed magenta suitcase, Sara's old navy satchel with a plumed gold *S* on the side—and beside them, a few books and the newspapers that had been languishing on her desk. As cars bumped past, Magda crumpled the papers around Sara, then buckled the seat belt around her, looking sideways through the rearview as she merged into traffic. She caught her own reflection in the mirror: brow knit, tightly focused. On her right cheek glowed pops of silver: Sara, there, in the reflection.

Magda flipped between radio stations: newfangled pop, an angry commentator espousing on the state of politics (too liberal), another commentator (the House was at risk of being turned over to the Republicans; true American values had been abandoned), more about the never-ending war, more pop singers crooning about heartbreak. In Hoboken, she inched past a parade; the gays were furious—they demanded to be heard. Farther south, people with a van full of rescue puppies pleaded for animal rights to be taken seriously. Farther still, and it was families again; there was a measure of quiet.

When Magda next pulled over, it was for a deli. Family-owned, all-American, boasted the signage, the surly teenager manning the register reluctant to let her use the bathroom. An SAT vocabulary prep book with a cracked spine sat beside the register, and he tapped a finger on it while sputtering about protocol. "We've had a lot of problems in there," he said. "With drugs and *fornicating.*" This was what it had come to, Magda thought in the bathroom: persuading a teenager to let her use a dingy and suspicious-smelling toilet, the mirror of which had motorcycle club stickers wilting from its frame.

From the counter, Magda ordered a coffee, medium, with a dash of whole milk. She had to be specific about ratios, she found, because more and more often, baristas thought if she asked for coffee, she meant decaf, that of course she wanted sugar; if she hadn't asked, it was by mistake. They handed her, as the teenager did just then, extra napkins. There seemed, always, to be extra napkins.

Annoying to be treated with such condescension. Sara hadn't been irked so much as resentful of their aging, and the fact that people just weren't listening to her anymore. Those same gallery assistants who had once sat ramrod straight upon seeing her enter a room now simply smiled, trilling their hellos with a little wave. Even the unflappable Boomer had slumped into the office one day to say that someone, upon seeing him board the subway, had voluntarily given up their seat. Their *seat.* Practically jumped away from it, as if the bench were aflame or getting older were a condition that could, somehow, be contagious at close distance.

They were becoming less relevant, was Sara's point.

The fear had spurred on panic. Sara, those last few years, grew frantic: canceling plans hours before they were meant to meet, changing tacks at the last minute. An aberration, Magda felt, Sara's becoming steadily less available to her. She had quit the gallery, telling Magda that she wanted to devote more time and energy to travel, and yet those plans seemed never to materialize. Plane travel became a bone of contention between them, because no matter the plan, wherever they were meant to go, Sara burst out angrily at some point asking how they'd ever get to Tuscany in this lifetime if Magda wouldn't get on a damn plane. But they weren't planning a trip to Tuscany, Magda would say—that was her and Fred; *they* were figuring out how to get to a certain part of Manhattan.

Fred had generally ceded to Sara on vacations and most plans. It was inevitably easier to let Sara make the calls, because she *was* difficult when bored. A lack of other things to feel launched her straight into apathy, pocked with casually cruel remarks. This happened in the later years, especially, Sara so consumed with analyzing and dismissing the choices they had made—and then about extending her own longevity. "I feel ten years younger," she would say, shaking a canister of murky water doused with cayenne and lemon in Magda's direction. Another week: reams of kale, or a thermos full of chalky protein shake. She scoffed when Magda refused them, repeated herself: "Ten years younger."

Magda couldn't bring herself to state what she felt was obvious: to feel ten years younger did not mean they would be granted such additional time. Sara's face went temporarily lopsided from the fillers, her sink awash in thermoses rimmed with some green-brown scrim. Perhaps she couldn't change the outcome, but she felt, a bit, like she had. Magda understood. It didn't seem that there could be a conceivable end of desiring one thing or another, no point at which one could say: enough, now, enough. "We could be happy instead" was what Magda said, after one skin treatment that left Sara raw and peeled-looking.

Sara had rolled her eyes, shot back, "I *am* happy." As she said it, white flecks of skin fell, ghostlike, from her chin.

All considered, it seemed unlikely that, had Sara survived, the road trip would be happening at all, given how things had been between them toward the end. Which was something that Magda tried very hard not to think about.

Back in the car, after some fiddling with the dial, Magda settled upon public radio. A host, prompting callers to detail their problems on-air, was sparring with a local man over a neighborhood dispute. The caller said that his neighbors had the smelliest trash in their neighborhood—it was a fact, and everyone agreed—and the stench crept into his home, into those of the other neighbors. He and a few local crusaders had crept to the trash cans at night, found them brimming with untied bags, raccoons neck-deep in banana peels. They couldn't manage to tie the bags? "I mean, this is *America*," the anonymous local sputtered, to which the host tutted, said,

"Hey now, ain't that the truth. Land of the free, people! Weather forecast coming after this break. And then hang tight for our recap of the Red Sox game."

At this, Magda's stomach pitted and she changed the station. She couldn't think about Boston, not now. A sip of her coffee, which was as expected: too sweet, the milk forming a thick skin across the surface. She rolled down the window and let the coffee skitter across the pavement, running in thick lines below the car. She shifted into gear.

To patients, Magda spoke of grief as a wild animal. An unpredictable beast, she'd say gently to Gwen, who murmured that she was out of sorts. Magda assured her that grieving became easier after the initial aftershocks. After a death, there were innumerable firsts to contend with. She, for example, had burst into tears when the server at Two Wok asked after Sara; and, later, when she found he had slipped an extra egg roll into the bag, with a smiley face drawn onto the wax wrapping, had cried again.

The first holiday season, the first birthday: those, also, were bad. It wasn't that these events were especially significant—that wasn't why they became unbearable; it was that, in noting their passing, Magda had to remember again that it was real, that Sara was gone. Magda's seventieth birthday would usher in a new decade—the first that she hadn't spent with Sara in thirty years.

Rarely was an unmooring a collective grief. The last Magda could remember was 9/11, after which she noticed a similar tendency in patients: timidity, people increasingly less able to make decisions. Some patients drew their curtains, and still others took on somber surveillance. Every street corner bore attention; no person escaped scrutiny. Whatever danger lurked could easily reappear, could be magnified, could *evolve*. They were realizing that danger wasn't just the big and obvious; it could be smaller. It could be deciding to take a flight, deciding to go to work. Those decisions, on the whole, were made up of risks.

People needed help more than ever, was the consensus—and they *wanted* it. Patients came to Magda after depleting retirement savings on cruises, slumped onto the couch with their Norwegian Cruise Line T-shirts and the grim deliverance of news: they had spent all of it. The three psychiatrists were hardly able to handle the influx of patients. "Help me," everyone kept saying. "Please, just tell me what to do."

The fears discussed in sessions became smaller, too, a combination of inertia and indecision. Patients told Magda that one bad event could only conjure another; they told her about calling the airlines and trying to cash in on frequent flyer miles, but by then it was too late. The lines were always busy. "If the world is in need of more help," Theo posited, "the three of us are in a good position."

Terror, that was it. Magda drafted pages of letters to her sister, Hedda, but they never struck the right tone. They sounded frantic, overly dramatic. *Too much*, she'd think. But then she would switch on the news, see the pile of rubble and ash still smoldering. The reports grew bleaker; politicians said it was under control; TSA said no more tweezers, no more scissors, no more lighters, absolutely no cigarettes; the situation was under control; it was getting better; it would only get worse.

What if the threat was among us? the people wondered. It was a question, Magda thought, that circled the same end. Was it death that served as the underlying fear, or was it that after being conditioned to fear, the human mind could not recalibrate?

Magda found herself doing what she usually did: penning notes in her and Hedda's native Swedish, asking after the weather, her nephew, her grandchildren. When Magda tried writing about what was happening, pen fell from paper. What she did instead was fold the drafts into tiny squares, place them in her desk drawer alongside the other letters, to return to at another time.

Winter descended on the city, the papers forgotten.

The drive continued. The radio host implored everyone to be safe, reminding them to use fireworks properly during the holiday weekend, and Magda reminded herself: an aberration. What had been happening toward the end with Sara was a fluke; what had happened since even more so.

The rest of it, that was what it had been like between them. Wordless conversations at dinner parties, the way her legs jellied upon walking into a room and finding Sara already there. How often, when coming home after a long day, the tape machine would be blinking red, a whispered message left during Sara's lunch hour about how desperately she needed a drink, or decent conversation, and was Magda free that evening? The sheer relief that came from that message, and knowing, of course, *that* was what she needed, of course Sara had already known.

Plenty of things to dread, Magda concluded. Terrorism, the heat death of the universe, global warming, coffee milked to oblivion, waking up one day to find the world indelibly changed. Not knowing when an unmooring was upon you, when the phone was ringing and it wouldn't—couldn't—be the person with whom you most wanted to speak.

17.

IF MAGDA WERE ACTUALLY GOING TO OHIO, SHE WOULD HAVE cleaved the drive into two days: the longer, more punishing mileage on the first, a shorter jaunt on the second. Despite what she had told Boomer and Theo, she had no intention of stopping there; the route she had chosen would take her through Washington, DC, and then Virginia, sidestepping Ohio entirely.

Once she reached Virginia, the traffic ebbed. Ahead of her were long, winding coils of pavement, the banks of the road lined by trees. The cars that she saw were largely service ones—vans emblazoned with logos for plumbers and carpenters, trucks with open beds laid heavy with wood. Nobody seemed to be in much of a hurry, and in passing, offered whiffs of cigarette smoke, the riff of a country song. A wave, sometimes a honk. Every so often, she felt a bolt of panic—it was Tuesday; she had missed Bill's session—before remembering that, no, she was on vacation. The next month was meant to be uninterrupted.

Even so, whenever she paused at a gas station or some roadside harbor, she would call Boomer or Theo. She began each conversation with the same pretense: wondering if any of her patients had called them. Inexplicably, she found herself worrying over a patient who had only seen her for three sessions, a man who, though homely, was imbued with an unshakable confidence about his eventual Broadway success. He had auditioned for a number of plays, none of which had resulted in callbacks—and yet. "Things are going well," he told her each visit. "Things are *moving*." He sang to her during their last session, a wavering glissando whose effort mottled his neck and cheeks a spotty pink. Later, Theo popped in to ask if she'd heard it also, the feral cats screaming? *Mating season*, he had said, shaking his head.

When she wasn't talking to Boomer and Theo, Magda listened to the radio. She had found a station that aired readings of old Westerns: a scrappy cowboy approaching the town to which his betrothed had been disappeared; a wandering priest bent on finding the meaning of his own raggedy life. The characters became real to her, enough so that she would remark aloud at their follies. The priest misread a map and missed, by minutes, his long-lost sister at her local church. The cowboy couldn't help but be bold and brash with his enemies, conflicts by which he inevitably became so enraptured that he missed his fiancée being secreted out the back of the general store. A faint whisper as she was whisked away in a caravan: *Help!*

Theo did not remember the glissando, but assured her that the patients were all fine since they had spoken that morning. "Enjoy the time away," he said, but in hearing that, Magda felt the prickly resurgence of panic, the sense that perhaps she had erred in taking this road trip, when she couldn't properly complete it. Ohio flashed against her mind, and she pushed it away.

Theo was saying he had gone for a drink just the other night with a woman he had met at a show—"the one I told you about, with the sequined costumes and bawdy dancing"—only to find she was newly widowed. "*Weeks* prior, I mean," he told her. "And I had absolutely no idea what to say, other than to ask whether the death had been . . . expected."

"Was it?"

"No," he said. "That was the part I couldn't wrap my head around. She was out, seeming perfectly fine, with a man she'd met during intermission, and three weeks before that her husband had had a heart attack in a cab. I kept thinking, *Well, I can't be with someone like that.*"

Magda said that perhaps the woman wasn't the one for him, and Theo laughed and said perhaps not, but wasn't it odd, that someone could be so muted to despair after the loss of a spouse. "But then," he said. "You remember what it was like after Sophia died."

Which she did. Just a couple of years after Theo's wedding, Boomer had delivered the news over coffee: Sophia had taken a handful of her new boyfriend's sleeping pills and chased them with window cleaner. No note. Boomer had missed a call from her a few hours back, but that wasn't so unusual—they were at the stage where both believed some sort of relationship might be possible, yet felt no urgency about developing it. He sporadically mailed her cartoons from *The New Yorker*, and she left tedious voicemails about the Broadway performances she had seen—all productions of *To Kill a Mockingbird* were overdone, she felt. The last cartoon he sent her was of a couple, newly divorced, emerged from their lawyer's office. *Breakfast?* said the caption. He had found it funny, both because of their continued friendliness and because they had never separated legally; he still checked "married" on medical forms and continued to list her as his emergency contact.

He was placid for weeks after her death, then stopped eating. They noticed his wedding photograph back upon its usual perch, Sophia's wedding band on his pinky finger. It didn't fit past the knuckle, and he took to touching it when the three of them were talking, as if it were some sort of stabilizing force. He started eating again within the week, but never stopped wearing the ring.

Magda thought also of Gwen, who had missed four subsequent sessions after her mother's death. When she returned, it was with a shadowy expression cloaking her face, shed when busying herself on the phone. Two sessions passed with Magda waiting, jiggling a foot, as Gwen texted and browsed clothes online. Then, when she finally spoke, she did so with a frenzied, buzzing fury; the grief made her dyspeptic, nearly rabid with anger. It wasn't about her mother, she explained, but the impossibility of confirming shipping options; she was doing *fine*. That annoyance was one which Magda experienced keenly herself, irritability rising in her chest at even the smallest of setbacks. A feeling that metastasized, and that Magda, by then flooded by unease, would shunt to the side.

After Sara, at Boomer and Theo's behest, she had taken a week away from the office. Time meant to collect herself, but it wasn't bad, really, until she had to return to regular life. Her patients weren't aware of what had happened, didn't know to treat her delicately, but she resented them, all of them and their little problems, until the anger began to fade. Before that, her palms were corded by half-moon indents, the places she'd held nail to skin until the feeling in her chest was no longer the most prominent one.

That feeling was swelling when she reached Shenandoah, Theo chattering on about Boomer's new girlfriend and her studies. "Something about youth and technology-related injustices," he said. "I couldn't make heads or tails of it, to be frank."

Magda pulled Sara free from her newspaper bundle, and Theo said, "Boomer showed me the photos of the bed-and-breakfast—nice place. Why did I think you'd be staying with your sister? Are you not in Ohio?"

"Oh, I'm not sure I'll make it out there. Complicated the route and all."

"When else will you be out there?"

Looking around, Magda thought that Virginia wasn't so unlike Ohio: bright green trees crowned the roads, neighborhoods opening up into rows of clapboard houses banked by large expanses of field. They weren't visible, but Magda knew there would be tractors tucked away and rusting in the tall grass. If she were to inhale, it would be the same dense, earthy scent she remembered from her father's farm, one that clung not only to his clothes, but to all of theirs as well.

For years after Sara asked that they visit Ohio, Magda had this recurring dream of driving there. Always summertime, the mellow unfurling of a summer breeze through lowered windows, Sara's voice rising over the radio. Never did they go inside, nor did they see Hedda. The dream ended as they clomped up those front porch steps, found the screen door ajar. From inside, Hedda's voice called them in. Sara went ahead and Magda, idling on the porch, heard someone say, "God, I've been dying to meet you," never sure who had spoken first.

Magda forced a laugh into the phone. "Oh, one of these days."

18.

April 1988

Dear M,

Do you ever think about how awful it is, going home? To your own home, sure, but also to other people's. We're in Connecticut, visiting with Fred's parents, and most mornings I gaze at the little egg cup and wonder whether the spoon could cleanly scoop out my eyes before anyone noticed.

It's an odd thing, returning home with an adult husband, only to find that, here, he is very much a child. Subject to the whims of his parents, automatically adapting to old routines. It's a strange sort of feeling, waking up as an adult in a child's bedroom (their guest room is being renovated, so I'm left to sleep in his sister's frilly pink bedroom, while he dozes in his childhood bunk bed). His mother suggested that we later look through his childhood artwork. "Oh, he was very sophisticated. I bet there's stuff in there that's better than the pieces at your gallery!" That's a direct quote.

I know, I know, I shouldn't complain. Some parts of being here are fine, though two weeks for a visit is far too long. (I have thought each morning about the egg spoon, which is how I can confidently offer that conclusion.) I told Fred, before we left, that one week was the absolute longest we could stay. He nodded, said sure. And then, as we were taking our coats off, his mother asked how long we were staying, and he turned to me and said, "Two weeks, aren't we?" And they all looked at me with all the hope in the world, so it wasn't like I could say otherwise. Whether he planned it this way or did it by accident, I don't know. In any case, it's done, so I don't feel the need to ask.

His father did, at lunch, tell this funny story, about how he used to drive around with little Fred. He would've been two or so, and his aunt had given him a toy steering wheel. So he sat in the front seat, holding it, and then when his father honked, he honked, and when his father turned, he turned, etc. One day they were stopped at the corner, his father looking around before moving forward, and then all of a sudden, there it was! A truck speeding through the stoplight, Fred's father jolting to a halt as he extended his arm flat across Fred's chest.

He bounced forward, then back, his father yelling, "Son of a bitch," as he hit the horn. (You know Fred's father, so you can appreciate how out of character this is. He is an angry person in the same way as Fred: stern, demanding. But never one to make a fuss.) Well, at that moment he was especially angry, and when they got home, Fred's mother asked them how their day was, and Fred's father started explaining. Apparently that was when Fred went to the living room, still clutching the plastic wheel, and began hitting it, yelling, "Summa bish! Summa bish!"

Which is how I feel, a bit, being here. Better than I would feel being at my own childhood home, I'm sure. But it made me think of something you said ages ago, about how after your parents died, you decided you'd never go home again. You said it without any kind of malice, but in a way that made me think you had known, even when they were alive, you wouldn't go back to Ohio. I don't know why I thought that—I really don't—but I had felt very sure, for some reason, that you had hated it there. I'm not sure why I remembered it, other than hating the thought of you being lonely or unhappy.

But I think the truth is probably that we all hate how we grew up, to some degree. (A real psychiatrist could confirm this, of course. Know any good ones? Ha.) I just mean that whether it's our parents or our hometown—whatever it is, really—it's easy to blame parts of childhood for making us unhappy as adults. Maybe it's better that we stick with blaming our parents, those summa bishes.

Yours,

S

19.

AS IT TURNED OUT, THE HOUSES HAD BEEN BUILT OUT OF ORDER, with each owner free to designate a number of their choosing. The range of them plastered to the mailboxes confused Magda—going from seven to eighteen to two hundred and twelve—who thus drove past the bed-and-breakfast three times before correctly identifying it as her destination. When she finally eased into the driveway, she saw the wide expanse of her hostess Barb's rear bobbing, buoylike, as she rooted through weeds. The growl of tires kicking up dirt led Barb to stand, hoisting the pants above her waist as they threatened to fall down again. She waved merrily at Magda, running a gloved hand across her forehead. It left, in its wake, a smudge of dirt.

Barb, recognizable from the website, was glad to see a guest. "I would normally be fully dressed"—she indicated the dirt-stained pants and top—"but it's been one of those days. One of those *weeks*, if I'm being honest." She pulled the pants up firmly, so that the ends rose above her socks, which were mismatched—the left maroon, and the right a nubby peach.

Magda held tight to the bag with Sara tucked inside. "I know what you mean."

The house, so striking in photos, was in something of a disarray, clapboard shutters partially eased off of the second-story windows, the mismatched woodwork of the front porch more readily apparent upon closer inspection. A tool kit toppled on its side, and from inside rose the sound of barking. Barb motioned for the keys, then rustled around in the back seat for Magda's bags before ushering her toward the backyard. The cottage stood there, nestled against the back fence, weeds pruning its sides.

The hot water was finicky, Barb warned, so Magda ought to let it run a few minutes before showering, but there were otherwise no issues with the cottage. Barb's partner, Nancy, had renovated the whole structure a couple of years back, and everything was in good, solid condition.

"Better than the house, probably, but we're getting around to that," Barb admitted, plunking Magda's bag to the ground. "Are you here to see family?"

"I used to live in Ohio," Magda said. "But this time I'm on my way farther south."

"Sure, yeah," Barb said. "We rented in Lorain County for a few years, until the college drove prices up. They bought out most of the owners there, so we had to move; you know how that is. Your family still live around there?"

A pause, and Barb added, "Well, God knows everyone moves on— can't stick to one place forever, can you? That's what I told Nance, about getting this place up and running. Night or two in one place, that can be enough. Especially a place you know well, huh?"

Magda swallowed, hard, and when she spoke her voice was thick. "Sure."

Barb cocked her head. "You got plans? You could join us for dinner, if you wanted to."

The ache behind her eyes intensified, and Magda, feeling like she needed to sleep, said she would. Barb told her to meet them on the front porch at five, where they might have a little cocktail before dinner.

"Door's open in the cottage, let yourself in. You just let us know if you need anything." Wheeling around in the driveway, she called back, "Hey, you like vodka?" and Magda nodded yes. Barb, pumping a fist in the air, continued home. Magda went inside and fell asleep, immediately, atop the sheets.

The salad dressing was sharp, a balsamic cut with lemon and olive oil. Murph and Soldier, the shaggy retrievers, cut paths in the air with their tails as they paced before Magda. Placed their wet snouts on her thigh, noses twitching toward the card table laid with picnic cloth. "They'll try to charm you," Barb said, her mouth full of chicken. "So just be warned."

Magda had been late to walk over, waking with a start just after five. That happened more and more frequently after sixty, that the afternoons felt like something she was wading through. Her vision, when she woke, felt surprisingly clear, and aided with a few eye drops, she felt well enough for dinner. She did double back, having left Sara behind, and when Murph got too close to the bag, she nudged him surreptitiously under the table.

Nancy was in construction. "One of the only forewomen in the county," Barb added, patting her on the shoulder.

"It's a nightmare job," Nancy confided. Men were constantly undermining her efforts, talking about her behind the scaffolding—and sometimes, right in front of her. All under the guise of desirability, whether or not she was really as great as she thought she was.

None of which, Barb added, had anything to do with the job, which Nancy was in fact very good at—"You're more than just good looks." She served a casserole: lumpy chicken mixed with red sauce, white flakes of cheese wilting against it. Sara, during one of her rare bouts of cooking, had made a similar attempt at manicotti, nearly setting the kitchen aflame. Fred had caught Magda's eye: takeout, they had decided wordlessly. It was one of the few moments in which Magda had felt any fondness for Fred.

"And you're an analyst?" Nancy asked. "Sounds horrible to me. What? It does." She glared at Barb, rubbing her forearm where it had been pinched.

"I bet it's an exciting job," Barb offered. "Do you meet a lot of interesting people?"

"It's not so bad," Magda demurred. "When the clients actually want to be treated."

"Right," Nancy said. "But that's the tough part to get to, isn't it? The client *wants* a clean, contemporary kitchen, up until they have one. Then they go over to visit with a neighbor, see the wood beams, a whole house done rustic, rustic, rustic. And then, what do you know, whole room needs to be scrapped."

"There's always something," Barb agreed, before turning to Magda. "You like it out in New York? We were so excited, me and Nance, about the marriage act getting passed. I was sitting back on the couch thinking, *No way, it won't happen.* But Nance here said it would, and you know what, she was right. We've got half a mind to go out there and get hitched for real when they start doing weddings. When's that again?"

65

"July," Magda and Nancy said together. Nancy cast a sidelong glance at Magda before getting up and going inside.

After dinner, Magda ferried dishes to the kitchen. Barb stood by the sink, her hands red and angry from the hot water, passing the clean plates to Magda to dry. "Nance likes to run them out before dark," she said, indicating toward the front door. A whoop from the front, a dog barking through a wet mouthful of tennis ball. "Less energy when they're neutered, but me, I couldn't do it. I'd planned to be a veterinarian, up until the day I sat in on one of the operations. No, thank you," she whistled. "That dog saw those surgical tools and just bolted off the table."

Barb laughed then, shaking her head. "Young nurse, didn't understand how to work the anesthesia levels yet. I thought she was gonna lose the whole arm, but it was just a bad bite. Didn't even get infected. But that was it for me. I decided to figure something else out, and then, you know, I met Nance. You can't blame him, though, you know?"

Magda put down the dish towel. "For what?"

"Well, biting. I mean, they'd brought him there to have his *balls* chopped off, and no one guessed he was unhappy? It felt obvious, afterward. Of course he wanted to get off the table."

Nancy entered the kitchen, bent over a liquor cabinet. She poured a measure of vodka into her own glass, topped off Magda's as well. "Doctors are there to make you miserable," she said blithely, to which Barb grunted, "You stop that."

Ignoring her, "Time for dessert, I think," Nancy said. She pulled a pitcher of water from the refrigerator, swirling packs of lemonade mix into it. Murph nosed at her legs, and Soldier, from the hallway, emitted a low growl. Nancy held her own glass between her teeth, and in both hands held the glass dish of pie. Cocked her head toward the door, was on her way.

Once she was out of earshot, Barb leaned toward Magda and lowered her voice. "Conversion therapy." Jerking a thumb toward the door, she added, "Didn't work, obviously."

20.

IN THE MORNING, MAGDA PEERED OUTSIDE AS BARB AND NANCY said their goodbyes. The truck had coasted down the road before returning, again, to the driveway, where Barb met Nancy. She rushed from the house toward the car, one hand to the waistband of her pants, the other brandishing a sack. *Lunch*, Magda thought.

She had decided to book two nights at the bed-and-breakfast, thinking that if she were to change her mind, it would be easier to reach Ohio from Virginia than if she were to, say, turn around closer to Nashville. Waking up, though, Magda had found herself as ambivalent about that deviation as she had been since first reading the journal. She'd not known how to frame it to Theo, who had regularly returned to Minnesota until both of his parents had died. Even after that, he went home sporadically to visit with neighbors, who reliably offered him spare bedrooms or couches.

The whole day ahead of her, Magda decided to go into town. It was a short enough walk, a mere fifteen minutes to its center. The heat proved to be a familiar animal: a rough tingling at the hairline where sweat beaded, a heaviness to her upper legs. Twigs underfoot as she made her way to the main drag. The town echoed her own, a sameness to the clean and cracked sidewalks, and the lean, open storefronts. What was a confectionery store in Ohio was a pizza shop here. Beside it, a specialized and expensive general store: there were nondairy milks and low-sugar desserts, chips made of vegetables that promised more energy and less brain fog. Chips that claimed to taste of chilis, ranch dressing, dill and garlic. One whole refrigerator teeming with drinks that would keep the consumer awake, without the threat of intense sugar crash. A sustainable kind of caffeine, the label promised. A+ ENERGY, GO HARD!!

It felt eerily familiar to walk those streets, Magda having a sense that she was moving parallel to her childhood. Above, the sky was a dense, clear blue, the color heavy enough that if Magda squinted upward she could imagine being underwater. One didn't look up that way in New

York, where the pollution fogged the skyline; she had done so in Ohio, where the night sky was freckled with stars. When she'd been small, and lonely for Sweden, her mother had ushered her to the porch and pointed upward. It was the same, she explained, as what *mormor* and *farfar* were seeing, the *kusiner* as well. She'd shown Magda the constellations, including her grandmother's favorite, Cassiopeia. Whenever Magda felt lonely, she ought to remember that she and anyone she loved might be looking at the same sky.

The morning was brushed blue and cloudless, and Magda found herself veering down the various side streets. The houses were pressed close together, each with a square of yellowed grass out front; the cars lining driveways were in various states of disrepair, most of them clean-looking, notable not for sleekness but for functionality. The homes, too, were modest, clapboard and wood. Squirrels gamboled about on the rusted drainpipes, pausing as Magda went on by.

She couldn't quite shake the feeling of déjà vu. That morning she had looked up her former home, where Hedda still lived. Grainy online, it was immediately recognizable, the exterior repainted a thick, buttery yellow. The shutters and doors appeared new, but the lawn was unmown. No car in the driveway, nothing to indicate someone was home. Tucked under the porch was yard furniture, all of the plastic painted forest green; only the flower beds on the left side of the house had been planted. To the right, dirt was piled high, and loosely; beside that was an unopened bag of potting soil, a tearstain of pollen frozen onto its surface. On the porch: lopsided plastic trucks, a plastic pitcher toppled onto its side. Planters lined with wildflowers, sharp lavender and pink. She imagined ducking between the slats to observe them, how she would find the scent muted—a bit like citrus, if anything.

Magda could picture Hedda moving through those familiar rooms, had thought for years about how her life inside of them might look. That if, say, Hedda had a cold, Magda knew the path to the bathroom where the medicine was kept, could walk blindfolded to the linen closet for a fresh washcloth. Anything Hedda needed, Magda could help with. At night, sometimes, she imagined going through the house, room by room. It felt critical to remember how to do that. *Just in case*, she thought. Just in case something went wrong.

The backyard, still, would be overgrown with dandelions. In the middle of the green there would be a children's playset, for Hedda's grandchildren, a pile of plastic toys at the base of the slide. There would be a pail on the lowest step leading to the back porch, where a book had been splayed atop gardening gloves. Hedda would have found a more efficient way to garden; if the front porch was any indication, the backyard would be similarly lined, perhaps with potted herbs in terra-cotta pots along the far side of the fence. Surely, Hedda would have removed the chicken wire mapping the parameters of the property.

Those links had been so clotted by rust, that, after storms, a thick metallic tang rose to one's nose upon leaving the house. Flecks of that oxidized metal shaking loose and littering the garden—cucumbers, dusted in it. Remembering it, Magda could smell the metal. Remembered also the wildflowers her mother had grown, how patiently she had weathered Magda's frustration over their scent—or lack thereof. The flowers weren't meant for humans, she explained, but for *bi*: the pollinators.

She could picture it all, from the way the floorboards rattled to that smeared yellow glow the streetlights cast into the living room. How Magda would open their window on fog-dense mornings, sit on the roof waiting for it to clear, for the neighborhood to reveal itself. Hedda, when she woke, would lean out the window and into the craggy morning light. Magda leaned forward, knees dampened by dew, to help Hedda out.

Sara, raised an only child, found the relationship between sisters—so close in age, practically *twins*—to be endlessly fascinating. She wanted to know everything about Hedda. Were they similar? Did people think they looked alike? No, not especially. People looked, mostly, at Hedda—at first, because she was cute, with wide eyes and plump cheeks, and later, when she became beautiful. Even in childhood, Magda had a serious countenance: a furrow to her brow and wide, impassive eyes. An intensity of expression that indicated she took it all in with the utmost gravity. It was different to have been raised aware of one's own intelligence than of one's beauty, for it not to be an essential fact of one's existence that people were compelled to look at you. Magda, their mother theorized, appeared more stoic because she had been the one to emerge first, spent a few years appraising the world before Hedda was born, at which point she began screaming. Wouldn't stop, for another year yet.

Magda didn't say any of this to Sara; what she said was that she and Hedda had been each other's mirrors. Even if other people didn't recognize their similarities, their mannerisms were identical. Was Magda herself beautiful? If she were to come across her own reflection in a mirror, she would think no, turn away, but in happening upon herself in, say, a storefront window, it would not be immediately apparent that it was *her* and not Hedda. To catch herself unawares, performing Hedda's gestures, Magda would think yes, perhaps she had been wrong.

This was not enough for Sara.

"Come on," she would wheedle. "Tell me more, tell me *everything*. Start from the beginning."

21.

WHERE TO BEGIN?

The first wave of Scandinavians had settled in the Midwest many years prior to the arrival of her own family. Magda's parents were ushered over in 1935. *Det fanns så mycket potential*, a friend had written to her father. Renovation on the local church had finally been completed, there was a true sense of Lutheran community. *Det är hemma nu.* Then, in scratchy English: *Here, is good.*

Magda's mother had been pregnant as they journeyed; some weeks after their arrival, she no longer was. Magda's father planted crops. It was a long winter, at the end of which she found herself, once again, with child. In May, she would lose that one as well, and her father would finish the year's harvest and prepare for the next one. Long, sullen months passed, the heat stretching and breaking like taffy. When they finally tried again, and she became pregnant, Magda's mother was wholly devoted to the church: attending weekly Mass, volunteering most other days. The only Sunday Mass she skipped was when her labor began, there, on the sidewalk, mere blocks away. A few years later came Hedda.

There were multiple churches: one for the Swedes, a second for the Norwegians, a third for the Americans. The groups were civil to one another, bound by a mutual respect for Christianity and education. At home, Magda's family spoke only in Swedish, and the integration of English proved difficult; it roused from Hedda a protracting, agonizing stutter that Magda could not stand. Hedda was three, an age at which language didn't yet solidly belong to a person, so whenever she felt uncertain, or could not quickly enough find the words with which to express herself, she sputtered or froze. Magda took more readily to English, rushed to speak for Hedda in those situations, after which Hedda would blink up at her gratefully. At home, though, Hedda was bubbly, talkative. It was only outside of their house, and when forced to speak in English, that she latched herself onto

Magda's hand and looked about, worrying her thumbnail between her front teeth.

Magda acted as translator for both Hedda and their parents, neither of whom became more than conversational in their second language. She'd feel a bolt of shame in watching them try, the heavy accents shrouding their intent; they would get flustered, turn to her, and ask, in Swedish, for assistance. Going into adulthood, Magda's own familiarity with Swedish would lapse into something less than proficiency, a base conversational aptitude. But she could understand enough to carry on a conversation, and sometimes, still, as an adult, thoughts occurred to her in Swedish before they presented in English.

She remembered her parents as stoic people, tethered close to routine. Each morning they sojourned to the front porch with their chipped coffee mugs. Magda and Hedda's room looked over the porch, Magda's bed frame flush to the window, and she heard the slap of the screen door as they went out there, dawn just beginning to brighten the sky. They didn't speak until the cups had been drained, and even then they often stayed quiet, simply rotating the mugs in their red, chapped hands. Magda's mother waited for her father to rise, and then, as he plodded toward the road, toward the farm, she would return to the house. Magda remembered her mother like that, watching until her father was out of view, only then shuffling inside. Her arms were hung low, with both cups held loosely in her left hand, the ceramic clinking against her wedding band.

For them, the world was composed of three things: earth, crops, and God. Her father brought home the musky, damp scent of the fields, intermingled with sweat; when he and the other workers stayed late, there was a tang to him that Magda would later learn to recognize as alcohol. Her parents saw their lives with clear parameters: what physically lay before them and the almighty kingdom. They seemed to view each day as a task, and each other as the silent partner in accomplishing whatever required doing; only in church could Magda perceive a softening to their relationship. Then, and only then, would the space between her parents be closed, when, at the end of a psalm, her mother would place a flat, cool palm against her husband's back. Not in the same way she did for the children when they were ill, keening on about fevers or a stomach bug, but with a certain pride, knuckles whitening as she gripped her husband's arm. He, though, rarely touched the children, the act of petting their heads or holding them in his lap baffling, unnatural. He would startle, slightly, when one of the children ran toward him, a flinch that momentarily shook his features before he remembered to rearrange them. Magda had been the one to notice it first, and tried to direct Hedda elsewhere, toward their mother or into the yard. As a child, Magda imagined some far-flung past in which her parents were talkative, chirpy; it was easier than to consider that they had perhaps exhausted their joy too early.

At home, their parents didn't touch, merely orbiting around each other. When there was physical contact, it seemed perfunctory: her mother's vein-striped hand laid briefly atop her father's, a moment in the kitchen when they brushed against each other. When other couples rose and swarmed the floor at church mixers, her parents idled back in their chairs; it seemed to Magda that all of the farmers did. Her mother was measured and bored-seeming, sipping only from one powdery cup of lemonade drunk slowly over the course of the evening. Conversely, her father would swill yellowy beers, the rings of the cans growing steadily wider as the night went on. By the time they left, the paper covering the table would be damp and shredded. When he drank, the conversations with their neighbors grew more animated, him gesticulating wildly as he described the flailing wheat of yet another bum harvest. If he had drunk quite a lot—which was often the case—Magda would hear only her mother in the kitchen the next morning, the familiar rumble of her making coffee before bringing a cup to father, still in bed. She did not sit alone on the porch, even then.

They were serious people, and only later would Magda think of this with a certain reverence. She couldn't imagine living as they did, viewing their bodies as instruments, if not necessary indignities, vessels meant to be used in service of something more noble. Their way of living did not account for the individual experience; she could not imagine her parents meeting Gwen or Bill with anything other than bemusement, at best, or judgment, at worst. Her parents would have found them grotesquely selfish, their obsession with minutiae and cataloging their own lives. This fixation on wants and desires, rather than necessities. Weren't they safe?

Magda could imagine her mother asking. Didn't they have exactly everything that they needed?

Magda had ventured to Cleveland for college, and then to New York for medical school. After the first year out there, Magda found herself thinking steadily less of her parents. Sometimes, though, following a session, she would glimpse herself in the bathroom mirror and be reminded of them. This happened more through the years, and especially after they both had died, when she reached an age that surpassed their own. She saw them in herself, then: the flat, unrelenting expression, her mouth tightly set and brow hung low. She could see what they would have looked like had her father not gotten sick, her mother following him two years later. There was significant research, she'd find later, about spouses who were unusually dependent on each other, and how the survivor was wont to follow the deceased. But to think of them as unusually dependent upon each other did not feel strictly true; those rules seemed to apply to romance rather than to their resigned approach to life. Then Magda would think of herself as being uncharitable. She had not once seen her father make coffee, and Hedda had said, in the months following his death, that their mother continued to brew two mugs each morning. It was upon waking that Hedda would empty the second and usher their mother in from the porch. Magda called more regularly after he died, but in those final two years her mother did not ask her to visit, and Magda did not offer.

There did not seem to be a way in which to explain this to Sara, and while Magda thought the answers might come with time, that was the thing they would, in the end, not have enough of.

22.

MAGDA RETURNED TO THE HOUSE SUN-TIRED AND PERSPIRING, to find Barb busying herself in the garden.

"The rain! Look at these plants!" Barb called out from the porch, brandishing a zucchini nearly the width of her forearm. "You've got to help us out; no way we can eat all this on our own. Do you have dinner plans?"

The light had shifted by dinnertime, a glossy pink undercut by orange, Magda glancing skyward as she trundled past the dogs, one prying her fingers apart to deliver a gummy tennis ball, nubbed with dirt. With the other hand, she clutched Sara through the fabric of her bag. "Oh, Christ, Murph," Barb said, and Nancy disappeared inside, returned with hand sanitizer.

"Don't worry about them," she said, looking at Magda's hand, the knuckles white around the bag. "They're dumb but friendly."

Nance had had a terrible day, Barb speaking extra on her behalf, but nervously, which led Nance to annoyedly interject. Magda sat across from them, listening to their increasingly urgent diatribes. About the weather—fickle! Reality television, and how bad it was—but how good!—and how straight it was—but even so, that's what the people wanted! With each point came its own contradiction, Magda assiduously chewing and, when she remembered, nodding.

It was a familiar dynamic, being with them, and not unlike being in a session. Magda's posture required a level of openness, indicative of active listening—decisive nods, slow turns of the head, a sporadic tut—but hardly any talking. Something that, at any rate, Magda was accustomed to. A role she could take on despite the clutch of roiling feelings in her stomach, the part tempted to peek into the windows of her old life. An intensity built in her limbs that did not dissipate through dinner or dessert, as Barb and Nancy carried on their conversation. "The thing is," Barb said, "it's not like you can just up and go, right? This guy, if he wants the tile done that badly, he needs you, babe. He can't just . . ." She flicked her wrist skyward. "You know? Nobody else does it as good as you."

Back in the cottage, Magda watched three episodes of a soap opera. A debonair man with expressive eyebrows was in serious romantic trouble. His wife and mistress were one secret away from finding out about each other, his own deception magnifying in response. He would do anything necessary to keep the truth hidden, anything, because as much as he'd loved his mistress, he was beginning to love his wife again. The only way out, it seemed, was away. His brows went up, down, knit together in sadness. He was cavorting across Miami, trunk full of cocaine, when Magda nodded off, but she was stirred after midnight, an owl hooting just outside the window. Through the curtains, moonlight landed on Sara, who seemed to be winking. *Do something.*

Out of bed, then, pulling from the closet a flannel shirt to wear over her nightgown—Nancy's, she guessed, because it was folded with a degree of care Magda supposed Barb didn't take to her own clothes. The shirt overwhelmed Magda's frame; though tall, even in old age, Magda knew herself to have comically long arms. Her wrists jutted out at least two inches past the sleeves of the shirt as she reached for Sara and moved toward the front door.

On her walk earlier, she had found herself moving parallel to a park: there, she decided. She lit a cigarette. The smoke whisked itself into the bruised light, the chirring of crickets in the distance, all things soft and slow. Voices from the television nudged out the open window, a guffaw as the talk show host revealed the truth: Marcus was the father; he had been *all along*. Barb cawed at the reveal, Nancy saying, "I *told* you. It couldn't have been more obvious." One of them set down a glass, grunted.

At the sidewalk, Magda told Sara she wasn't sure the women would stay together. "Between us, of course," she said.

Sara had been deeply nosy about patients, most often asking Magda about their future prospects. Would the one she couldn't name actually leave his wife? No, Magda didn't believe he would. Could the other one who couldn't be named realize that it wasn't her marriage causing the problem, but her expectation of it? No, Magda didn't think so.

When they had been at the farmers market, many years prior, Magda had seen Bill by the bread vendor. Magda looked over but said nothing—it was policy to allow patients to approach, if they felt so inclined—and the moment would have gone by unannounced except for the fact that Sara saw him wink at her. The last session had been a productive one; he felt he had nearly quit smoking, and he was falling back in love with his wife.

"God, he's handsome," Sara said appreciatively. "Classic good looks, like a superhero or an opera singer—like José Carreras! Is he your lover?"

Magda, examining a green onion, had waved her off. "He's nobody."

"Mr. Nobody," Sara had crowed loudly. "Come on, who is he?"

Magda could not explain to Sara how she knew Bill, Sara in turn going dark and glum. Broody, asking, "Why?" and, "That? It's not a *real* rule." Sara announced a forgotten errand, and they had parted ways early, before the movie. Magda went alone, left the bag of green onions under the seat. That night, she waited by the phone, and Sara did not call. As with her own childhood, she had wanted to say more than she found herself able to.

As she walked along, pulling from the cigarette, Magda explained to Sara that Barb and Nancy ultimately wanted different things. "Take the bed-and-breakfast," Magda said. "Nancy never wanted to do that; Nancy is looking for any excuse to find quiet. *Any* excuse."

And, Magda mused, Barb had a fixation with improving their lives. It was a tendency that played out over and over again with her younger patients: studies in single-minded pursuit, disappointment. Chasing off that perfect partner, who upon closer inspection had a lackluster flossing routine and sweated profusely. The dream job, which really wasn't so great; actually, it was quite a lot of work. That gorgeous apartment—oh, how they had dreamed of those windows!—but the heaters banged at night, and the neighbor played trombone. But the next job, person, apartment—surely that would be the one.

Barb, Magda felt certain, had insisted upon the bed-and-breakfast, likely because she believed Nancy would enjoy the repair process, because it might bring her some degree of satisfaction. Nancy did it because Barb had asked her, and she had dwindling reserves left for conflict. She was already tired enough with work, just trying to get through the day so she could get home. At some point, the dissonance in what they wanted was bound to weigh heavily upon them, the center unable to hold.

When it came down to it, Magda believed, Nancy would have far preferred the company of her partner to any strangers, and she almost certainly would have preferred that their money go toward their own home rather than the backyard cottage. The dinner had been Barb's way of saying that short-term rentals *were* a good idea, and while Magda felt Nancy didn't mind her—liked her, even—she wasn't vain enough to think she had irrevocably shifted Nancy's perspective. The end result remained the same: a stranger in the yard; more responsibility. Whether it was an old lady like herself, or someone else, it was yet another thing Nancy would have to take care of.

Sara would have disagreed; she would have said that the caregiving was what held the two women together. Barb in perpetual need of a project, Nancy quietly enjoying the attention—like positioning herself in the hot, warping glow of a sunbeam. Magda and Sara had often argued about those things, though. What held anyone together? Desire and need, insisted Sara. Familiarity, retorted Magda. Love.

The park was a grassy knoll, its center semicircle of dirt for playing baseball or kickball, a scrappily walled fence encircling the playground. It was on the slide that Magda sat, smoking a second cigarette, stubbing the end on the plastic and then burying the butt in the cedar chips below. She smoked like it were really Sara beside her, like the owls cresting overhead were not the rustlings of suburbia but the sounds of her childhood street just after sundown. There was the rustling of the heavy denim overalls, the clinking of lunch pails against bruised legs, shards of beer bottles glinting in the fading light. She would watch, sometimes, from the roof, as the women peeked anxiously from the kitchen windows, waiting for their men.

Magda smoothed the plastic with one hand, ash sticking to her palm.

Magda thought of Hedda, of how when they were very young they had sat in their neighborhood park speaking in Swedish, like it was a secret. Their father, an American, eager to have them learn English, insisted that would be all they spoke in Ohio; their language, already, a ghost. But he was rarely home, and in his absence the girls were indulged by their mother; she let them speak Swedish in the hopes that she would eventually learn enough English to enforce their father's wishes.

By her third cigarette, Magda began to feel queasy. She turned back again toward the big house, where the downstairs lights had been dimmed, the only one left illuminated on the second floor. Frosted, a bathroom window. Barb seemed like someone who would listen to the radio while showering, who, blinded by suds, would yell for Nancy to come, because wasn't that the song on the radio the one they'd heard five years back while pulling out of that one gas station in Michigan, wasn't it the one from Grosse Pointe?

When Magda fell asleep, it was close to four, golden streaks of sun just starting to lighten the sky. Already she felt the pinpricks of a headache behind her eyes, and when she woke just after eight the pain was full-blown, stars dancing against her vision. The water glass standing sentry on the night table remained full. She had stirred to the feeling of a palm, which, upon waking, had turned out to be only a pillow warmed by her own cheek.

It was, Magda realized, her birthday. It was time to leave. She remembered leaving Ohio, for school, and how Hedda had run the length of the driveway after the car, waving and then standing in the middle of the street until the car was out of sight. Magda's stomach had dropped, she had turned away, straightening her back. This time, the only witnesses to see her off were Barb and Nancy, waving from the front porch.

"They might make it," she said to Sara, and it sounded like her friend guffawed, but it was actually Barb yelling goodbye, Nancy's hand moving to rest at the base of her spine—to quiet or comfort her, Magda couldn't say.

23.

MAGDA LISTENING TO THE LOW THRUM OF THE CAR'S AIR CON-
ditioner, the sporadic clattering of her belongings as they were jostled
in the back seat. Even with sunglasses on, she found her eyelids creased
with heat. It did not feel particularly different, being seventy.

She did not feel different for having decided to take the trip, either.
Knowing Sara's plan had been enough to prompt that familiar, keen sense
of gratitude toward Sara for telling her what to do; and she had, without
question, trusted it was right. As she always had. Perhaps that was the
more impulsive action, in the end—that, to her mind, it had seemed easy.
That she would proceed on the due course, forge ahead. Finish out the
road trip she'd promised Sara and simply return home. She had not considered the possibility of new experiences dragging her deeper still into
the old ones, nor had she considered that—even in a new environment—
she would remain herself. History had a way of repeating itself; she had
undergone similar negotiations in leaving Ohio, holding close the furtive
hope that, in New York, she would be different.

Manhattan had been, at first, an utter sensory overload. The intimacy of
daily life proved astounding. Magda would idle outside a deli and watch
as two men passed back and forth a cigarette, fingers briefly twined during the transfer. On the same block she would see a woman kiss a man full
on the mouth, his hands snaked around her waist. Another student who
gripped the arm of his friend while recounting a shoddy lecture, while,
behind him, a hand rose along the slope of someone else's thigh. Magda
felt stiff and heavy inside her body, watching as affection was treated as
an afterthought; she couldn't figure out how to respond to that kind of
spontaneity. When a classmate, say, leaned in to hug her, or a date bent
down for a kiss, she tried emulating people she had seen on the street

responding to that sort of touch; in any event, she found her own arms leaden, mouth and forehead pinched in anticipation. Already, she worried over what might go wrong, how she might embarrass herself.

At home, nobility came from serving God, and following His word. Hedda was as dutiful with religion as with coursework, puzzling over a psalm in the same way that she might complete a grammatical exercise. Hedda seemed never to doubt the verity of what she was absorbing, would not think to question something an authority figure told her was correct. Piety came naturally to her, the motions intuitive in a way that Magda could not quite imitate. In elementary school, Hedda broke free of her stutter and, her English well improved, began making friends. Magda struggled to do so, worrying terribly over her clothing and her accent. She feared that she carried with her the smell of the fields, musky and of the earth like her parents, as some of the children claimed she did.

Making friends had come more easily to her when young, the insecurities blooming alongside adolescence. She had grown tall, quickly, her front teeth bucked. The girls from the church clustered together, their ringleader a girl named Lucy. Magda and Lucy orbited each other in a way typical to a small town. Lucy, dark-haired and slight, reminded Magda of the angels cast in stone outside of the church; she had tried to say as much to Lucy, once, who frowned at her. Ever since, Magda's face had burned upon seeing Lucy; she wanted so very much to be liked, and thought obsessively about what she did and said, how she could be different. Better. Lucy was spontaneous, and laughed loudly, and while Magda wanted to make her laugh, she could tell that she was too slow and stolid, perhaps, to be a potential friend to Lucy. They had had moments together before—grouped among others at the church's annual picnic, or in the schoolyard jumping rope—during which Magda felt a bubble of hopefulness in her chest. But it was easier, of course, with the cushion of other people; rarely, if ever, did they find themselves alone.

It was the weekend before Thanksgiving, the annual can drive petering off. Donations had slowed, the basement brimming with shelf-stable items. The men had secreted beers outside, drinking them while trimming at the hedges, mowing the lawn. Inside, in the kitchen, the women bustled over a few turkeys, poured brine onto green beans before baking them. The teenagers were bothersome, the boys sent into the front yard to assist their fathers in weeding, Magda and Lucy left to stand uncomfortably by their mothers. "Shoo," Lucy's mother said. "Make yourself useful: organize the food." Magda's mother had nodded in response, pointing Magda toward the basement with one firm movement of her chin.

Downstairs, they surveyed the mountain of cans before dutifully marching to opposite sides of the room. Lucy eyed the cans before sighing loudly. "Boring," she said, turning to Magda for affirmation.

Magda's stomach dipped—she hadn't realized it was boring; she'd been having a fine time. "We could make a game of it," she offered. They began stacking cans into increasingly elaborate lines of defense, the tuna and tomato soup tipping over as the speed and urgency of their builds increased. Magda's chest was tight, nearly breathless with laughter, when Lucy pronounced herself the victor. Only then, after toiling with her stack, did she see it immediately collapse. The floor was flush with cans, the hollow thunks and low rolls barely audible over their laughter.

It was a moment that struck Magda, even then, as temporary. She had watched her mother and father long enough to see how whatever she felt would be eclipsed by the realities of her future, unknown as they were. Her life would shift toward a catalog of other things—not farming, hopefully, but a family and raising children—and the sweetness of something as banal as this competition wouldn't prove to be the best part of her day. Without knowing why, exactly, she understood that bursts of romanticism and excitement were somehow shameful, evidence of a fickle constitution.

Magda walked toward a dented can of black beans, wondering if her mother had felt such joy before, if she'd ever been without the serious, pinched expression shrouding her features.

"Do you smoke?" asked Lucy. She rummaged in her pocket, before triumphantly brandishing a lipstick-stained cigarette. "Lifted it from *mor*."

Though Magda didn't, she nodded. Lucy motioned her toward the little basement bathroom, a grimy cube with a window gone milky with condensation. Magda's first inhalation proved too casual, and, panicking, she inhaled too deeply, at which point it felt that her throat had been set aflame. Lucy laughed as Magda's vision blurred, eyes wet as she squeezed out thick, bronchial coughs. She felt lightheaded, spinny, a tight pressure in her forehead. Even with the window closed, she could smell turkey wafting down from the kitchen, could catch tidbits of the adults' conversation.

Magda would first remember it as Lucy dropping the cigarette; later, she would suspect she had been the one to do so. Each would blame the other for the moment that the flame met the bathroom rug. Both frantically stomped upon it, the toe of Magda's loafer caught under Lucy's heel, her own body buckling as Lucy bent to keep her from falling. The blame proved impossible to delegate, both of them certain that the other was at fault, and while they wouldn't discuss it, each quietly blamed the other for the next moment, in which Lucy's hands were on Magda's waist, and they were kissing. Then Magda's spine pressed catlike against the wall, Lucy's mouth on hers. Were they still laughing then? Yes, the thin beam of Lucy's breath was smoky and dense, her tongue insistent as it roved in Magda's mouth. Magda was made entirely of liquid, a substance that would take on the shape of any container that Lucy offered her. There was a fevered intensity that muted Magda's sense of speech; it seemed that all she could be asked to do, ever, was kiss Lucy, be kissed by her. It seemed impossible that she had, only that morning, donned stockings and brushed her teeth, when there was only this one thing that mattered. How long it went on for, Magda couldn't say; she was undone by this person, her heart tripping over the realization: Lucy was her friend. The categorization felt murky, but undeniably true. It wasn't until Lucy gasped that Magda saw they were not alone. There, in the doorway, was her mother, silent and horrified.

Though she tried, Magda couldn't remember what happened next. She was ushered away from Lucy, that was certain, but whether her mother then verbally reproached her, whether she was slapped, she couldn't remember. What Magda knew was that she wasn't allowed to see Lucy again. At church, Lucy sat resolutely straight two rows ahead, unwilling to look at her. And when Magda tried at school—just the once, but she couldn't help herself—to pass a note to Lucy, one of Lucy's friends simply tore it in half. Magda picked up the shreds after class; she wouldn't try again. Magda watched the part in her friend's dark hair, willing Lucy to please just turn around. She wouldn't, of course; she never did.

Magda's mother refused to speak of it, and, for the rest of the time Magda lived at home, refused her much else. Magda did not attend the school dances, nor was she allowed to stay over at the houses of other girls. She was rarely invited, anyhow, Lucy having told the other girls what she, Magda, had tried with her. Magda went to the library, and read about the aftermath of World War II. She read about the mounting Cold War tensions, she read about missiles, and she read about psychiatry. There were articles about electroconvulsive therapy, and how it might be the solution to malignant health conditions; that was what one piece said, that it could be used to solve for "queer, disallowed behaviors." The electrical activity would trigger seizures, which, in turn, would relieve severe symptoms. Magda spoke of this to Hedda, the only person, really, who still made time for her. And while Magda worried over whether her mother had told her father, or Hedda, their behavior toward her did not change, and she was left to wonder what she had done wrong.

Seasons passed. She was accepted into community college, and though her father had suggested she live at home, her mother had somehow convinced him otherwise. December came and went, the slow ticking down of days until holiday break lapsing into a cold January. A cool rain came down, hissing as it wicked snow into slush. February stayed damp and unhappy, and, through all of it, Magda stayed inside. When she first saw Lucy outside of school and church, it was in the local park. Lucy was holding hands with a boy, one about whom Magda had heard the other girls squealing. Lucy had looked up and caught Magda's eye, and for a moment, stopped moving. She waved. A flat smile, lips cinched tight, and then she was gone. Spring passed, then summer, and Magda applied to medical school. She thought often of currents zapping through her own brain, the prospect of lifting herself from the table as a changed person.

24.

MAGDA DID NOT KNOW VIRGINIA WELL ENOUGH TO RECOGNIZE
when she missed the first exit, or the second. Banked at a gas station,
Theo's voice warbling through the static: "How was it? Did you make it
back to see your sister?"

"Oh," Magda said. "It was exactly as I'd expected."

His tone was mild, warm with surprise. "That's nice. Never happens
like that, does it? Knowing what to expect, I mean."

Magda drove another fifty miles before she realized that the route
and the fact of her location were incongruous. Of course, a degree of that
could have been avoided if someone else were in charge of the navigation, but Sara had been disastrous with maps, and with most planning.
By nature, Sara was inclined to press against what she saw as arbitrary
deadlines until they punctured, or until she arrived at the gate to see the
plane veering upward and away.

Magda's body was tipping toward annoyance, her fingers taut
against the steering wheel. Had she left earlier, paid more attention,
pushed back against Fred when he insisted that she watch Sara. The
counterfactuals stacked together, building to the largest: Why had she
gone on the road trip at all? She pulled over on the side of the road.
Especially dark on those long stretches of country highway, lampposts
infrequent. There were rarely signs indicating where one might next find
gas, shelter. One seemed promising, but upon closer inspection was a
handwritten screed: HONK FOR FREEDOM!!! Magda tapped the base of the
cigarette pack, which made a hollow shaking sound. She pulled out one
of the remaining three cigarettes.

Ahead of her was a motel, with sagging discount signs perched out
front, and sat opposite a strip mall, halogen advertisements for REAL
CHICKEN!! and TATTOOS FAST blinking against the windows. Across the
road, opposite Magda's window, a door was propped open to a pizza shop,

casting out clouds of doughy air. Two doors down, people were milling about a tattoo parlor. One woman—the artist, she suspected, though it was difficult to tell from such distance—had black and white needlings up her arms and pulled at the hem of her sweater like those threads were the last thing tethering her to the sidewalk. A larger, balding man emerged sporadically from the store to check on her, and each time she held a cigarette in offering, and he shook his head—*No, no.*

The teenager who checked Magda in wore a patriotic shirt: an American flag inexplicably wrestling a tremendously muscular bald eagle. A low rat-a-tat of fireworks spattered outside as he looked at her ID. "Happy birthday," he said without looking up, and she said, "Thanks," noticed the peanut butter stuck to his braces. He squinted at the card before handing it back. "Fourth of July," he said. "Nice."

In her room, Magda stubbed the cherry against the windowsill, waving out the smoke before she latched the screen. Over the bed, a print of a winking cowboy gazed down at her; a miniature plastic spurred boot dangled loosely from its perch over the mini-fridge. She had opened it, releasing a shivery chill, to find two water bottles, a few domestic beers with a sticky note affixed to one damp label: *pay up front.* In the bathroom, there was a grainy framed photo of a sailor tipping a woman back for a dramatic kiss. *WE <3 AMERICA*, proclaimed the notepad by the bed, in stocky, loose handwriting. A scratchy rendition of a firework exploding atop it.

"I think it's more of a thing that townies do," the cashier was saying when she walked in. He picked at a dry piece of skin on his cheek, expanding on that idea, before noticing Magda. "Oh, sorry." He handed her a menu flecked with dry bits of tomato sauce. "Half-off small cheese pie today, you know, for the holiday."

The cashier resumed talking to the girl working behind the counter, who had long fiddly fingernails painted a bright blue. She was refilling canisters of sugar from a large paper sack, the length of her nails requiring her to move impossibly slowly, tethering one bottle to her palm, then reaching for the bag. The boy watched her as well, then peeled off to take

Magda's order, leaving the slip on the shelf connecting the main room to the back kitchen. "I mean, it's cool," he said. "Like, the fields all lit up and shit. I bet you'd like it."

Focus taut on the canisters, the girl barely took notice. "Yeah, maybe. Could be cool."

He nodded effusively. "Super cool. I go every year."

"Do you think I can bring my boyfriend?"

His shoulders sagged, and, when he caught Magda's eye, he pretended he hadn't. "Oh yeah. Totally."

Outside, the hot cardboard leaking oil onto her palms, Magda looked over at the motel. The setting sun melded with the red roof, the parking lot bathed in a hazy warm light. There was the spitty crackle of fireworks; somewhere, bright streaks were rattling across the skyline. Her admiration was broken by the woman outside the tattoo parlor asking if she didn't have an extra cig, did she? "Slow night, smoked straight through my pack."

Magda pulled the remaining menthols from her bag, tapped the bottom of the pack until one cigarette jutted out. "Did it hurt?" she asked, indicating at the woman's neck, where AARON snaked around in script. Gwen had a number of tattoos, had told Magda that they gave her a sense of ownership over her body. "I didn't feel like *me* until I had them," she said, rubbing the spot on her wrist where her mother's name pressed atop her skin.

The woman lit the cigarette, grazing the area with her fingertips. "This? Nah. Ribs are the bad spot, for most folks. Neck's not so bad, 'cause you can't see it happening. Like a shot, you know? It's worse if you're watching." She exhaled, pointing the lighter at Magda. "You got any?"

"No."

"You want one? I can get you in now; it's no problem. There's a book in there, lots of options. Just give me five minutes."

The man behind the counter was drinking diet soda, watching a video on his phone. Something he should not have been, based on how swiftly he stood up and brought the laminated booklet over to the waiting area.

Hearts bedecked with flames; roses twisting upward, their thorns dripping blood; a skull with smoke blooming from its eye sockets. "You see anything you like?"

Not on that page, or the next. Magda wondered how long it would take before she could make an excuse to leave, and continued turning the sticky pages, finding herself surprised by the last one. The man leaned over her shoulder. "Yeah, that'd be good. You thinking face, or . . . ? Nah, I'm kidding, wherever."

As the woman sat her on a chair, the pizza box on the floor beside them, Magda asked if it would hurt. "Here, I mean," she said, rubbing at her left wrist, then, gesturing behind her ear, "Or would it hurt less here?"

"Nah," the woman said. "Not worse'n most other stuff. The thing is, you want something you can look at. Any special meaning to that one?" the woman asked. She nodded toward the booklet, wiped her nose against her forearm.

Magda shook her head. A cold wipe against her skin, followed by a light pinch, the hum of the machinery, the feeling that she was lifting out of her own body. Then the woman said it was over; she had done great. The skin was reddened, and the woman laid cling wrap over it, reminded Magda not to expose the tattoo to sun for at least two weeks.

At the front counter, the man gave her the price, then said no, sorry, and knocked it down. "You gave her a cig, huh?" He said it as if it were very funny, and as she pushed the front door open he called out, "Hey! Happy Fourth."

Back in the motel, Magda ate the cold pizza, slowly, with her right hand. She had not remembered to ask who Aaron was. She watched a sitcom in which a woman chased after a man, ignoring the other man who had been chasing her all along. Everyone was blond and funny. The low hum of pain in her wrist felt like an anthem, something on which to focus her attention.

Even to look at it felt absurd: thick black lines of a four-leaf clover, skin around it red and swollen. Absurd, but it made her want to laugh. Want to go back and tell the woman, actually, it was significant, to find that all this time there had been a way to create her own luck. Hedda had been masterful at finding four-leaf clovers, seeming to pluck them from anywhere. Magda's jealousy abounded, her own searches futile. It hadn't mattered, though, because Hedda didn't hoard the clovers; if she found one, she went in search of another, which she'd place in Magda's palm. Really, the clovers hadn't been the prize, so much as the expression on Hedda's face, as if she couldn't believe their collective luck: *Look*, another one.

Magda placed a hand over her heart, pressing it taut against the collarbone until her heart slowed. She moved the palm upward along her neck, to the point under her jaw where her pulse darted madly. The skin felt papery, thin. She could touch herself like this, but she became awkward when other people made similar attempts—or any attempts, really.

Theo was the first of her classmates to notice how she stiffened at the touch, and rather than hugging, he chose instead to jauntily salute at Magda. He made a joke of it, referring to her stellar grades as the reason he called her The Colonel. Because Theo did it, other people caught on, and it wasn't long before—without ever having to ask for it—people stopped spontaneously touching Magda. She still had to manage those negotiations while on dates, of course, feeling the familiar panic rise in her chest as the pasta dishes were cleared, as her date paid the bill. It seemed an inevitability then that they would stand and he would walk her home. Even anticipatorily, she felt confined to her body, and resigned to the moment at which a man would press his lips to her own. She would think then, *Ah, kissing*, as if she were watching it happen to someone else. In these moments she would sometimes think back to the silliness of that day with Lucy, and how their mundane activity had shifted into something brighter and essential. There had been a terrific violence to their kiss, the need so sudden and overwhelming that it became a question that only one action could solve for. She would feel her body cleave against her date's, then, to respond in kind. But then, inevitably, Magda would recall the sound of the door opening and her mother's face—sleek mouth, the stony expression—and she'd make an excuse to go inside, alone.

She'd become less jittery about contact over the years; it was impossible not to, with a friend as expressive as Sara, who cemented feelings through touch. She'd crane her head over Magda's shoulder to read a recipe, pointy chin jabbing into Magda's collarbone, or grab her hand during the scarier scenes in a movie. Sara viewed the bodies of those she loved as extensions of her own, and it became second nature to assume some level of access. In time, Magda allowed it—craved it, even. She thought nothing of swiping a loose hair from her friend's face, or removing a fleck of pollen with her thumb.

But that, of course, had taken years. To think so far back was to realize she had made excuses for so much—herself, especially—and what, in the past year, she'd hidden from Hedda.

25.

MAGDA HAD MEANT TO TELL HEDDA, SHE REALLY HAD. IT WAS just that in the weeks following Sara's death, the act of answering her phone felt unbearable. She wanted to be called, but she found that, when the phone rang, she could rarely muster the energy to pick it up.

Even then, the hope clenched tight in her chest until the caller spoke. Immediately, the voice would be too high or too low. Hesitant. Bold. In any case: not Sara. It had just been one of those months, was what she told Hedda, the sort of thing someone said to avoid saying something real. They had talked instead about the weather and work, and when Hedda asked after Sara, Magda paused. She held the phone to one ear, the other scratching at her scalp. She glanced at her nails, the white flakes of skin embedded beneath them. *It's time*, she thought.

Hedda went on. "Is Sara still having trouble at the gallery, with what's-her-name—the lady with those shopping lists?"

Magda's heart drummed something fierce at the sound of Sara's name. Present tense, for the first time in weeks.

"Janet Yengelman."

"That's the one! Sara has the patience of a saint, doesn't she? I can't imagine putting up with that, and for so many years."

Mouth gone dry, Magda cleared her throat. "I could never. But she makes the gallery so much money."

Hedda laughed. "Me neither. I still think about the time she forced poor Sara to come over in the middle of the night because she needed help hanging a print."

"Of her own work, if you can believe that," Magda added.

"Has there been anything like that recently?"

Tell her now, Magda thought.

Then: *recently.*

Then: *Sara.*

"Well," she said slowly. "You know what, there was an issue just last week. Have I ever told you how specific Janet is about bleach?"

Magda hadn't meant to carry on with it, either. She'd intended to correct the record on their next call, only the relief at hearing Hedda say *Sara*—again, in the present tense—was so sharp and furious that lying felt better than it did lousy. Their biweekly calls resumed, Magda building on that original fiction of her own busyness, telling Hedda that she had finally, finally dug herself out from that hole. She was going to the theater; she was seeing Sara more often.

They tended to speak on Sunday nights, when Hedda watched her son's children so that he and his wife could go on a date. Magda spent the afternoons walking briskly in the park in preparation, oscillating between guilt and anticipation of being able to say *is* rather than *was*.

Next time, she thought. *You'll tell her next time.*

Months passed and the guilt began overriding the joy, a queasy feeling rattling around inside her, lacquered to her rib cage: she was too late to correct her mistake. It could not, at this point, be justified. One night, after unspooling a particularly elaborate fiction, Magda looked at her bookshelves, where five copies of *The Year of Magical Thinking* were pressed side to side, notes from the senders peeking up from the spine. Those had been mailed to her in the past six months, along with Boomer's annotated copy of *Refusing Heaven* and a copy of Kübler-Ross's *On Grief & Grieving* that had arrived, unmarked, along with flowers.

Could the deceit be justified by circumstance? To patients, Magda would say no; the only due course was to admit wrongdoing, make amends. It was what she told Bill: tell your wife, try to move forward. He could not manage this, and neither, it seemed, could Magda. It was she who had made it impossible to see Hedda; her sister would not forgive her this. Even if she did, Magda might not forgive herself.

Yet the anger teemed below the surface. What she was doing, Magda rationalized, wasn't lying so much as it was explaining how their lives would have been, *if*. If Sara hadn't been alone, if Fred had been there, if Magda had. If she had lived, they would have been waving their hands madly, trying to hail a cab. They would have been late to the theater. They would have been shepherding bottles full of bleach to Janet's studio. They would have been sharing cigarettes on the fire escape and imagining their retirement and dipping into the breadbasket at dinner, just for something to do. All of it, all of what she said, would have been true. In that, Magda could feel confident, justify the next phone call.

But she could not return to Ohio; that particular boldness could not be sustained if she were to see Hedda. Magda could not lie to Hedda's face, nor could she stand—she would simply collapse—if she were to see the disappointment flooding Hedda's features. To tell Hedda would make it true: Sara was gone, and she wouldn't be returning.

26.

ALONG THE ROAD CAME BELATED *HAPPY BIRTHDAY* MESSAGES from Boomer, and Dr. Stein, who said delightedly that Boomer had shared her cell phone number, another call at a rest stop as Magda was twisting the fuel cap back into place.

"I'm not interrupting you, am I?" Theo asked, over a faint dinging. *The grocery store*, she thought.

"I had to tell you," he said. "I ran into Marty the other day. Her husband is doing worse—no, she didn't say that, but it was . . . well, you could tell. She told me the diagnosis and said, 'I guess Harvard won't work out,' something like that."

"God," Magda said, opening the car door. "That's awful."

"Well," Theo said, "Yes, thank you—no, I don't need a bag, I brought one, yes."

In the background was the hush of someone else's voice, the sound of a receipt being torn from its reel. How like Theo, Magda thought, to bookend a sentence with affirmations.

A moment later he spoke again. "Sorry, Mags. I keep telling cashiers I don't need receipts—did you know they're filled with BPA? You can't avoid neurotoxins, but this is just—no, anyway, what I was going to say is that I went to this dating event yesterday, in a hotel, and it was incredible, actually. Fifty or sixty people with name tags on, like we were schoolchildren or something, but it was a school for people who were both very lonely and very old."

"Did you meet someone?"

"Well, yes and no. If you can believe it, that was actually where I ran into Marty. She was mortified, understandably, because I thought—we *all* thought—she had this husband. And it turns out that they've been divorced for two *years*, but she didn't tell anyone."

"She's divorced?"

"And now he's sick."

A steady exhale from Theo, like a hum. She leaned back against the car seat. The day was almost breezeless, air dense with humidity, the heat a flash against her skin. "So she's not going to Cambridge, then? She'll stay with him?"

"I think she will. It was strange, though, that it took so long for her to tell me the truth. We'd talked for maybe five, ten minutes before she was able to say that she wasn't out cheating, she'd just failed at marriage. That's how she put it, anyway: that *she* had failed. As if it weren't something that happens to thousands of people every single day, but some personal fault."

"I think you're right," Magda said. "She probably bought the tickets when she realized he would actually die."

She could hear Theo sigh, and he said, "Probably. It's just sad, isn't it? The stories we tell ourselves in order to feel better."

Magda took a sip of the lukewarm water in the cupholder, nosed the car away from the pump and into one of the spots directly outside of the gas station, as Theo interrupted himself, said they had added another two goldfish to the tank. "It's a troubling now that we've added Kübler-Ross and Kline."

"A troubling, is that really what it's called?" she asked, and he said, "Really. It was the birthday gift I thought you'd be least likely to balk at."

To which she sighed, and he added, "As if I'd forget."

Inside, she bought coffee, three packs of cigarettes. She had forgotten, she realized at the register, to ask after her own patients. She saw a little refrigerator magnet with an Ohio tableau: Cedar Point's roller coaster, a husk of corn swirled glittery yellow. With one nail she began to peel the magnetic strip from the back: *For the troubling*, she thought.

The man ringing her up looked so much like Bill that she felt her heart constrict. Impossible, for them to meet like this, and sure enough, when the man turned to scold the child lolling behind him, the jaw was softer, the hairline receding. That seemed to be the trick mirror of memory—how, in missing someone, they could briefly be returned to you.

"$25.93," he repeated, and then she paid, waving off the receipt.

"BPA," she said. "Very dangerous."

The child eyed her, lollipop in hand.

Magda's wrist ached, the plastic catching the light as she drove. Underneath the bandage, the skin felt pinched—not irritated, as she'd expected, but throbbing. More alive, somehow, the detonations of her pulse a reminder: still here.

And there she was, going south. The trees were large, green, edged with unfamiliar light. The sun dipped low in the sky, its light dimming to pink, then a hazy purple, which spread gently along the road. A pop song warbled out from the speakers, barely perceptible above the wind.

A night so peaceful and unremarkable, the destination seemed irrelevant. She could have been on her way anywhere. Not to Nashville, necessarily, but back to New York. She could've been on her way to Ohio. If she were to do so, point the car in the opposite direction and go along until the sky went inky black, a chirring of insects drowning out the evening. Her headlights a beam along dark country roads until she reached the town. If she were to, say, cruise past the familiar intersections and idle to a stop before the yellow house. If she were to do all that, there would be nothing to stop her from walking to the front door, pushing it open, and calling out, *I'm home.*

Night would fall soon, sweeping the road clean of blemishes. Only up close would the gummied tires and roadkill come into sharp, yellowed focus, but all of that seemed, temporarily, a ways away. For now, the sinking sun, the lively jostling between the radio host and his call-ins. Magda would be on the same route for a long time, and she kept the windows open, her cigarette smoke whisking into the breeze. The purple faded into black, and the host congratulated his listeners on making it through the hottest day of summer.

27.

October 2008

Dear M,
I love Nashville! Everything about it! A great city.

Yours,

S

28.

THE HUNDREDS OF MILES BETWEEN VIRGINIA AND TENNESSEE passed in a series of rote motions: accelerate, brake, check the rearview, shift from one lane to another, back again. Every few hours, Magda stopped for gas, each time buying coffee and water. She only ever finished the former, the soft crush of bottles ever expanding; those she left to cushion Sara on the passenger seat. Any sudden movement let loose a long hiss as residual liquid moved, settled. An overhang of branches cast sharp, lemony light across the road. Magda sporadically checked the map to see that, yes, she was still going in the right direction; I-71 S idled onward indefinitely. Her eyes were dry, the beginnings of a sunburn prickling at her cheeks. In Magda's sight line, it was all golden and emerald: hot sun overhead, trees, grass, the road bracketed by streetlights and telephone cables. Though Magda's skin was pinkened, itchy, and her nose tickly from the allergens—despite those things, she felt ever ravenous for fresh air. The farther Virginia was in the rearview, the more obvious it felt: the trip had been a mistake.

The furtive hope remained that, perhaps, Sara had linked these places with a greater goal in mind. That there was some truth for Magda to glean, something that had been invisible to her for the past years. It didn't seem that way; rather, that the trip was like any other one of the birthday parties Sara had planned for Magda, with the initial intention usurped by what actually happened. By what inevitably went wrong. Even though she had passed over Ohio, Magda had felt almost drunk with the hope that Sara would find a way to show her something, that she might—for one last time—make Magda feel seen, understood. That there was a link for her yet to discover.

Turn back, she thought.

She took another sip of coffee, looked carefully behind her. Toward the exit, which she continued past. For the next fifty miles the same impulse, steadily deploying her signals, and each time carrying on. The cup sat empty in its holder, Magda's tongue furred and heavy. *Turn back*, she instructed herself, and still she continued on. Returned to the middle lane until the signs for the next exit loomed large against her sight line.

Magda did not reach Nashville until very late, the man at the front desk bleary-eyed. His eyes on her license, the birthday already a thing of the past. From the back room, rustling, a tinny clink of metal as he dropped keys into her palm: "Here they are." The sprightly lobby music was turned low, the television blaring over it. A sports commentator said how that night's game had been revelatory, and from the panel came murmurs of agreement. "Frankly, Jim, that's about the best we're going to get from them this year."

Upstairs, Magda fell into a thick and dreamless sleep. She slept nearly until the next afternoon, and awoke groggy, at which point it seemed silly to get back on the road. She might have missed checkout entirely were it not for the woman knocking hesitatingly on the door, who offered room service in a delicate, lilting voice. Magda let her in to empty the waste-basket before calling the front desk to request another night's stay, and then getting back into bed. When she woke up, the light was thinning. Dinnertime.

The hotel was close enough to the city center so she could walk there, and the sidewalks became steadily more congested. Yet it felt like moving from a suburb very quickly into a city, albeit one with a different breath than New York. Whereas Manhattan felt tight-lipped, frantic, Nashville seemed to be in a perpetual state of exhale. A man in a cowboy hat was kissing a girl pressed against a lamppost; beside them were two plastic cups of beer. On the opposite corner, a drunk man offered free hugs. "Get 'em while they're hot," he shouted as someone tried to wrestle the bullhorn from his hands.

The streets became more crowded, people talking loudly about their plans for the evening. Magda walked by lampposts plastered with signs for a band that would be in town just the one night, a band whose name she remembered from a conversation with Bill. He had seen them at an event he and his wife attended, the one welcoming summer interns to the company. The lead singer had long, stringy blond hair, the drummer's arms lined with tattoos. She touched her own, the skin still angry and reddened.

She and Sara had talked about Nashville, during that miserable February when both of them were wrecked by a flu. Fred, traveling for work, had been the one to pose the idea: Why doesn't Magda stay with you? For days, the two of them had lain sprawled on the couch, the dim noise of the television rising over their conversation and snoring. Glasses of water cooled on the surrounding tables, a mess of tissues balled on the floor.

"Pneumonia can kill you, did you know that?" Sara said. Her voice was throaty, congested. "Geriatrics, I mean."

Magda groaned. "We're in our fifties."

"I would kill to be young again. *Sexy.*" Sara began coughing, a thick, phlegmy sound. Reached to the side table for a bottle and swigged directly from it. "Want?"

Magda swallowed deeply, the syrup cherry-flavored and heavy. "Once we're better, we'll get a time machine. How's that?"

Sara cleared her throat. "Or we can try for osmosis. Try some trendy city—Seattle or Nashville, maybe. I keep trying to convince Freddy to go—no luck."

Magda settled back, eyes clouding over as she resumed her position. The apartment was warm, her breathing slow and regular. Sara, supine, feebly raised her arms. "Get over here—let's nap."

Magda crawled over, and her friend pulled a heathered blanket over them. It smelled of lavender, whiskey. Magda let her head loll against Sara's shoulder. With the rise and fall of Sara's breath, Magda heard the sounds inside of her: a slow rush of blood and oxygen, the gurgling of her stomach. This entire universe, she marveled, inside of one person. When Sara began snoring, Magda felt the vibrations in her own chest.

Their fevers broke the next day. Magda's first, Sara waking to find her removing the snot-laced tissues from their posts, scrubbing a purpled scrim of cough syrup from the table. Sara's voice was still dry and low as she said, "We'll have these as a memory of the worst flu ever."

Magda laughed, the lightness in her chest a relief. "We won't want to remember this," she retorted. One of them—she couldn't remember which—stumbled into the kitchen to brew tea. Later, they would watch a movie.

That, at least, had proven a happy conclusion. But Nashville? Why would Sara have wanted to return there? That letter had been deceptively cheery, Magda turning the page under the assumption that, surely, Sara had forgotten to attach the rest. That intense, loud enthusiasm—no, that wasn't Sara. But she couldn't know. The spectrum of possibilities had collapsed in on itself: neither of them young, only one of them still alive. It was this dissonance, and the lack of understanding, that made Magda so uncomfortable; she couldn't understand what Sara had meant. What she had wanted. Why she was seventy, alone, and currently at a restaurant with Sara nested between her wallet and loose receipts, her pill bottles. She couldn't shake the feeling that they had not known each other as well as she'd thought, if Sara thought she would go to Ohio, if she would have insisted they come here, to Tennessee. To look around the restaurant in Nashville felt an exercise in futility, observations gleaned for no purpose. There was no one here to appreciate them.

Magda wanted, badly, to transmit such moments to Sara. She would send her the posters, the young waiter's triumphant uncorking of the wine bottle, the couple arguing at the adjacent table over something silly (it was always, it seemed, something silly). She would send her the stripe of dusty pink sunset; from the main stretch, sounds of exclamation over the night ahead. She would send the cowboy hats and the tall boots, that *tick* of stilettos upon pavement, the fleeting scent of someone's perfume, or a truly excellent laugh. She would send the rumpled white sheets of the hotel bed, and the way, earlier, light had beamed through the curtains to cast shimmering lines in the places where she had dreamed.

Together they would look at the group of young women tottering in their high heels, one in a short white jumpsuit with BRIDE bedazzled across the rear; they would buy those women a drink. A pitcher of something fruity; Sara would know what to choose. At some point, the bride-to-be would offer Sara her veil, but people were always offering Sara something, and Sara, mouth to her straw, would be saying, "Mags, do you remember? The story I was going to tell, do you remember?"

A story she never told: their reunion after Nashville.

Sara had called, hiccupy and gasping: Fred, another woman. Magda had told her to calm down, to come over. Sara kept repeating *Nashville*, said she was flying back that night; they would meet the next morning.

Magda was early to the café, jittery with caffeine by the time Sara arrived. As they drank their coffees—Magda on her second—Sara explained what had happened, and Magda said to leave, leave, leave. Sara went practically mute with the distress of it all. "It's *marriage*" was what she eventually said. "You wouldn't understand." She stood, and rather than see Sara walk away, Magda stormed off in the opposite direction. At the bike path, full of regret, she hurried back to the café, nearly losing her hat in the process; the table was empty, a dollar bill tucked under Sara's half-drunk cappuccino.

The whole way home, Magda had cursed herself: she could have been more sympathetic, she could have slowly brought Sara toward the realization that she ought to leave Fred, she needn't have been so assertive. Sara was still processing the indiscretion; she couldn't be expected to move on immediately; she had only just been betrayed.

On the stoop, Magda smoked a cigarette. Then another. As she stubbed the second onto the steps, Sara emerged at the end of the block. In her hand, a plastic-wrapped sheath of bodega flowers. She held the hand over her head, tentatively: an apology. When she was close enough that Magda could see her red-ringed eyes, she opened her mouth.

"I'm sorry," Sara said first, hurriedly.

"No," Magda said. "I am."

Sorry and annoyed, perhaps in equal measure. While it was true that she couldn't understand—she hadn't been married; that was indisputable—she had seen enough to understand what marriage ought to be, and that shape seemed closer to what existed between them than what pulsed between Sara and Fred.

"Stay with me for a few days," Magda offered, and Sara squeezed her hand, came upstairs. They ordered their usual scallion-dotted sesame noodles from Two Wok, ate so much that their stomachs ached. Fred called that evening, and Sara, after listening for a while, agreed to return home. She offered to help clean up, but Magda waved her off, instead stacking the greasy containers on her own.

"I can't leave him," Sara said the next day, and Magda bit her tongue. *Give her time*, that's what she thought. What she said: "We'll be fine, really, whatever you choose."

The weeks unfurled into months, Magda continuing to meet Sara for dinners and gallery openings. In between, she demurred when Hedda offered to visit, thinking that any day Sara would file for divorce. Or that Sara would simply show up at her door, bags in hand, red-eyed but resolute. At the very least, that, while meeting at some coffee shop, she would set down her cup and say, "I think I need to leave him."

None of those things transpired. Whatever they talked about, Magda found a way to steer the conversation toward Fred, surveying Sara's face for signs as she commented on his late schedule, or a recent and demanding case. Was she waiting for the golden parachute, a reissued invitation to stay at Magda's apartment? Neither seemed to be the case, Sara unaware or unbothered by these insertions, pivoting from Fred's work difficulties to pointing out a particular sculpture she thought Magda might appreciate, which didn't seem like someone preparing to leave—or even adequately punish—her husband.

A groaning, unfamiliar distance grew between them. Sara's marriage was excised cleanly from conversation; around it grew scar tissue. Sara continued to call, and Magda begged off plans when she could—work, previous engagements, she said whatever she needed to. It was easier to do that than it was to see Sara, thinking of her in that apartment with Fred—holding hands, ordering in from Two Wok, glibly watching television—as if he hadn't been with another woman. Easier to busy herself with work than to think of the ways in which she was undermining the choice Sara had made. Saying that they would be fine regardless was the first lie Magda had ever told her friend, and she resented herself for it, but, in truth, she resented Sara more for going back.

Fall set in, red leaves shivering toward the ground. From her window, Magda watched Mr. Tyson lug a leaking garbage bag from the front door, and give up halfway down the steps. He scanned the street, lit up, and Magda's phone began to ring.

"Look," Sara said. "What if we did something fun—what if we drove to Boston?" Her voice chirpy, hopeful.

"Sounds fun," Magda agreed.

That was the second lie.

Magda ordered a second glass of wine, and through the open window she watched the bachelorette party clambering into their limo. The woman with the BRIDE sash flung her arms into the air, obliviously tipping a blue drink onto the sidewalk, her own dress. She dropped the cup and looked down, began to cry as she rubbed at the stain. "Babe," one of her friends said. "Babe, it's fine, it'll come out in the wash." When that didn't help, she added, "*Babe*, he's going to love you, like, no matter what." After some coaxing, the bride stumbled into the car, and a trio of men repaired to the space they had left, one pointing at his phone and then in various directions down the street. The swarm of people made it nearly impossible to see much beyond where one stood, and Magda leaned back in her chair, watching them.

The beginning of the end: that's what Nashville had been for them. Not four years later, and Sara would be gone. Sara hadn't asked for her advice—not then—but so many times a patient would ask Magda directly what to *do*. Take the job or not. Whether or not they should marry someone, break up. Whether a splintering or togetherness would be better. It was against protocol to offer that kind of advice, and so each time Magda steered the conversation gently back toward the patient, reflecting at them the question: What was it that they wanted?

A question she had nearly posed to Sara as they sat on the stoop, Magda thumbing at the petals in her bouquet; the sobs broke her resolve to actually ask. Days later, their hazy truce formed, the letter arrived. She disassociated in session, coming back to herself as Bill talked his way around an answer. "I should quit, right?" he repeated. "Everyone is saying how bad tobacco is for you these days."

Magda had blinked, Bill sharpening into focus. "That one, yes—it's a bad habit. Better to quit."

She ran a finger along the stem of the wineglass. The bachelorette party had disappeared into the night, the group of men gone not long after. There remained a few stragglers, stumbling down the street, drunk and happy. Their faces were flushed, open, bantering as they passed the window, none of them looking in. Magda signed the check, her signature sloppy. Her hands were shaking, badly enough that, once outside, the packet of Camels tumbled to the sidewalk. Tossed loose, one cigarette rolled toward the edge of the curb, sliding over and out of view. Farther down the block, a loud whoop. Laughter.

Magda followed the sound, found herself toward the back of a long line. A man ambled in behind her, laughing into his phone. She could smell his breath: beery. "They're, like, the *best*. They saved my life, honestly."

She stayed in line, at the front slipping cash into the bouncer's hand as he pressed a ticket into Magda's. She moved to enter, and he pressed a thick hand to her arm, motioning for her bag. There was a moment of confusion; he aimed the flashlight toward Sara, turned to Magda, whose face, she was certain, had drained of blood.

"I swear to *God*," the man behind her was crowing. "These dudes saved my life, man. You've gotta hear them. Are you coming or what?"

The bouncer stamped her hand, a giant heart blooming red over her tendons.

In the photograph on the poster, all five of the bandmates looked deadly serious, though most of the posters had been blighted by weather, their corners warped by rain and sun, the bandmates' expressions shadowy.

The band was already onstage, the doors revealing a crush of people, thronging closer to the front. Only a few others seemed content to dwindle toward the back: a bald man, furtively texting, and beside her, a blond woman, fingers entwined with those of a darker-haired woman, who was singing, loudly, along with the band. The blonde sang a few words here and there, more often turning toward the brunette, a dreamy expression blooming as she watched the brunette dance—a moment that, to Magda, felt achingly private, the desire so apparent she felt embarrassed for the blonde, who pushed a strand of hair behind the brunette's ear. The brunette's focus shifted then, and she leaned in, kissed the blonde, palm lingering soft against her cheek.

"They're a good band," Bill had told Magda. "But I can't really listen to them anymore."

Bill had been the one to introduce the band at the company party, afterward cutting his gaze along the audience: tipsy, excitable interns mingled with his colleagues, their ties loosened, cups sweating in hand. His wife was somewhere out there, nursing her second glass of wine; there had been one earlier at dinner, drained shakily after he said it wasn't time, yet, for them to have a baby. Ernesto was waiting for Bill offstage, his tie undone, mouth stained red at the corners. It was there, nestled in those black curtains, that he let Ernesto run a hand down his pants. Somewhere out there, Bill knew, his wife was dancing. Oblivious. Bill pulled Ernesto farther back, the curtains shuddering closed around them—concealed, he thought. Totally alone. Ernesto's fingers snaked down the zipper, the other hand pressed over Bill's mouth. The rumbling of the bass shook Ernesto's hand while he gripped Bill, both of them trembling. The singer called out, "I fucking love you, New York," and as Bill opened his own mouth he came abruptly, hot in Ernesto's palm.

Bill had gone quiet, rubbing at the same worn spot on his pants, just above the knee. He looked at Magda then, who asked: "What happened next?"

Scanning the wall behind her, he only sighed. "I went to look for my wife."

The beginning of the next song, and the blonde tapped one foot distractedly, offbeat. The *tsk* of drums and a thready bass line were a slow incantation as the singer said, "What, y'all want another one?"

The blonde twined her fingers with the brunette's, and from Magda's throat came a strangled sort of noise. She managed, as the blonde looked over, to turn it into a cough, smile apologetically. The blonde handed her a water bottle, saying, "Oh, I don't even need this," though Magda had seen her drinking from it not moments before.

The brunette's eyes remained fixed on the stage, wiggling in place as the singer crooned the final notes. He opened his water bottle and tipped it over his head, shaking his head so water beaded out and into the crowd;

they cheered, the brunette loudly with her high voice. Whooping, hands above her head, before she turned to the blonde. Said, "God, I'm so glad you're here. Don't you just love them?"

The blonde smiled toward her, eyes soft and damp-looking. "Oh, totally, yeah. I'm *obsessed*."

29.

October 2008

Dear M,

I lied in the last letter, I lied on our phone call. And I'm writing because what I said—it wasn't true, and I don't lie to you. Tomorrow, we'll see each other, and I'll tell you the truth, or as much of it as I can figure out how to tell you. And the rest you'll find out, I suppose, whenever this letter arrives.

Remember how Fred said he could take the weekend away? It wasn't true, about his being free. He seemed distracted, but we had a nice night out, and the next morning he went down to the hotel conference room, called up and said he only needed a few hours. But four hours later he wasn't back.

I went down there around lunchtime—crept in, really, thinking I'd surprise him—and he was speaking very quietly into his phone, nothing I could hear until I was right behind him and he said, "I'll see you on Saturday, okay?" Which isn't a suspicious thing on its own, but if you'd heard the tone—oh, it sent chills down my spine, M. Because who would whisper when they are alone?

Apparently it's been going on for months and she's—well, it doesn't matter who she is. I cut him off before he could say much more. I have a vision of this young (very young) and blond (very blond) woman, who doesn't believe in colors or art. A banker, an accountant, the very inverse of me. Or worse—and this part I can't bring myself to think of— worse yet, maybe she's someone he knows from work. A divorce lawyer, the kind of woman who hoists a glass and toasts, "To the dissolution of joint assets."

Like I said, it doesn't matter who she is, it doesn't. What matters, I suppose, is what Fred did. Who I'm finding him to be: the opposite of what I thought. The safe choice. I thought it walking down the aisle, yesterday morning as he made coffee. This, I thought, certain every time, this is a safe person.

You don't think of these things happening to you. But then they do! They happen with the person who sleeps on the opposite side of the bed, and you think, like I am doing now—him? That's who this woman chose? The man who has never once remembered to put the cap back on the toothpaste, who consistently forgets to pick up milk? You wind up despising this person you should be sleeping next to, because in the end you can't hate the other woman. Her mistake was only in making the same choice as you.

I thought tonight I wouldn't be as angry, but I was, still trembling with it as I left the hotel and went walking. Down the main stretch, all neon lights and restaurants with the windows flung open to the street. Every place packed with people, all of whom seemed tremendously young. I hated myself for noticing that. But I also thought, this is it, isn't it, if he leaves: old and alone, too late to make a change.

And then I thought, well, maybe I chose wrong. The evidence seems to boil up: the fact that I abhor his parents, that we don't laugh at the same jokes in movies, that he and I can pass an entire day without talking, that he thinks there's nothing wrong with that. I thought, fine, that's why he went after someone else, because I know Fred too well to like him anymore. Except that argument against myself splintered, because I've known you nearly as long and never liked you any less.

Do you know what else he said tonight, as I was leaving? That he had been meaning to end it. The same thing he's said about the toothpaste, the milk—that he's been meaning to get around to it—is now something he says to his wife, about another woman.

Yours,

S

30.

THE MARSHLAND BEAT THICK DRUMS OF HEAT AROUND THE CAR, the finicky air-conditioning no match for the muggy air. Boomer had installed it himself, with Theo's help, and the thing glugged before spitting out a few beats of cold, and then, from what Magda could tell, doing exactly nothing. She kept Sara wrapped in a sweater, for fear that otherwise the metal would become too hot to touch. With the windows down, the heat rolled in—a dense humidity that precluded hunger. There was only a light and persistent craving for cold: the crunch of ice cubes, or milkshakes that needed to be drunk in just a few sips. Since the concert, a thirst had overpowered her; Magda had flashes of lemonade, the sort that emerged from powder and was served in paper cups at soccer games. Lemonade and iced tea.

The stops along the way offered some relief. Though not all that long of a distance, it had taken her nearly three days to reach Louisiana from Nashville. A wall had been hit; she would drive two hours and find herself exhausted, the remembering of nonsense fights with Hedda and Sara a reliable itch, her thoughts in a current of what she might instead have said, done better. So: two nights of deep sleep in hotel beds, three stops at diners, where the people-watching was reliably better than the food, and the water held the particular taste of plastic. If Theo had been there, he would have commented on the material of those glasses, wondered aloud whether some particulate matter or bacteria had seeped into the water itself. *You see?* he would have said, dinging a thumb on the base of some plastic cup. *Botulism, no question.* Magda didn't mind, though, felt ravenous to overhear snippets of a dishwasher's life, or to get the waitress's opinion on why, really, the meat loaf was *the* special of the day. Easier to focus there than to return to whorled thoughts about her sister, about Sara, to think again of Lucy.

The air grew hotter and hotter as she moved through Alabama. Gas stations dotted along the highway, long-limbed boys with twangy voices who insisted upon pumping her gas as they asked after her trip. Where was she coming from? Where was she headed? Everything became more pronounced, be it laughter or sweat. Around her, everything lush and green and growing. So hot that even the sunglasses kept slipping from the bridge of her nose.

She called Theo and Boomer, but found she had little to say. They were fine, the men promised, they missed her; her patients were fine, they missed her; New York in the summer smelled of wreckage and potential; the city missed her. "It smells so bad this year I feel like I need to justify the choice to live here, if that makes sense. I've been mostly with my mother, out east," Boomer said. "Gorgeous by the water right now."

"No," Theo said. "We haven't heard from the patients, that's why we're saying they're fine. That's *good*." He chuckled. "Fred called to check in, from Venice."

"Everyone's fine?" Magda asked. She wondered whether Sharon was pregnant, or if Bill had decided to go through with the divorce. If people could simply stay unhappy in marriages, just carry on indefinitely. Theo said nothing, until she said, "Wait, he's in Venice?" and Theo added, "Some sort of vacation, with, uh—"

"Gloria," Magda said. She rolled her eyes. "Of course."

"Not that it makes it any better," Theo said. "But he called collect."

The last time Magda had gone to Louisiana, she had not technically been in Louisiana at all. It was Sara and Fred's honeymoon, the letters arriving with such regularity Magda could easily imagine that she, too, was walking the French Quarter. The letters themselves were loosely written, a drunken scrawl describing the sights, though every so often Sara broached more serious topics—how Magda was faring during her extended absence, mentions of the gallery show she was only too happy to be missing. The featured artist, Janet Yengelman, had for months thrown fits about what she perceived as Sara's lack of enthusiasm for her work. Sara, she claimed, did not *understand*. The lowest blow to a gallerist, that she or he was too dense to understand the art.

Explaining to Magda over dinner, days before the wedding, Sara had conjured images of canvas beat heavy with household essentials. Window cleaner, dishwashing solution, soap, salt, olive oil, vinegar, whiskey. Swirled and literally punched into the fabric. It was meant to be a rebellion against femininity, only, Sara said, the colors merged in such a way as to just become brown, and the whole of the exhibition reeked, worse by the day. She had said something of that effect to Janet, whose entire being seemed to swell with anger, and whose agent began to call the gallery under the guise of checking in. None of the coverage secured was enough, was *right*. They'd bought Clorox for the weekend show? *Clorox?* Janet's agent sighed at Sara. Obviously, that was the wrong call. It wasn't like Sara could fire Janet, though; the artist had become far too profitable to the gallery, enough so that she had returned the five massive bottles of Clorox herself, replaced them.

Promise me you'll go, Sara wrote from her honeymoon, and so Magda did. When the show was panned by the *New York Times*, and then later the *Post*, and then by most other outlets, Magda clipped the reviews for Sara and delivered them in unmarked envelopes to her doorman. *I must also admit I did not understand*, she wrote on the clippings.

Toward the end of the trip, on the cusp of Sara's return, they spoke on the phone. Sara, calling from the hotel room, was happy to come home, of course, but nostalgic as well. She hadn't expected to miss Louisiana, and wasn't it odd that she hadn't, not until she was there again. "I'm whispering," she explained, "because Fred is asleep. A few beers after lunch, and one of those drinks with the twirly straws. All rum, I think." They were meant to see a jazz performance that evening, but Sara wasn't sure he'd be awake in time—but had Magda made it to the show? Was it horrible? "From the silence, I can tell it was," she said. "Serves Janet right, that feckless snob." Both of them, in laughing together, felt another lift: they would soon be reunited.

"How happy are you?" Magda asked, and there was a pause.

"Oh, I don't know," Sara said after a while. "About as much as I'd expected to be, I think."

Magda's first time in the South was less romantic, overhung with the stale smell of the car, of her own skin. It being summertime, and being wholly without relief from the heat, she gave in to the discomfort. First a night at a motel just outside of Tuscaloosa, where the pool water was tepid and stippled with candy bar wrappers, the parking lot a sea of empty soda bottles and prophylactics slick and flattened by rain. Inside, a sense of an outer layer that needed to be shed, the decor several decades old and wizened, shrugging itself off the walls. Though the signage touted air-conditioning, the teenager at the front desk cringed in saying it was out. Had been for *weeks*. Well, not so much out as they didn't have it just yet, though they would soon. The vendor had been busy; the units hadn't arrived. He slowed his speech, realizing that perhaps these were things he ought not to say.

A shower proved paramount, though the relief was fleeting. Even as the droplets pelted at her, Magda felt herself overheating, resolving to find a better hotel for the next stay. After she dried off, she went to the lobby to use the hotel's computer, dangling her fingers over the sticky keyboard before giving in to the grime, pounding away in search of her next destination.

It took time to scroll through the listings, decide on a place, but even with a computer screen she had to squint, and also, she didn't trust the smarmy front desk attendants to quote her an accurate rate. Too easy to take advantage of geriatrics. They could quote her a price higher than the usual nightly one, skimming from the top before carrying her luggage upstairs, and hanging like wraiths from the doorframe before she remembered to search her pocket for a few rumpled bills. "All bargaining, really," said Bill, who traveled regularly, who had been the one to tell Magda that calling hotels and being able to reference their competitors' online discounts simplified the whole endeavor. By doing so, he and Ernesto had stayed all over the tristate area. He had called her once, voice hushed, from a bed-and-breakfast in Montclair, after narrowly avoiding a run-in with one of his wife's friends. "Idiotic to go to New Jersey," he whispered into the voicemail. "I can't believe how stupid I've been, but that's what people do for love, I guess." He startled. "Oh God, don't bring that up in the next session. I didn't mean it."

In the actual lobby of the hotel, the man behind Magda tapped his foot, sighing. A dour-faced man with a ruddy complexion and suit straining against its buttons. When Magda toggled between browser windows, he let out an impatient sigh. She could hear him, at the front desk, inquiring about another computer. Well, there was nothing he could do if some old lady was hogging the only available one, was there? How was that his fault if she didn't know how to type? The front desk attendant apologized; they were going to get another computer down the line—she would definitely bring it up to her manager. The businessman, scowling, instructed the attendant to call his room once the old lady was done, and to absolutely not let anybody else on, did y'all understand? "It's a real fucking problem, you know. You're lucky that this is the day my laptop broke, because if I *needed* to be online right now, if I wasn't just checking email, well, Christ, I wouldn't be so nice right now. You call room 105 as soon as she's done, you got it?" He said it again, slowly, from the doorway. "What, you need me to write it down?"

Magda, having found three possible hotels, waited until the man left to close out of the browser window. Six minutes left in the session. Theo had been the one to explain how computers held a record of what was searched; anything sensitive, you wouldn't want that tied to your own machine. Magda, with two fingers, typed into the search engine: *what happens to ashes in heat.*

One of the first results was a blog called DEATH FORUM. In queueing up the page, spectral mist curled upward from the bottom of the screen and along the margins. *Welcome,* swirled the mist, before dissipating.

ARE YOU LOOKING FOR A LOVED ONE? DO YOU WANT TO MAKE CONNECTIONS TO ANOTHER REALM? ARE YOUR "LIVING" LOVED ONES UNWILLING TO TALK ABOUT DEATH? LEARN HOW TO BE THE CONNECTION BETWEEN "THIS WORLD" AND THE "NEXT REALM."

where are the ashes now?! one post asked. The blogger supposed that, until submerged in water or fire, or otherwise dispersed, ashes held on to consciousness. *Think of it this way,* they wrote. *All of the ashes together, that's the whole of the person. Their entirety. Once even a fleck has disappeared, part of the person is gone, and it's impossible to say what, exactly, has disappeared. Right brain? Pinky toe? Who knows. You're not going to see spooky happenings with a half-full jar of ashes, not a chance. Who KNOWS what's left then. Me, I had big-time issues when my mom died—pictures falling out of their frames, light flickering out, freaky things. As soon as the cat tipped over the urn, it was fine; we just mopped up the spill, put the thing back on the mantel. The whole house relaxed.* Anyway, the post concluded, *figured I'd post in case someone else is dealing with the same kinda thing. My advice: if it gets weird, get a cat. Or flush a spoonful of the ashes.*

thanx, commented 917hotrod. *u can't believe how long we thot it was just us! Haahah*

Honestly, chimed in shoegirl821. *We thought we were the only ones dealing with a haunting. This totally explains it, thanks.*

ur fuckin kidding, rite? wrote realdennisjohnson. *you want a nice CAT to swallow the ashes? grow the fuck up!!*

Four minutes left. What else was there on the internet? She thought of the man complaining out front, how he hadn't even lowered his voice upon insulting her. She thought of internet viruses she'd heard lurked on sketchy sites, remembered Bill's sheepish confession of late-night pornography.

Upon further prodding, Theo had said that the internet did have a memory. "Whatever you type in, lives on. That's why you've got to be careful about what you search for, and where, but also what you click on."

When Magda keyed *pornography* into the search, thousands of pages populated. *Brunette gang bang! Multiracial facial! Uh-oh, sucked off in a cab— CLICK HERE to see more. Hot lesbian action, XXX! Sexy virgin plays with stepdad. Hot slutty redheads, NICE!!!*

With two minutes left to go, Magda clicked on thirty-seven of the links and slid the chair back. By the time she walked away, the pages were already reproducing, becoming *viruses.* By the time Magda let the front desk attendant know the computer was available, the atrium echoed with sighs and moans. "I don't know what I did," she said over the counter, the corners of the girl's mouth turning upward. "Perhaps," Magda suggested, "that nice businessman can help out?"

The girl's eyebrows rose, a smile creeping across her face.

Magda, entering her room, heard a shout.

It was already too hot again, and during her second shower Magda reminded herself of what needed to be done before leaving. She would call the next hotel; she would remove Sara from the mini-fridge; she reminded herself of this no fewer than three times, and also of the fact that, according to the blog, there would be no damage to ashes for being cold. *they're already dead tho lol,* wrote hector87. Which was all well and good, but when Magda emerged from the bathroom she had half convinced herself that Sara was already in her suitcase, she was already out the door.

A story she tried to forget:

On the day Sara returned from her honeymoon, Magda left the office early. From the usual grocery store she ferried home wine and a crinkly bag of underripe cherries. Though Magda preferred her cherries fit to burst, Sara liked them on the cusp of ripeness. If she left them to sun by the window, she rationalized, her half would be tender enough to eat by dusk.

By four, when Sara had not called, Magda called the airline. Half an hour of a droning busy signal and she hung up, tried Sara's doorman. He, too, did not answer, leaving her to wonder if the rest of New York had undergone some cataclysmic event—a silent bomb, an unexpected alien arrival. In looking out the window, though, the city looked the same. The old lady in the brownstone across the way was drinking and folding towels in her laundry room. The second driver in each lane still leaned upon his horn as the traffic light began blinking green.

Again Magda called the airline, and when an attendant finally answered, he confirmed the flight had arrived without issue. He seemed embarrassed upon saying no, he couldn't confirm a customer's attendance. "It's against policy," he said softly, after she asked for the second time. When Magda called Sara's home phone, there was no response. It could have been, she thought, that there was an issue during the taxi ride back to the building. Her television offered no news of sensational crashes, though, only a fire somewhere in the East Village. A gas leak, five casualties.

By nightfall, Magda had tried Sara's phone three times, to no avail. Only with that final call did she leave a message: it was her, she hoped they had made it home all right, would Sara be so kind as to give her a call?

Nothing in the morning, and Magda went to the office with a pit in her stomach. All through the sessions she listened for the communal phone;

when the police officer identified the bodies, she would be the first call after Fred's family, assuming that he, too, had died. The line stayed quiet, only once trilling, and though she all but ran out of her session, the call was for Boomer. A new patient of his—*Highly anxious*, he mouthed, motioning Magda back to her office.

"I'm sorry," she said to her patient, whose eyebrows were raised.

"It's fine," the man had said. "It's just that right now, everything is an emergency." He slitted his eyes at her, then continued on.

Not until that evening did Sara call. "You wouldn't believe it," Sara said, "but I fell asleep yesterday afternoon, and I've only just woken up. I know," she went on. "I can't believe it, either. And the messages—*oh*. Janet Yengelman called four times, and I somehow slept through it all.

"I hope you weren't worried," Sara said. Then, with a laugh, "I'm sure you have more important things to worry about, anyhow."

Of course, Magda allowed, of course—they'd see each other soon enough, and no, she hadn't been worried.

Placing the phone in its cradle, Magda had found herself ravenous. Bent over the kitchen sink, she ate all of the cherries, spitting the fleshy pits one by one into the drain. She assumed the cherries were ripe, but moments after eating them, she had already forgotten the taste.

31

MAGDA HAD ARRIVED IN NEW YORK AT THE OUTSET OF THE ANTI-psychiatry movement. Revolts against conformity and authority were gaining steam, and to be part of the medical establishment—or of any establishment, really—garnered a vague distrust from the public. Magda schlepped her textbooks to diners, eventually shrouding the covers with a newspaper so as not to reveal herself as part of the institutional problem. It was not all bad, though, and often intensely exciting to be—at that moment—studying the brain. Skinnerian conditioning offered the counterargument that perhaps behavior was shaped primarily by environment; it was behavior, he posited, that required control. Antipsychotics like chlorpromazine had proven to be a boon. Electroconvulsive therapy had been popularized as treatment for myriad issues—severe depression, of course, but also homosexuality. A professor, during a first-year lecture, espoused the benefits of such therapy while touching lightly upon the risks. He passed a stack of glossy photos among the students, Magda's stomach dropping at a shot of two men, hand in hand, being tugged into Bellevue.

Memory loss, hummed the dissidents. That was an underdiscussed side effect to repeated electroshocks.

The professor reminded students that, for all the complaining, many people regained their memory. Only in rare occasions were such lapses permanent. Loss tended to be short-term.

Magda thought often of Skinner in those days and the years to follow. To understand a behavior was to prevent it. To learn enough about oneself to be able to withhold harm, shame—it seemed nothing short of a miracle.

Talk therapy was the radical advancement. Magda, in approaching New Orleans, worried after the patients who wouldn't feel comfortable calling Theo or Boomer unless something was so wrong that there wasn't any

other recourse. Unless, say, the floor had shattered, they were wholly un-
moored, they were in emergency brain surgery or been institutionalized.
Bill wouldn't file the divorce papers without her; Gwen's anxiety would
continue to drive a wedge between her and her husband. A sheen of anger
rose like nausea, Magda thinking of Fred lolling about on a gondola. She
imagined him pitching forward into the canal, Gloria toppling overboard
in her attempts to rescue him. Magda's breathing slowed.

It wasn't a real job, living in other people's minds. That's what her
mother had said, as the final stragglers got onto the bus. Hedda and her
father were walking back toward the truck they had borrowed to bring
Magda to Cleveland, and her mother stood there, looking at Magda, until
the driver honked. She moved forward, as if to touch Magda, and seemed
to lose her nerve. *"Säkra resor."* Magda was only a few miles closer to college when she decided she wouldn't return for Christmas. She'd go to
medical school, and she'd be gone for good.

Magda's chest ached, and she peeled onto the side of the road. A van
screeched past her, honking, as she waited for her vision to go back into
focus. Not just Fred, but Sara—she was angry at Sara. Magda hadn't refused
Sara's invitations to travel because Sara wouldn't drive on highways, or because she could barely read maps. She had refused, ultimately, because to
go anywhere with Sara only made her think of Boston—oh, but she would
have to think of that eventually.

A story that neither of them ever told:

How Sara, in the shaky aftermath of the indiscretion, had decided to
surprise Fred with a puppy. "Come with me," she pleaded, and Magda reluctantly agreed. She was waiting, still, for Sara to admit her own unhap-
piness. It was late summer, humidity glove-like around them, the city so
swollen with heat that irritability rose to its surface like sweat. In retrieving
the car from the garage, they saw two fistfights. Magda accelerated through
a yellow light to avoid the howling, the bloodied noses. They discovered too
late that the car's cooling system was broken. "This was a mistake," Sara
said, pushing the hair from her forehead, and Magda agreed, without being
sure to what, exactly, Sara was referring.

In the days leading up to the trip, Sara had called each morning with
weather updates. "Brisk," she said on Monday. "It should be fine." Progressively more grim as the days dragged on, and upon getting into the car,

she said, "We shouldn't have planned for a windy day," though, really, there was no way to have known, and it wasn't windy in New York, not at all.

After sweating through an hour of traffic in the city, they had found themselves surly and overcaffeinated, bickering most of the way to Boston. As had been the case since the affair was revealed, they were less likely to speak of anything with real substance. Lipless conversations with no teeth. Toward the end of the drive, Sara began complaining about Fred, for having once again forgotten to empty the dishwasher, but whenever Magda chimed in, Sara grew more angry—and at her. "You're avoiding the issue," Magda said.

"I'm avoiding it? God, you're so smug," Sara said, to which Magda replied, "Don't tell me about this if you don't want my advice." She drummed her fingers against the wheel.

"Of *course* I want your advice," Sara said. "It's the condescension I don't need."

It was the opposite, really, of what Magda had been trying to do. "Look," she said. "If we're going to argue, maybe it's best we don't talk about this right now."

Sara, looking out the window, didn't reply. She examined her nails, adjusted the volume on the radio, smoothed the legs of her pants. Hours dredged by, the arrival at the hotel a relief. Parked in the garage, Magda thought, *Finally, it's over.* Which wasn't the case, because when Sara called the woman with the puppies she said she wasn't going to be home at the agreed-upon hour—could they come by around dinnertime instead? Magda then had to call the restaurant and cancel their dinner reservation, Sara flipping through the newspaper to figure out what they might do in the meantime. She had planned her day around the dog, and where they might take him, and, as was typical, had not accounted for disruptive variables. "Are dogs even allowed in the hotel?" Magda said at one point, to which Sara's eyes widened. Another thing she'd not considered.

Having another place to which they could direct their annoyance was helpful, at least, Sara suggesting they might take an afternoon walk along the Charles. The humidity had broken, a cool breeze wrapping around them as Sara encouraged Magda to tell her about work. "I've barely seen you," she said, as if that weren't her own impetus.

Magda spoke about a patient she'd met with recently, who was professionally accomplished and yet mired with anxiety about decisions outside of work. She had a sense of ambivalence toward children and marriage, wobbling between wanting and avoidance as her boyfriend urged her toward both. He was more than happy to offer her those things, the patient kept saying, and yet that offering felt akin to pressure.

"Tell her not to" was what Sara said. "Doesn't have to be a crossroads."

"I can't tell patients what to do," Magda reminded. "That's not how it works."

"But that's what people want; that's the whole point of them showing up to begin with. How is she going to figure it out, if she hasn't already? She wants you to tell her."

"I can't."

"Well," Sara scoffed. "You *should*. It's not fair to him."

Sara's jaw was set tight, Magda's face tensing in response. "Relationships aren't often fair."

"No, but they should be."

"But they're not. You know this."

Sara frowned. "So you think she should just, what? Carry on and pretend like she's happy?"

Magda felt the pinpricks of a headache coming on. She was tired, overheated, and didn't mean to, but said, "Isn't that exactly what you're doing, with Fred?"

For a moment, she thought Sara hadn't heard; the silence bloomed between them, the first time in weeks Magda had said his name.

A belt of laughter burst out, then another; a group of runners swerved past, red-cheeked and panting.

Sara's eyes narrowed, her mouth a slit. "If you're so bent on analysis, you should just say what you think. It's cowardly not to. What would you say, if I were your patient? What would you tell me to do?"

Magda acutely felt the heat below her arms, the skin of her face smarting against the wind. *First, do no harm.* "I would—oh, I don't know ..." She trailed off.

"Come on," Sara taunted. "What would you say?"

"I'd say leave him, I guess, marry someone else. Marry me."

She hadn't meant to say the last part, wasn't sure she had until she saw Sara's expression: eyes wide, mouth ajar. Sara eventually saying, "My psychiatrist? I can't imagine that's ethically sound," and Magda quickly replied, "Right, of course, not me, but someone else. I'd tell you to marry someone who really loved you, who wouldn't . . ."

She gestured vaguely, and Sara turned to face the water. "Right," she said.

Magda, flushed, worried that Sara might find cause to be annoyed with her. But her friend said nothing of the sort, and the silence was not resentful or unkind. It felt that they had reached some sort of conclusion, though what that was, Magda couldn't quite discern. By the time they returned to the hotel, it was nearly time to pick up the dog, and so they brought the car out from the garage, drove as the traffic grew sticky and relentless. They talked about other things: weather, minor annoyances at work. The constrictions in Magda's chest grew less intense; she imagined an electrical current flooding her brain, and Sara's, wiping clean that afternoon's conversation.

When they reached the house, the woman brought the puppy to the car, passed him to Sara through the window. Thick drum of a stomach, his arms and legs so spindly it looked as if they had been affixed as an afterthought. "Yeah," the woman said fondly, looking at him. "That's Ringo." To their blank stares: "The Beatles litter? This one is Ringo."

Dirt kicking up behind them, house fading in the rearview. "He's obviously not a Ringo."

"No, decidedly not. Harry? Spot? What do people even name their dogs?"

"He's so serious-looking, like a person. A poet, maybe. Or, do you remember Eugene O'Neill? The playwright?"

"My mother liked him, I think," said Magda. A car cut around them, and she honked. The dog startled, growling meekly before burrowing back into Sara's lap.

Sara nodded. "Brave boy, there you go. Well, he wrote mostly dramas. Serious, serious, serious. Sad plays, and then there was this one—what was it called, ah . . . *Ah, Wilderness!* That was his one comedy."

The dog began to pee on her leg.

"Eugene," Magda said. "It's very nice to meet you."

Sara cracked the window, groaned very softly.

The next plan to be foiled was that of dinner. Upon arriving to the restaurant, the maître d' had scoffed at Eugene in his drool-soaked carrier, let Sara know that there were no animals allowed. No exceptions. Magda felt prickles of annoyance at Sara's lack of foresight, but it seemed a useless argument; she suggested instead that they order in-room service and wine.

Eugene's teeth were fine needles upon their suitcases, shoes. Sara blocked Magda from the bellboy's vision when he arrived with their food, as Magda was mopping up a small pool of Eugene's urine, from which he could not be discouraged. As Sara unpacked the food, Magda held him under the shower spigot. He yowled at her, baring his tiny teeth, even though the water was hardly lukewarm. They turned on the news, and by the first commercial he was asleep, small pink tongue flopping out of his mouth, only waking at the end of the hour. By then Sara, too, had drifted off, and so Magda took him outside, where he stood, shaking, impossible to coax into peeing. Not on the trees, the pavement, nothing until they were in the lobby again, and then came gold puddling along the carpet. The doorman grimaced, said it was fine, he could handle it. Upstairs, Eugene whined until Sara awoke, rubbing the grit from her eyes.

"Should we open a bottle?"

"Why not," Magda said.

They drained the first and opened a second. The overhead light blinked hotly against Magda's vision, the bottle of wine tilting forward in Sara's hand, as she refilled Magda's glass. On the bed, Eugene gnawed at the corner of a pillow. "It's the principle of it," Sara said, teeth purpled and bruiselike. "'Til death do us part.' I'd been so sure with him, about our life. But now I think"— and at this she paused, drank deeply from her glass—"I think that it wasn't so much that we saw each other so much as we convinced ourselves that the other person was the person we thought they were. So we deferred ourselves from the, from that feeling, of *being* ourselves. Deferred. That's a good word, right? *Deferred*."

"That's not so uncommon," Magda said. Her tongue felt heavy, brackish, her head aching. The hangover was imminent, but she was too drunk to reckon with how she might prevent it. "To romanticize a person's potential, that's not so uncommon." She took another sip.

Sara shook her head. "No, not that. It's that he didn't—well, you know I always wanted to be a mother?" When Magda said nothing, she continued on. "My whole life, I wanted a baby. But what I never told you, is that Fred said yes, and then he said let's wait until he's made partner, and let's wait until he's been partner for a few years, and then is it the right time, and then it had been five years and then ten years. Then we were in our forties and it felt too late, and by our fifties it actually was."

"But you said—"

"I didn't care about travel, Mags. That, the work, it was all *fine*, but it wasn't a child. I saw them everywhere, out on the street, at restaurants, in someone else's arms. Can you imagine? Seeing the thing you want and knowing you'll never have it?"

Magda looked at her friend. "I can."

Sara reached again for the wine to top off her already-full glass. "I've spent my whole life longing for something I can't have, because of a choice I made. It just, every New Year's Eve, I'd get this silly twinge of hope: *It'll happen this year; we'll figure it out.*"

"Why stay?" The room was spinny, words fleeing from Magda's mouth before she realized that they had. Eugene pressed his head to her leg, dug deep with his teeth. She twisted a hand at him and he flipped onto his back, the lump of his belly rising and falling.

"Because the fact is that I chose to stick with him even as he pushed off having a baby. And I just thought, *What if he does change his mind? What will this have all been for if I just leave him now?* Because I'd made the choice, hadn't I? And I remembered how it had been, early on, before we needed things from each other. Before those resentments built up, calcified. *Calcified.* That's another good word, isn't it? And I did love him. So I assumed it would work." Her eyes were bleary.

Magda's mind turned to Bill, the careful machinations about his wife. How he loved her best from a distance, at which he could convince himself that this, here, was what he wanted. "Over time," Magda hedged, and Sara's eyes returned to focus.

"No," she said. "I pretended to be someone else. The fun wife, the happy one. And that's—that's marriage. It's about whose fault it is that we can't afford a better place, or to retire, whose fault it is that the 'someday' issues are now present-day. I acted like we had all this time, and we didn't. And then I didn't get my baby, and I didn't get the husband I wanted."

Magda regarded her friend, saw with new clarity how wan she looked, how sad. The bags under her eyes were mottled, mouth twisted downward. She looked into her glass, watching herself, and chuckled sadly.

"It's not easy," Magda said. "Longing for something."

Sara's eyes were watery, and she flung her arms around Magda's neck. She smelled sweet from the wine, her skin underneath damp and slightly sour. Sara kissed Magda's cheek. Magda wrapped her own arms around Sara's waist, felt the shuddering breaths thrum through her friend's chest.

"It was a mistake," Sara said, sitting up and pressing her back against the headboard. When she yawned, the movement gave her a soft double chin, the bottom dropping out from Magda's stomach as she watched Sara rub the grit from her eyes. Her breasts shifted as she sat up, nipples taut against the thin fabric of her dress. She surveyed the mess, mouth turned down. "You wouldn't—you're too smart to make mistakes like that."

Magda's vision clouded. She thought about Lucy, and Thanksgiving, the weight of another woman pressed snug against her, and then, in looking up, did she realize she had said this—all of it—aloud. Sara sat very still, eyes wide, and Magda, with no idea what else to do, leaned forward and kissed her.

What was it, then? Atoms vibrating in place. A meteor rocketing across the night sky. The second or third cup of coffee. A bouquet pulled from behind someone's back. It was Sara's mouth opening against hers, Magda's tongue roving against Sara's molars, it was her hand against Sara's expectant nipple, Sara's hand against her own chest, it was Magda climbing atop Sara, whose hips rose to meet hers. Then it was Sara pulling away, her words indecipherable as she wobbled toward the bathroom. Magda clambered into bed, the room rotating around her. *It was a mistake*, she remembered Sara saying, and then she fell into a thin, fitful sleep.

She woke, anxious, to find Sara sprawled atop the fainting couch. A sharp, foul smell rose to meet her: Eugene, snoring atop a yellowed stain. Magda's head ached, a knifelike pressure as she tried to sit up. Her stomach lurched with movement, and with memory—surely she hadn't? She pretended to be asleep until Sara woke, a sinking sensation in her chest when she saw Sara cull her clothing into her arms before going to the bathroom. Sara had changed in front of Magda any number of times, utterly unselfconscious; Magda had not changed in front of her, but this difference seemed significant.

They were quiet on the way to the garage, Eugene in Sara's arms gnawing against bread crust. He growled every so often, prompting Sara to touch his head; he met her fingers with teeth. As Sara waited for the car, Magda bought their coffees from a nearby bodega. She bought a banana, which was heavy and sludge-like in her mouth. She threw it away. They began the drive home, coffee bitter and sharp against Magda's tongue. At one point she said, "Sara," and her friend, either asleep or pretending to be, did not respond. "Sara?" Magda repeated, and though Sara's head turned toward her, her eyes remained resolutely shut.

In the following days, Magda thought about Sara obsessively, cataloging her litany of faults and imagining the conversations they could have, at the end of which Sara would admit it had been a mistake to return to Fred, who didn't and couldn't possibly appreciate her. Sara, appearing with her suitcase at the base of the steps. Sara, hair mussed, with a duffel bag in the waiting area. The imaginings sent happiness flickering through Magda's limbs, a gentle, slow pull of it coursing upward until she looked around the steps, into the waiting area: empty.

In Sara's later retellings, the drive to Boston would take on new forms. In one, it took seven hours. In another, eight. The woman had delayed their retrieval of Eugene by nearly a full day. The dog had had violent bouts of diarrhea on the pillows as they slept. A drunken waitress had mistakenly sloshed hot coffee upon their laps, rather than at their feet.

In none of those retellings did they argue. In none of them did Magda, bleary with wine, kiss Sara. Even if she had, in no retelling would Sara have kissed Magda back.

32.

November 1997

Dear M,

Mary Magdalene! I think is what I said, upon meeting you. You looked puzzled, and so I tried to explain: The Sea of Galilee? You started to back away. Magdala, I tried again, and you shook your head. Magda, you repeated, emphasizing it—mag-DAA!—surely thinking I was drunk, and I said no, it was an old fishing town. The Bible? I said as a question, and then you nodded. Oh, you said, okay.

For a while, you know, she was considered a prostitute, and then the currents turned. I don't remember why, honestly, Sunday school so far behind me, but that's all that matters: that people changed their minds. A savior, they decided—a saint!

There's a point to this rambling, I promise.

I write this because the apostles and Mary Magdalene were what my mother spoke of in her last days. Even before that, the nurse says she was fixed on religion, insisted on going to Mass, though she hadn't been for some time, not since she had gotten sick. She kept trying to go back to the old church, the one in New Orleans, but couldn't quite remember how to drive.

The house is utter chaos. Dishes brimming the sink. A closet full of clothing, tags still on, one pair of underwear and a few plastic bags in the hamper. She always wore the same outfit, the neighbor said, and I find myself wondering if she changed out of those overalls, or if she simply fell asleep in them each night. Did she make herself tea? Did she remember to brush her teeth?

It feels disloyal, maybe, to share these details, but I can't stop thinking about them. I can't. Because I should have been here sooner. A form of penance, maybe. The nurse said she kept talking about the apostles, focusing on Paul, who was originally a Jew named Saul. He called himself the apostle of the Gentiles. My mother, who took some issue with anything progressive—Jewish tradition, homosexuality, liberal politics. This one, this was the person my mother was fixed on—but why? And why is it only now that I feel the need to know why?

I found one of the Mary Magdalene statues in the bathtub, her nose poking out from a few murky inches of water. It is worse, I am finding, the knowledge of how my mother lived. Another one of the statues was sidelong in the oven, coated in ketchup. The spoons are in the underwear drawer; the freezer is full of socks. That clean pair of underwear, folded, at the bottom of the hamper. A stack of programs from the church, weekly up until last month. Blood clotted in the carpet from when she fell climbing into or out of bed.

Sometimes it's abrupt, is what the nurse said. The change from coping to not. Fred said he will fly down at the weekend, and I feel that he can't see me like this. Me, the house, none of it. But of course I worry, in my self-involved way, what if this happens to me as well? What if I wake up one day and think the world is fine, when I've become this other person—a shell of a person? What do we do then? I just need you to promise you'll look after me, you'll make sure Fred makes the right decisions.

Yours,

S

33.

NEW ORLEANS WAS SO HOT THAT MAGDA FELT ANY ALERTNESS slipping away, replaced by a dull complacency. If she tried focusing on anything, the pangs of guilt poked at her again: your fault. By noon, Bourbon Street was a hum of noise, and drinks slipped away as people adjusted their sunglasses. "Hot, isn't it?" she heard a man say, waving the menu at his beard. "Should we get another round?"

Noise ballooned from every corner. The whole city felt sensationally tactile, heat and noise and sights converging in such a way that Magda felt consistently aware of her whole body and overpowered by its needs, all of them urgent. Every few blocks, she found herself tucking into a bar for bottled water or a glimpse of air-conditioning. New Orleans was a city that Sara had warned wouldn't be accommodating to age; it was a place to be during the years when sleep could be replaced with caffeine, when the soft animal of one's body was the answer to every question.

Sara had also spoken of Bourbon Street as the tourists' thrum, described how during Mardi Gras the streets were so congested one couldn't move without touching someone else's arm, upsetting their drink or chain of plastic beads. In the summer, with its oppressive humidity, Magda found it easy enough to weave through the groups, but she was moving aimlessly. Perspiration beaded on her eyelids, weighing them down. She went into a gallery that smelled thickly of lavender; she went to a bar. She went to another bar, and while the bartender poured her water, she looked up to see a cross hanging above the clock.

Outside of the bar, Magda's eyes welled up. The pavement went wobbly before her. She had been fine, and then she was not. Back again: the unexpected bite of nostalgia in an otherwise ordinary situation. That feeling was familiar enough, one that had encroached upon her when Sara was alive, during a time when they were together—say, at a dinner, approaching dessert, Magda growing desperate to extend the evening. In such a way that she might, before the check arrived, suggest that they walk home together through the park, and when Sara pointed out they lived in different parts of town, Magda would say it was fine, she would just take a cab home from Sara's. Five more minutes, she would think, then she would be fine.

In front of her: a street sign teetering against the breeze. Inhale for three seconds, exhale for five. Repeat. Slowly, it began to come back to her. Edges sharpening, the world tilting into focus. By the time her breathing slowed, Magda's throat and eyes had gone scratchy.

When Sara died, there was the immediate shock, flanked by this suspended disbelief: Surely it wasn't true. A mistake, some clerical error. It couldn't be that Sara was dead when they had plans for the following weekend. That was what Magda first thought, that Sara wouldn't have died before their lunch. Sara wouldn't have died before they could talk things through. She had experienced a similar, sinking sensation upon hearing about the Twin Towers; believed ardently that someone had misspoken, that all was fine. She remembered the previous fall, when Bill found out that one of his summer interns had died, the seam of his sleeve pinned between his fingers as he told her the news. "It's not like I would have seen him again, probably," he said. "But I liked knowing he was out there, going to make something of his life." He, too, had plans: an MBA, a wedding, all of it felled. Easy to think of the counterfactuals. Had Bill done something different, had he asked the kid to stay on through the fall semester—if Bill had done that, perhaps he might still be alive.

In the after: Magda reckoned with her decisions. Each morning, fiddling with the rounded edge of her subway card, she would consider whether it was more dangerous, then, going underground than it would be to walk. Were something to go wrong, it seemed that there was a better likelihood of escape were she to stay aboveground, but that didn't account for the cars zipping by, for bikers, for everything ahead and above.

A thick, cool fog as people spoke to her, the voices coming from some far distance. She walked the same path home, ordered the regular food from their usual places. If she kept going, she thought, if she just kept going, it would be fine. So how was it that the impulse to continue kept nudging itself into her, that she kept thinking if she clenched tight enough, if she kept moving, at some point she could understand?

What she knew was that there remained grave, unchartable distances between people—what was said, and what wasn't, and, between those things, the wobbly horizon of longing. A bridge with its support rails missing.

What else she knew:

That time with the two of them along the Charles, hair skimmed by fierce wind, Sara in that awful oversized coat she loved so desperately— Magda had known then that, no matter her protestations, she would go again to Boston. Provence. Tuscany.

That when Sara had told Magda that one day she would be preposter- ously happy, that it would make her miserable, she had added something else, afterward, to the proclamation. "You're looking for things to go wrong," Sara had said, her voice very quiet. "And that doesn't have to be the case."

There, Sara had been wrong; Magda knew this to be fact. The misery came from those shadowy glimpses at happiness. Preposterousness from the belief that happiness could be held indefinitely, that any one person could.

That there were plenty of reasons for it not to be Sara: her relentless tendency toward lateness, for one. How she was prone to disappearing, those vicious mood swings. But there seemed to be an inverse as well, for each negative a thousand positives: because there wasn't anyone with a sharper mind, because she was beautiful and intelligent in a way that demanded more from those around her. Because she was afraid of noth- ing, and encouraged Magda to be brave. Because she called with weather updates before a big storm, knowing Magda wouldn't have watched the news. Because she was, actually, afraid, and brave in spite of that. Be- cause whenever she merged into traffic, she thanked the person behind her, even though they couldn't possibly hear. Because she always, always made the bed, and that was the kind of thing you learned about a person over time: how, even if the world was on fire, they would turn up the sheets before stepping toward the flame. And because it would be those things—the catalog of what they did and loved—that would endear them to you completely, make you wonder how you had ever loved some- one who didn't pull the sheets up or say, "Okay, then," before leaving the house, make you wonder if you ever could again.

34

MAGDA WASN'T SURE QUITE HOW LONG SHE'D BEEN STANDING there when a man bumped into her. "Hey," he called out. "Watch it, lady!"

Magda found the cobblestones troublesome, and found it more difficult still to dodge the other tourists. Their shirts were stained through, and they pointed at window displays, foisting their drinks on the nearest or least drunk friend—"Take my picture, take my picture!" The ankle Magda had twisted decades prior while chasing after their family dog throbbed on occasion—it had healed improperly. Dr. Stein had reminded her that some injuries didn't allow for total recovery. "It's not always about the severity of the injury, but the formation of scar tissue," he had said. "Mysterious beast, that." When Magda was reminded of her head by a trickle of sweat, she was pleasantly surprised to find it without pain, just a mild fogginess. Even cigarettes were unsavory, that joy of that particular heat lost to the humidity. Each time Sara crossed her mind, that queasy feeling returned: *Water*, thought Magda, and went in search of another bar.

It was with a sweating bottle in hand that Magda began making her way out of the French Quarter. Sara had been raised well away from there, in a neighborhood on the cusp of corporate infiltration. Walking along, Magda noticed the haphazard homes on one street, the gyms and clothing stores on the next. Some stores had COMING SOON signs on the windows: chain coffee shops, specialty sandwich places. Most of the residential buildings held their original charms. Others, decked out with hanging ivy and plants, looked well attended to; others were in a ramshackle state that in summer seemed almost romantic. It would be different in winter, lush greenery withered and stems dry and curling, gaps between the windows and the world. Then, they'd be fending off drafts.

Sara had described her home as a yellow two-story, with a porch wrapped around the whole first floor, and a massive tree just beyond the sidewalk that cast shadows into her bedroom. When her parents had taken it over, they had rented the first floor to a young couple from the church, who were not even ten years older than Såra herself. When she, in adolescence, wobbled home drunk from parties, it was Mrs. Morton who gave her water and aspirin, and brought her around the block to share a cigarette. Mrs. Morton, in her twenties, had seemed unfathomably old.

Sara told Magda there was no chance the Mortons would still be there, or that the new owners hadn't repainted; the yellow hadn't been butter, or bumblebee, more like the yellow of a cold white wine that, upon sipping, tasted grassy; in thinking back, then, it would be remembered as green. A color that shifted in the light, revealing without modesty the places where light and time had warped it.

On Bank Street, there it was: a house so liquid blue that it appeared, at first, black, like the first second of opening your eyes underwater. Blink, and the true color disappears, blooms into something else. In front of the house were a bumpy sidewalk and a magnificent oak, its branches mostly bare. On the porch were strewn plastic toys—a child's tow truck and lawn mower—and two rocking chairs, linked by a thin silver chain. The humidity seemed to break, for a moment, in ascending the steps. Eyes aching, Magda settled gingerly into one of the rockers. Just a moment's rest, and she would be on her way.

Magda startled awake to a woman yelling.

Before she saw the woman, she was apologizing, and as the shape came into focus she saw the woman wasn't afraid, she was simply confused. She was standing closer than one would if the threat of her body felt pressing. Magda knew she was too old to present a physical threat. The woman, in considering her, seemed less worried, and yet there she was quietly saying that she would call the police.

"There's no need," Magda told her, voice crackly. She cleared her throat, which felt full and heavy. "A misunderstanding."

She stood slowly, the swell of blood causing stars to pop before her eyes. For a moment she held her place, waiting to open her eyes until the stars blinked back into black.

The woman, inexplicably, put a gentle hand to Magda's shoulder, easing her down into the chair. She went inside, the screen panel creaking shut behind her.

Through the window, a view into the kitchen. Bright, crowded, a mess of pans stacked beside the sink. Atop that, the thin damp plastic of a baby's tub. Magda watched as the woman pulled a cup from the cabinet, squinting before wiping the edges with the seam of her shirt. If Magda looked past the woman, she could see the corners of a living room: bright yellow couch, a red afghan laid out along the back. A pillow, or a rumpled sweater, had fallen to the floor.

"Mango juice," the woman said, when she reemerged. She hadn't brought a cup for herself, and didn't seem concerned with whether or not Magda finished her cup—which she continued to drink from, pulp tethering itself to her teeth. The juice was as thick as the humidity, and Magda thought of saying as much, but the woman was looking toward the road, where two children were biking lopsidedly. The larger one said something like *hurry up*, and the little one *I'm trying*, before the little one swerved, and the larger had to circle back. The woman rocked back and forth, an afterthought. She smoothed her hair, startling when Magda complimented the chairs.

"A wedding gift. You married?"

Magda paused. The memory flashed before her as if it were her own, Sara's tone furtive: *About as much as I'd expected to be.*

"I had my honeymoon here," Magda lied. "Many years ago."

The woman nodded. "It's a good place for that."

She fussed with her hair, where the humidity had already caused blond strands to rise. With both hands, she halved and tugged at her ponytail, revealing half-moons of sweat ringing her armpits, light fuzz pocked along the seam of her shirt. Neither hand held a ring, and Magda felt the other woman's gaze run across her as well, her own ringless fingers. "Seven years," the woman said, shaking her head. "Still feels like he's here."

Magda contracted her hands into fists, let them expand until her fingers felt loose enough to slap against her pants. With forced cheer, she said she probably ought to be on her way. She swilled the last of the juice, resisting the urge to bite into the cup's thick plastic rim. Leaning against the railing, she turned back to the woman.

"I came here looking for someone," Magda said. "Do you know a Mrs. Morton? In the neighborhood?"

The woman furrowed her brows. "Morton? No."

When she reached the base of the steps, the woman called out, "Hey." Then again: "Hey. I'm sorry about your loss." She motioned at Magda's bare ring finger, before running her right hand across her own.

Water, thought Magda.

Boomer called later on, when she was walking through a quieter neighborhood where the sky yawned open into a bright, spotless blue. Nearby, a trio of boys clustered around one smaller one on a bike. "My turn, my turn," one howled, as another pushed the boy from his seat.

He had called to tell her about an article he had read, a piece on reductionism in schizophrenic patients. The psychiatrist had tried segmenting the different personalities, which was interesting in conceit, but of course, Boomer conceded, flawed in execution. "For all of the other issues," he said. "All of those withstanding, the man chose a *violent* schizophrenic, and is using him as a case study for this logic, which, frankly, makes no sense at all. No consideration of hereditary correlations, emergent properties, nothing. And this piece," he went on. "It was *published*."

Magda shook her head. It reminded her of a course during medical school, so many years ago, when the professor lectured them on common reductionist theories, all of which seemed to hinge on the assumption that any one thing could be thought of in terms of its constituent parts, no matter how tiny or fragmented. Even at the time, she had considered the idea implausible, that constituent parts could be considered individually, without acknowledging other factors of import. And yet at some point those tiny pieces were all that was left, and what else could there be, really, to consider?

35

AFTER HER HONEYMOON, SARA DIDN'T RETURN TO LOUISIANA until her mother began cursing at the neighbors. By then her father was gone—a heart attack, unexpected—and her mother lived alone in a three-room cottage in Baton Rouge, half an acre rimmed by a high, wobbly hedge. This was shared with the neighbors, the branches overgrown enough that all either side could see of the other was scraps of driveway. It was this neighbor who called Sara after her mother left the car running one day. "It might have been hours since she went inside," he said, "I'm not sure." He only knew that the tank had been idling on empty, the keys still in the ignition, and after turning it off and knocking on the front door, he had walked in to find Sara's mother staring at a burner on the stove, flame leaping about, no pan in sight. "She called me by the wrong name," he said to Sara. "She's . . . she's not herself lately." It was with some hesitation that he repeated the other things her mother had said, the list of flatware and plates that she had lobbed at his head. Plastic, he rushed to say; that was lucky.

The diagnosis arrived before Sara did. It made sense, the doctor said: there was the forgetfulness, and then the slow deterioration of memory, the increased interest in flame, in heat, prolonged periods without activity. Difficult to say how long it had been going on, but the fall was swift. For the first few weeks after Sara's arrival, she allowed her daughter to brush her hair, dress her in the morning. She talked about church, recounted Sara's favorite sermons. A few weeks later, her mother believed her to be a childhood friend, the mailman, her own father. "Please," she'd say, placing a hand against Sara's, which cupped her elbow through the shower curtain. "Whoever you are, please don't make me."

She didn't die right away, but the person Sara had known was gone.

On her last day in Louisiana, Magda stayed in bed until noon. Sprawled in the tangle of cotton sheets, it occurred to her that there was another place she might like to see before leaving. She remembered Sara keying up the for-sale page online, the days since listed only ticking up. She felt a bit dizzy. Best, then, not to drive.

The cabbie drummed his fingers against the dash as they idled on the bridge, teeming with cars. "Not many people gonna take a cab an hour away from New Orleans."

Before them swelled Lake Pontchartrain, which looked more like an ocean than any lake Magda had seen—sprawling, boundless. Looking in the rearview, he asked, "Some people, they get to a certain age, they don't like being behind the wheel. That like you?" he asked her, in the mirror.

"Sometimes," Magda said. The odometer continued to tick.

"Not me, I'd be happy driving 'til the end. Something peaceful about it, just getting people where they need to be. Anyway," he said. "It's a beautiful lake. One of those sights that just—woosh. Right in front of ya. All road, and then just water. Ya think for twenty minutes people could just slow down, but they can't. All rush, ya know? No lingering. Ya don't see anything that way." He shook his head. The furrows grooving his forehead were deep, cloaked in shadow.

He left her at the driveway of the little house, where a weathered mailbox stood sentry. Farther back from the curb were hedges, yellowed and over-grown, lopped off unevenly at the tops. The result was a jagged border, as if the hedge itself had swerved in trying to ward off intruders. The place had been repainted since Sara's mother died, a boisterous lavender that matched the lilacs bedded out front. Hedda's favorite. A house that had been reupped, claimed, made to be cheerful, not a place that the owner had inadvertently almost set aflame.

The neighboring house, separated by a tall white fence, no longer be-longed to anyone. Sold and then sold again for parts, then seized by the bank and left to languish. One of the first-floor windows was split open, cracks spidering up the sides; a hole gaped in the center. Grass grew wild, dandelions sprouting through cracks in the fence.

The backyard was in further disarray. A swing set overrun by weeds cast its shadow over a lawn mower, the handles and blades all rusted. Farther back, a watering can tipped on its side, half-buried in the ground.

The neighbor had eventually moved to Metairie—closer to his children, away from the memories. That's what Sara had told Magda, anyhow: that the neighbor had been the one to go over, daily, after the diagnosis. Sara would have been hovering somewhere over North Carolina when the neighbor's wife walked upstairs, clutching her swollen belly: "Honey?" Still another minute before he bolted outside, where Sara's mother was sitting placidly on the lawn, naked. He gingerly approached, and she turned to him: "There you are, Sara. About time."

The real Sara was in the sky, pulling from a tepid bottle of water, thinking of how lucky she was to arrive when she did. Before it got bad.

It was dreadful, Magda agreed, when parents died. And it was—the worst part came after the news was gently delivered, silence creeping in to blanket the loss. Through the gaps in sound came a particular relief that her parents' wishes were no longer hers to carry, and with that came fear: her little defiant life could topple over for having no opposition. When Magda's own mother died, the tension dissipated from her limbs, yes, but so did the resolve.

"You wouldn't have even suspected she was sick," Sara said. In her hand was a scrapbook, a photo of her face and her mother's pressed together. *A carbon copy*, Magda thought. "She wasn't that old yet; she wasn't even seventy."

The first page of the scrapbook had been left blank, a laminated funeral card pressed against the blank page: St. John's Church of the Divine, Baton Rouge.

Back in New Orleans, the horns arrived just after Magda did.

A low blast, and from the street corner, a man appeared with a trumpet in hand. Behind him, another trumpeter and a trombonist, followed by another twenty or thirty people dressed in black. En masse, the mourners moved slowly, many singing, and others talking softly among themselves. The trumpeter stood out front, sweat skittering like spiders down his neck. Magda, on the sidewalk, was tugged in by someone. It could have been easily assumed that she had stood there in wait for them, to join the march.

The singers in the back were saying how they wanted to be in that number, oh Lord, when the saints go marching in. The brass brand holding steady in the front line, the second row somber. *Family*, Magda thought, watching the back of a child who was clutching a much-older woman's arm.

As a child, Sara had sat between her mother and father during Sunday services. She squirmed in the pews, mouthed the hymns instead of singing along. In adolescence, Sara was more interested in the altar boys who smoked behind the building, and so when one of her friends, who was going steady with the taller one, invited her along, Sara said yes. The first time she had held a cigarette, first she had ever inhaled smoke, been this practically close to fire. After that, she skipped Sunday school. The religion she held closest was in her own yard, throughout which her parents had laid a number of small stone statues. All of them depicted Mary Magdalene, in various states of prayer. Sara couldn't look out a window without seeing Mary's clasped hands, the modest bow of her head.

The woman who had tugged Magda, who was still holding her arm, continued to sing and stare ahead. Her fingers edged along Magda's arm until they reached her own hand, held fast. Up and along the wide expanse of the avenue, moving past the street-side vendors and their wares. The vendors paused upon their passing, waving them along, or nodding until they forged ahead. Magda nodded in recognition. Her gaze trained on the ground, the mourners every so often breaking free with cries of "She's home now" and "Praise the Lord."

Jazz funerals were also symbolic of rebirth, Sara had told Magda. Slow dirges segueing into joyous, up-tempo songs. Dancing. The body, separating from the soul. Ascension. Their home, well along the route, meant that what she saw from the living room window was mostly dancing. She had thought, for a long time, that the people were glad to see their loved ones go. That if the mourners were smiling, the dead weren't, in fact, truly loved ones. "If I die," Sara had solemnly told her mother, "I want you and Daddy to cry." Shortly thereafter, she had been sent to her room without dinner.

For another five blocks they walked and sang, people joining from the streets as they moved. Magda's hand stayed firmly in the grasp of the other woman, who said and sang nothing. Onward they went, and the music lifted. "Onward," they were singing, onward in the glory of the Lord. Magda's eyes were wet, and lifting a hand to her face she discovered in her hand a thin gold chain. A cross, speckled by thumbprints, a metallic tang in her mouth as she held it to the light. The woman who had pulled Magda in, whoever she was, was gone.

The pastor raised his hands, indicating that they sit. Around here, the mourners bowed their heads, settled into their plastic chairs. The people who loved her most moved slowly toward the front, to carry her into the ground.

The woman emerged by Magda's side, leaned heavily against her friend. "I just need to know it gets better," she mumbled. Magda didn't realize she was laughing until they turned to her, eyes swollen.

Better? No.

It went like this. To be young meant ambition, years of thinking ahead, during which the question and answer were often the same: *When?* This golden question running a parallel line to its inverse: time, and the steady depreciation during which those dreams could yet come true. It was simple math, really; the sum total of years would, at some point, be lesser than what had already unspooled. Less time than life to live. When that happened, the answer changed, became *while*. While I am, while I can. Still the years ticked away, until the rules of the game were changed, the cards face-up on the table, revealing their fate: *until*. That was the key word, tucked away inside what had already happened, huddled in a corner waiting for its moment. All good, anything possible, *until*.

What proved devastating was the fact of death's lurking, the perpetual surprise of an unexpected passing. Age and freak accidents and cancer and drunk driving and suicide: it all *happened*. But that didn't mitigate the feeling of choice for those who grew still older, knowing that—despite the protein drinks, the regular exercise, those reams of kale—still, it would come. The cards would again be flipped, returning to the origin point: When I had time, I didn't know it. Had I chosen right, had I done things differently while I had time, how much is left until—

This woman whose casket was, at that moment, being lowered into the ground, Magda's own parents, Sara's—they had wanted that same thing people always did: for their lives to be good.

The church bells tolled, a shovel dug deep into the dirt. Pain sharp in her hand, the cross's edges digging into her palm. A refrain echoed in her mind: *May the Lord bless you and keep you.* "The priestly blessing," Sara had explained. "It's sort of a catchall for the end of services, worship, baptism, marriage. Beginnings and endings."

Magda was laughing, still, but her eyes were wet.

"Hedda?" she said, too loudly. A roar of traffic surged, and Magda repeated her sister's name into the static.

"Mags, is that you?"

"I know I missed our usual call, it's been busy, I've been . . . well, I've been so busy."

"Oh, Mags," Hedda said. "I was getting worried after you didn't call me back. Are you away? You know, I thought I—"

"*Ja*, no, at the beach house. Boomer's. Helping with his mother, who is *sjuk. I huvudet.*"

"*Det är sorgligt.* And what did you do, besides?"

"Nothing," Magda said. "I'm just coming back to the city now. And you?"

"Oh," Hedda sighed. "A regular week, nothing special. A little party, a dinner. Really, the prospect of hosting was the kick I needed to finish repainting the house. It's done now, finally."

"Is it now," Magda said softly.

"I know, I know, it's been years of saying I would. But it's done now. Finally. Yellow."

Magda traced the seam of her pants. "It's funny, I always imagined it like that. Buttercup. Or dandelion."

Hedda's laugh rang out. "It's more like corn, but it's nice. Of course, with the grandchildren here, it's impossible to get much done. They're like we were, always getting into something. And speaking of, I need to go to the corner and meet the camp bus—will you call again soon? Or I can call you at this number?"

"Yes, of course, either one."

"Well, gosh," Hedda said. "You, traveling. Next time, maybe you could even visit."

"I'd like that," Magda said. "See the house. You, Daniel, the kids. It'd be nice."

"Send Sara my love, will you?"

"I will, I will."

"*God.*"

The dial tone cut in, sour and sharp.

God. It amused her, still, that the English word signifying the utmost deity, had meant, in her first language, only *good*.

That was what Sara used to say, that she couldn't bear knowing how good it could be—*had* been—and for those things to be taken from her before she could make her mark. It seemed cruel, for the world to slowly retract itself, to find themselves with funerals penciled alongside movie dates. Nestled in their little constellations at a wake, one would have that thought, catch the other's eye.

Another widow to whom food must be sent, another visit or two or three spent exalting the deceased's virtues, and yet streaked indelibly across Magda's mind was that feeling of luck. She had experienced it with Sara, as they sat with a widow's hand cupped in each of theirs: Thank God it isn't us. Thank God it isn't you. Thank God it is good.

A mark, Magda thought. Her whole life had been imprinted with Sara's, and still her friend wanted to leave a mark.

36.

FARTHER AND FARTHER WEST MAGDA DROVE UNTIL SHE REACHED Texas, where the gas station attendants welcomed her with a low drawl. She drove past abandoned fairgrounds, Ferris wheels rusting in the sun. Sagebrush shifting in the breeze, dead armadillos humped along the road. Past restaurants, their wide swathes of dirt lawn dotted with tables, dust flecked around their legs. The men hunched beneath the umbrellas, playing cards; women kept their noses upturned, crisping in the sun. Steepled white churches dotted the horizon. Magda stopped at a gas station flanked by mobile homes, where the sun was harsh and the light flat, rendering the shadows deep and sweeping. Before the pump stood the metal overhang of one trailer, which cast its small yard into murky shade, left the two white plastic chairs gleaming. A tiny brown dog ran in circles, barking toward one piece of cacti.

From the shade, a man bellowed, "Don't you fucking do it."

The dog yipped and ran, circles widening until he reached Magda's side, took her pants between his teeth. Growled until she followed, then darted ahead.

Beneath the cactus, a scorpion was flexing its pincers. The dog snapped its jaw, barked again. Magda reached for its collar, pulled him back. The man, by Magda's side, said, "Sorry about that. Fucking Chance. He won't do shit, just barks a big game."

He wore a sweat-stained shirt, ripped at the collar, the hair on his chest damp-looking. Swept aside to reveal a puffy red scar. When he noticed Magda looking, he pulled the shirt lower, revealing the scar that split his chest. "After the first heart attack, my daughters got me the dog. Said it'd keep me active. Second chance . . . Chance . . ." He shrugged, scooping the dog into his arms. "Pain in the ass."

Another chance.

Some months after Boston, Sara and Magda shuffled along in awkward silence at the Whitney. Magda had tried, a few times, to broach the trip with Sara, who'd interjected with how phenomenally *drunk* they'd been. She couldn't remember anything. Not a thing.

They took in multiple installations by Félix González-Torres, one of which spanned an entire stairwell, a chain of twinkle lights descending for three floors, pooled at the bottom. In another room, a pile of candy pressed into the corner of a wall, pieces wrapped in Technicolor cellophane. Magda cocked her head, leaned closer. The plaque read: UNTITLED (PORTRAIT OF ROSS IN L.A.).

"A hundred and seventy-five pounds," Sara said, sidling up alongside Magda.

"What?"

She gestured toward the pile. "That's the weight, I mean, of the installation. It's what the artist's lover, Ross, weighed as he began to die of AIDS."

"God," Magda said.

"We tried to get this one, for the gallery, but the boss didn't want it. Said he thought it was a bit reductive. Of course, he had awful taste and was fired a few months later, but by then it was too late." Sara stepped in to pluck a yellow pastille from the bunch. Magda put a hand over hers, and Sara shrugged it off. "No, you're allowed to eat them. I don't know who, but there's someone who's been replenishing the pile for years."

Magda blushed, stepped aside. "I never would have thought that."

"That's why I love it," Sara said. "Looks saccharine, but it's just . . . it's brilliant, really. And lasting. You know, their love didn't even end there. Félix kept making art for Ross, for *years* after Ross died."

Sara rubbed at one eye, the bags pronounced beneath it. Her hair was shot through with gray, the familiar crow's-feet widening as she smiled, saying, "But you know, there's something beautiful about the story, sad as it is. I mean, the rest of his *life* he made art for Ross. He talked about it to an interviewer, once, who asked about his process. How do you create your pieces, who do you make art for, that sort of thing. And you know what he said?"

"No."

"That his public was Ross. The rest of the people just came to the work."

"God," Magda said again. "That's terrifically sad. Was he ever happy after that?"

Sara, catching Magda's eye, went, "What, what?" Ran a tongue across her teeth, and touched a hand to the creases in her cheeks. "Oh, these? I know, I need to get them taken care of."

"No," Magda said. "I was just thinking about the piece. Wondering if he ever loved again."

"Oh, sure," Sara said. "Though I don't think he ever got over what had been stolen from him, and from Ross. He had more chances to love, and he did. But what I mean is that, probably, it wasn't the same."

In Texas, Magda spoke too quietly for the waitresses, who leaned in while asking her to repeat what was it that she wanted, hon. Often misunderstood, Magda ate the things her orders sounded like—steak, creamed corn. A low-stakes endeavor, but each time someone got her order wrong, she thought: *I'll try again.*

Second chances.

What people held on to were the memories, clutched tight to remind themselves: *This is the way we were.* Magda could think one thing, believe in it wholly, and yet to the other person—to Sara—the relationship was a different animal. That was the nature of memory. It became slippery, deceitful even, bending itself to the whims of the story someone was telling.

The part Magda had not previously considered—and then puzzled over while she nibbled corn bread and sipped sweet tea—the part she hadn't thought about, was her own mind obsessively coursing the grooves and, in its effort to protect her, overwriting the past. How ultimately it could be worse, being the one who survived and had said nothing, the person who couldn't know anything for certain. *You might've asked her,* Magda thought.

What had happened next in the museum was this: Sara's eyes went stormy, damp. She turned and said, "Magda," and in response, Magda's whole body tensed. In lieu of response, she shoved into her mouth five of those candy pastilles: red, two pinks, yellow, purple. Sara had closed her mouth, then, the tide of her expression waning. A soft smile, her lips tight, as she said, "Never mind," and began walking toward the next room. Cellophane crackled in Magda's hand then, louder than her own heartbeat. Jaw aching, she followed.

37.

April 1991

Dear M,

You were the one who said don't do anything too elaborate—this time, don't take it too far. And at the time, I didn't think I was. Genuinely. I thought of course Fred will want to take a trip—it's our tenth wedding anniversary, how could there be any question—and you had been the one to point out he was still in the running for partner at the firm, he wasn't necessarily going to be present, you said all that.

But you know me, I couldn't help it. Out came those old planning instincts, an itinerary. We're going to Lisbon, I announced last week, all cheery, and he said nobody had time to go to Spain. That's fine, I told him, because Lisbon is in Portugal. I said it smugly, so as not to become angry. He didn't care that I'd planned the trip, he kept saying he was too busy, it would be too much to take on, why don't we go some other time. I told him I'd be damned if we spent another anniversary in the same apartment in the same city, doing what—getting takeout from a different restaurant?

Well, I should have called you before we left—I meant to, I did—but there was all the complaining and the wheedling and, eventually, the packing. And wouldn't you know it, two days before we were supposed to leave, he said no, there was no way we could make it to Spain. Portugal, I corrected him. And he said, can't go there, either. Let's just stay close.

So guess where we are?

Amarillo, Texas.

We're here because after all that planning, I needed us to do something. Go somewhere. We got to the airport and guess which flights were the cheapest? But Fred hasn't settled into the trip at all. Two days in, and he's spent most of the time fielding business calls from the hotel lobby.

Here's what I can tell you:

The city wasn't always called Amarillo. Supposedly in the spring and summer there were droves of yellow wildflowers lining the land (before it was city). But there is also a nearby lake called Amarillo Lake, speckled with this bright yellow soil along the banks.

Once, the city claimed itself the helium capital of the world. You wouldn't think helium is produced, would you? I didn't. Frankly, I'd never thought about it. But if I had, I would have thought it was naturally occurring, not manufactured here, in Amarillo.

This part you'll hate, but Amarillo is home to a nuclear weapons facility. The only one in the country, apparently, that both assembles and disassembles nuclear weapons. For a while, people called it Bomb City, but that nickname didn't last.

Have I learned these things from being out, seeing the city? No. I have been lying flat on the hotel bed, reading pamphlets and waiting for Fred. I told him last night about the nukes, making some joke about how he had brought us accidentally to one of the most dangerous places on earth. Then he said that few things are more dangerous than I am when bored. I wasn't bothered at the time—it was easy to laugh off—but the comment has been eating away at me ever since.

You know what's interesting, though? Most of the songs I've heard about Amarillo are about driving up from San Antonio, or along Route 66. They're songs about the road, not the city—it's one of those places you wind up in on your way someplace better. Maybe I'll tell that to Fred.

The danger is inherent to marriage, I think, not one person or the other. It's the romanticized tedium. The feeling that you know how someone is feeling, what they want, without ever asking.

What are we doing if we aren't talking about helium fields, places to pass through?

Dreaming of where we want to be, I suppose. Writing letters.

In boredom,

Your S

38.

THERE WAS A SLIGHT CHANGE IN ACCOMMODATIONS, THE FRONT desk clerk told Magda. A large group had taken residence in the hotel, the turbulent weather having forced them out of their desert yurts. "They need bathrooms," explained the flustered clerk, and the storm wasn't meant to let up for days, leading the group to hastily book a suite of rooms at the Stetson, and so, he finished, "There's a problem. Well, not a problem, exactly, but an *issue*..." It appeared that Magda's room, the only one still available, shared a wall with the conference room where the group would be congregating.

"It's fine," Magda said.

The weather had turned. Local weather forecasters proclaimed hurricane season had arrived late that year, an unexpectedly mild June giving way to a rough-and-tumble July. The forecaster suggested that unnecessary travel be avoided as the first front rolled on through. The windshield wipers had done little to improve visibility, and Magda needed on multiple occasions to pull over and drudge bits of debris from their antennae. A headache beat low and steady against her forehead, pain rattling at the base of her spine. She had taken to napping on the lip of the road, or, as the aches intensified, pulling from the omnipresent well of iced coffee in the cupholder. One couldn't avoid sweetener in the south, and so the coffee tasted of hazelnut or French vanilla or cinnamon, until the straw met knobs of sugar along the bottom. Magda needed the hotel because it felt like days since she'd last brushed her teeth, or dreamed without waking to the phone's jittery alarm, or the churn of another car coasting by. Upon placing her bag beside the bed, though, she regretted her decision. From the neighboring wall came a low hum and a man's instruction: "Repeat after me."

It was just after three in the afternoon. Too early, Magda thought, to sleep, but what else could be done besides rest? As she waited for the shower water to warm, occasionally dipping a hand behind the curtain to test the stream—still chilly—she retrieved the toiletry bag from the side pocket of the suitcase. Ten purple capsules to alleviate pain, which, Dr. Stein had reminded her, were incredibly potent. For someone of her age and build, they would double as sleeping pills. Even half of one would be enough. Emergency use only.

From the neighboring room, a chant: "I am enough."

"I AM ENOUGH."

"I! Am! Enough!"

Cupping a handful of sink water, Magda swallowed two pills, and when she woke, it was on top of the bed, just before midnight, no noise besides the dripping water. In her sleep, she had shrugged off the towel, the whole of her exposed and inclined toward the windows. She hadn't closed the blinds, but the view looked out onto an underutilized part of the parking lot, lined with trash bins. In the darkness, it wasn't clear. A steady stream of water in the bathroom: the shower, taps still open.

After turning the water off, Magda carefully halved a pill with the car key's jagged edge. She anticipated a liquid center, but it was dry, powdery, and she swallowed quickly, wiping the excess dust from the table. She slipped into her nightgown, left the curtains open, and drifted back into the ether.

Magda was roused by the sun plying its way through the window. Without the blackout curtains, she learned, the room became not just bright but hot, and so she woke with the urgent need to shower once again. It was too hot to smoke, but she tried for half of a cigarette before giving up and pressing the cherry against the window frame so it could sputter out. She went to the breakfast hall feeling even more out of sorts, and as she fiddled between canary-hued eggs and a platter of slick and sweating sausage, a woman approached and introduced herself: Judy.

"Oh!" she said, when Magda demurred: not there with the group, no. "I was going to say, I *thought* I'd met everyone."

They had gathered in Amarillo for a women's retreat, planning to stay for four days. Outside of the lectures—which happened twice daily—they would paint; those who were menstruating were encouraged to apply their own blood to canvas. "Putting it simply," Judy explained, "this retreat is meant to unleash one's divine feminine energy." There were other extracurriculars, including peyote and meditative treatments. Magda was welcome to join in on any of the sessions, or activities, if she was interested, so long as she committed to abiding by the rules of the group: no photography, no negative self-talk, absolutely no videography, no toxic male energy—no toxicity, actually, of any kind. Drugs were fine, if pre-approved or taken in a supervised capacity, and for the right reasons, and not by someone who had previously abused them. "It's an honor system," Judy explained. Magda thought fleetingly of one of Boomer's patients, a young man who had grown a patch of hallucinogenic mushrooms on his parents' roof. How angry they had been to find their town house desecrated, and for such an ignoble reason.

Judy was by no means the mastermind behind the clinic—"That's Gardee," she said, pointing at the brochure—but she, having completed some psychology and biology coursework during her undergraduate studies, served to monitor the peyote. And the marijuana and mushrooms. Not all of the women had fully experienced the power of recreational drugs— "Most don't until middle age, if you can believe that"—and the retreat offered not just a vehicle for doing so, but a safe and monitored experience. Judy espoused that shutting off the mind was nearly impossible for most women; that proved to be the issue they encountered time and again. Too much worrying over spouses or children or family, and they couldn't *relax*. Magda would be welcome to join them for workshops, or meditation— "Are you on vacation?" Judy asked. "In transit? Working?" She wrinkled her nose at that. Tough to get away these days, wasn't it? No matter, though— Magda was welcome, if ever and whenever she cared to join.

"Maybe," Magda said. "That could be nice."

There was something familiar about Judy: the mountain of hair, the gasp of intensity with which she spoke, and how, in listening, she cocked her head just slightly. She was very good at her job, Magda determined, though she was someone who likely would have been successful at any job requiring her to interact with people. Ask something of them.

"What kind of training is required? For your role?"

"None in particular," Judy said, and then, to Magda's nonplussed expression, "I know! It seems like there should be some training, right? I guess the training is just common sense, really. I wouldn't try any of the drugs myself, but, you know, I needed a change." Someone gestured at her, and Judy waved back. "Find me anytime, okay? I'll be around here somewhere."

Judy ambled toward a cluster of women in the corner booth, and Magda felt compelled to trot along behind her. Judy, like Sara, had a way of holding eye contact that felt near and distant simultaneously, a look that said, *Follow me or don't, the choice is yours,* when in fact the choice had been made upon Judy's entering the room and deciding upon what she wanted, and from whom.

By afternoon, Magda had watched two hours of treacly soap opera and weather reports. The meteorologists said the storm was brewing and that with a developing situation, the safest solution was to stay home. Hunker down. The retreaters had begun taking their drugs; Magda could hear, through the wall, the sound of someone gasping. A rainbow! Another woman rhapsodized about the tree frog climbing the walls, kept asking whether anyone else could see his progress, if anyone was scared of him leaving with their secrets in tow. There had to be a doctor present, Magda thought, turning up the volume.

A rattle, the radiator kicking on. Magda called the front desk, and the clerk apologized once and then again: an old building; the vents were sticky. The clerk was sorry to hear it was getting hot—really, very sorry— and noted that while their maintenance guy was temporarily off-site, that she would call him and explain the situation.

Another shower, and when Magda emerged from the bathroom the missed call light was flashing on the phone. "Yeah, so, sorry," said the message. "There seems to be, ah, an issue with the pipes in the guest rooms, and, well, we can't get anyone there until tonight, with the weather advisory and all. So, yeah, I would head into town, or you can move to a common space until it gets sorted out. You're, uh, a lady, right?" the clerk finished hurriedly. "'Cause if you are, there's a place you can go ..."

In the banquet hall, Judy pulled away from her group to hug Magda, grip her arm. "Well, this is perfect, isn't it? You actually arrived just in time for Gardee's introductory speech."

In saying so, Judy pressed a pamphlet into Magda's hand, upon which was an image of a short man bedecked in jeans and a silvery linen tunic, his hair somewhere between loose and ponytailed. "The introductory speech is always so special," Judy said. "But especially during a session like *this*, when the plan has been, well, indelibly changed—and by something so simple as weather." She leaned over Magda, curls brushing her shoulder as she indicated the first page. "See, here."

"Makes you think," a lady beside her said solemnly. "About cosmic forces beyond our control."

Judy raised an eyebrow at Magda. She was younger than Magda, but notably older than the rest of the women—early sixties, maybe.

Magda leaned toward Judy. "A cosmic blip, maybe, having a man in charge."

Judy didn't respond. Someone was loading baked goods onto a folding table. Another person, speaking into their phone, said the delivery had to arrive on time. It *had* to. No, they couldn't hold, the person didn't understand—there was no plan B, there was only plan A. Something, also, had not arrived, and it was Judy who took the phone from the assistant and pressed it to her own ear.

Perhaps Judy had not found it funny, or perhaps Magda had spoken too quietly, but there wasn't time to ruminate on either of those things because the women began to arrive: young, and in droves. She wouldn't have been surprised to see Gwen break loose from the crowd, wave her down. The early arrivals came in alone, each eagle-eyed upon entry: Gardee wasn't there yet, okay; now, where to sit. One lady, in sitting beside her, offered no greeting but promptly began speaking.

"Shitty weather," she told Magda. "Really shitty, even for hurricane season. The other ladies, they're all out-of-towners, but not me—no, ma'am. Born and raised in Texas." She smiled, a flash of long, white teeth. "Corpus Christi, way out there."

"The workshop was a gift," she went on, rolling her eyes. "Kids could've paid the electric bill with that, but you know, they keep saying I need to get out there since Carl left," the woman said wearily. "I'd always *known* he would leave, but you know, I'm doing all right. I keep on working, keep my head above water, keep up with the payments. God knows what comes next," she said, blessing herself, and, after a moment, Magda as well.

It would take Gardee some time to reach the stage. The crowd, undulating, pressed ribbons of handshakes upon him, and he, in turn, gripped each reachable arm in response. Magda, who had been pulled by Judy toward the front of the auditorium, saw that Gardee wore a wide and unwavering smile. He moved leisurely along the aisle, at various points raising his own hands to his chest, overwhelmed, it would appear, by the audience's passion.

The women seemed frenzied by his arrival. Those who couldn't physically reach Gardee gripped the backs of their neighbors who could, as if whatever power he held could be harnessed through the muscle of someone else's shoulders.

Upon the stage—a raised podium draped in carpet—he removed the microphone from its perch, asking the women how they were doing. Amarillo, he went on, was usually beautiful in the summer, but not all that glittered could stay gold, and surely, not all workshops could occur without some strife. How many of them, he asked, were focused on the reality they had imagined? Was that version better, really, than what was before them—would the current reality be remembered as simulacrum?

"I ask the tough questions," Gardee said, "because someone has to." By ignoring the fevered grip of expectation, by waylaying its demands, he would disappoint them. But, he explained, this version of the trip, the one derailed by weather, *this* was the one that most closely resembled the world itself. A perfect mirror showed the viewer's flaws, after all. And here they were. The world was unpredictable: a series of surprises that landed one in unexpected situations. A motel in Amarillo, Texas. He rolled his eyes amusedly, and some of the women laughed. "How did we end up here?" he asked, and when there was no response, lowered his voice, added, "Exactly. How does anyone wind up anywhere? The real trips happen here, in our heads. In our hearts."

Magda thumbed through her brochure. Gardee's training, from what she could discern, was experimental in scope. She could imagine her father's voice: a hack profession. *Quacks.* Gardee had been raised outside of Denver, in a town where strains of marijuana were part and parcel to local medicine. As a youth, he had taken a few courses at the local community college focused on human development. The brochure said it was there that he had realized the failings of conventional medicine, specifically as it impacted women.

Nobody thought about *women*, the pamphlet said, the most powerful people of all. Divinity in their motion, and in their action. Their ability to *create* and *grow* life. *Nurture* and *evolve*. But until women were empowered to harness the loveliest aspects of their being, they would continue to be overlooked—often, even, trod upon—by society. The back of the brochure showed Gardee flanked by women, one of whom was young, pregnant; another woman, significantly older, clung to his shoulder, silvery hair tossed forward and obscuring her smile.

Upon the podium, Gardee was still speaking. Raising his hands, he said the name again: Amarillo. As if by doing so, the problem and the answer could become one. He raised his hands higher, opening his palms to the audience. They said it with him: Amarillo. The women raised their palms skyward. Magda thought of the time Sara had visited the city, how she mentioned the facility just north in which workers were, at that moment, dismantling and assembling nuclear weapons.

Judy, who had once again materialized by Magda's side, squeezed her arm. Whispered, "Something, isn't he?" Her eyes widened, pupils expanding.

Once more, they said it: Amarillo.

Onstage, Gardee had pulled his hands together. He was thanking the women for their bravery, and for their willingness to engage with him on this journey.

Magda felt nauseous after the session. The cooling system was still on the fritz, and opening her window did little good; there was no breeze. Outside, the rain was still beating upon the parking lot, but bright swatches of sky peeked through the clouds. Magda crumpled the brochure and tossed it into the trash can. Ridiculous, that man leading a workshop. Ridiculous that she was there at all, which wouldn't have happened if Fred had simply handled the situation. If he had, just the once, been able to manage his own life.

Magda pushed the window up still farther to find the air was hardly cooler. Not dark, but soon, the streetlights only just switched on. She cried—unsatisfying, dry heaves—and looked over the parking lot. A woman and her dog paced in the purpling dusk. The dog, arthritic, could only hobble. The woman was saying things Magda could not hear, but could guess at. The issue, it seemed, was that the dog wouldn't pee. And so the woman veered away, briefly, and then back under the light, the dog following, and Magda crying for her, too, this woman who wanted badly to go inside. The dog, its snout illuminated by the thick yellow light, raised a leg, and the woman yelped, bent down to praise him. Yelped again at going to the bins and finding Magda, red-faced, watching her.

Years ago, she had gotten in a real argument with Theo, who believed everyone was inherently capable of true change, Magda arguing with the conditional statement that they had to *want* to change. Boomer, this being not too long after Sophia's death, said he didn't believe people could change who they were at the core. But, Theo argued, people tended to compartmentalize the different parts of their lives—desires, fears—in such a way that it was possible to focus on a single element, render it differently in the retelling. Which Magda, at the time, had balked at. She told Theo it was a superficial way of healing, that hyperintense focus on a singular thing was just that: a distraction.

They were at a restaurant on Second Avenue, seats facing the sidewalk, which was where Magda directed her focus then. A slow stream of cars going past, and how extraordinary, really—all of those people with whom her life would never intersect. A man tugging at his tie, a teenager hauling a skateboard, a woman checking her phone, a man in a fluorescent green running shirt, a lithe and coltlike woman, who even in walking seemed to be tripping over herself. All of those people—people distracted and hungry, people who couldn't keep the radio tuned to one station, who were constantly in pursuit of something better, people who couldn't wait to get home or to fall in love or to fall out of it. All of them, just out of reach! She had wanted to believe Theo then, that on a whim any one person could decide to become better. That just one decision could be enough that they *could* become better.

Boomer had been the one to bring up that argument, in the first year after Sara died. "You're not trying anymore" was what he told Magda as they left work. After seven in the evening—something she hadn't considered strange at the time, his being there then—hovering around the sixth floor. The elevator continued downward, and she had shrugged it off, holding up the waistband of her skirt as they left the elevator. Not until getting home did the strangeness reveal itself: Boomer, there for a full day, without any patients coming or going.

Magda was no longer crying, her eyelids gone heavy with exertion. She was nearly at the point where she could return home, but the prospect felt heavier than it had even at the outset. She knew less than she had at the beginning, it seemed, Sara's intentions still maddeningly vague. All those indications of where she ought to go, but nothing to indicate what she should actually do. How she might bring herself to change. After Texas there was New Mexico, the museum. After that, just the road. Though not immediately, it was somewhere along that path she needed to decide what to do with Sara once they got back to New York. How she would have to return her friend to a man who would stow her in a side closet, leave her under the bathroom sink.

The only urgent question, that evening, was what Magda wanted, and that answer felt obvious: a strong drink.

39.

THE FLOOR WAS GRITTY WITH PEANUTS, SHELLS HALVED AND quartered by wayward feet. A squeak to Magda's own shoes, the puddles of rainwater having leeched through the heels. Behind the bar, the walls were emblazoned with pictures of local royalty: Big Bud, who had downed fifteen beers in just as many minutes, and Ol' Jim Dale tipping his cowboy hat behind the bar, soda wand in hand. Homerun Hank with his wide arms and tattoos, replete with a thick mustache and fitted plaid shirt. Magda imagined that half of the men there had at one point or another ridden mechanical bulls—real ones, even. They were men who, upon seeing a bear, would not panic, needed only to loose a pistol from its holster: *pow.*

A bar for men, Magda thought, and felt a tap on her shoulder. "I *knew* that was you," Judy said. Her eyes went wide. "Do you want to sit together? Should we find a booth?"

Magda nodded, though Judy was already tugging her along. She had thought that women like Judy were rarely alone at bars, women who entered like a storm towing everything else in their wake. Women who were never alone, really. Like Sara, they enjoyed the world more for showing it to other people, and so with them always was a friend, a lover, someone who absolutely just had to see that one thing, go to that one place.

"What a day," Judy said, easing onto the cracked pleather seat. "One of the women fainted after the event—just keeled right on over when she tried to stand. Dehydration, probably, but the radiator situation certainly didn't help. Is yours still on? Mine is, just drumming out heat. The person at the desk said this was the only bar that definitely, definitely had air-conditioning, and so . . . here we are, I guess. But it's not much better, is it?"

Judy raised her shoulders, hair falling over her left eye. She combed it behind her ears, leaned forward.

"Maybe a little bit," said Magda, adjusting her collar. "But not much."

The bartender made his way over, Judy ordering a gin and tonic and then, waving at Magda, whatever her friend was having. Magda chose a whiskey sour, which arrived in a small plastic boot topped with a purple straw. On the accompanying napkin was scrawled YEEHAW, a cartoon of a cowboy solicitously touching the brim of his ten-gallon hat. Magda, under the table, readjusted her flannel shirt where it sagged at the waist. Instinctively, she sucked in her stomach, the waistband of her pants loosening in response.

From the bar, men glanced suspiciously at Judy. It was her smile, Magda surmised, because Sara had had the same problem. Slightly crooked front teeth, the way her lip tripped over them on its way to a smile. Messy, her loveliness undeniable and somehow slightly out of focus. Another man looked over, turned when Magda's gaze met his own. Men did not trust beautiful women, but oh, how they longed for them.

The ice in their drinks nearly melted, Judy told Magda more about herself. Judy, short for Judith. The nickname came from her high but quiet voice, and how, upon introducing herself, people heard Judas, expected betrayal. Newly divorced, and thus, Judy supposed, newly free of expectation. "I guess it was exciting," Judy doubled back. "I mean, it was *really* exciting to punch out of that old job and find my way into something else. You don't think that'll happen after sixty, but you know, you think your life is completely sorted, and then suddenly you're not someone's wife and you don't have to be a pencil pusher in DC, you get to be . . . whatever this is." She waved a hand above her drink, eyes glassy.

Gardee's retreats had gone national, taking Judy from Amarillo to Portland to Oklahoma City to New York. "Not the city," Judy clarified, but farther upstate—Albany, or close to it. The travel didn't matter to her so much as the reliability of not belonging to any one place, but with the next destination always in sight. "It's a summer gig, but it's good for now, while I get back on my feet."

Judy ordered another round, and the second drink had an herbal bite: gin. Judy apologized—she shouldn't have assumed Magda would want the same, but it was habit after living in DC: a drink for each hand before returning to the table. Bars in Washington were horrific, perennially crowded, and her ex-wife—"girlfriend, sorry"—had a penchant for lateness. At best, she would arrive fifteen minutes after the dinner reservation, after Judy had ordered the appetizers and their mains. At worst, she didn't arrive until after the food. By the time she arrived, Judy was usually two drinks in.

"It wasn't a bad relationship, at the beginning," Judy said. "More that the value depreciated over time. My value, I mean, to her. God, sorry. She was in finance, and I still catch myself talking in numbers."

Magda had to remind herself that it was fine to fiddle, that she could take sips of her drink, that she shouldn't take notes. She didn't *need* to fix things for Judy. It had been so long since having a drink with a veritable stranger that she felt herself lapsing into therapist mode: listen, analyze, solve. She sucked the last of the whiskey sour, by then runny with melted ice, out of her straw, reached again for the second drink.

"But listen to me, rambling away. I'll shut up, you tell me about yourself," Judy said.

I live other people's lives, Magda thought. She exhaled instead, said, "Hm."

Judy sipped at her drink, tugged at the neckline of her shirt. Sweat bloomed beneath her arms, and one piece of hair had fixed itself to her forehead. Magda, without thinking, pushed it away. She felt a bolt of retroactive panic before looking up to see Judy's expression was unchanged. "Thanks," Judy said, reaching a hand up to ensure the hair was then in the right place.

"I'm on vacation for the first time in years. I'm driving to New Mexico next, and then back to Manhattan."

Judy's eyes went soft. "Very romantic, isn't it?" she said. "I mean, driving across the country alone. It's the sort of thing I'd like to *think* I'd do but never actually would. How did you decide to do that? And you're from New York, aren't you? What do you do there?"

"Well," Magda said. "I'm a psychiatrist."

Judy laughed. "Oh God. If I'd known that, I wouldn't have told you anything."

Magda waved a hand at her, the gin warming its way to her stomach. "I don't notice more than anyone else."

Judy held the glass flush to her mouth for a moment before taking another sip. With her teeth still on the rim: "I don't believe that for a second."

There was a third drink for Judy, and while she settled the tab, Magda went on to the bathroom. There, she pulled two ibuprofen from her purse, swallowed them with tap water cupped in her palms. Before unlocking the door, she surveyed herself in the mirror: old, still, but younger than she looked in more unforgiving light. Sixty, maybe.

Even so, she looked at herself for another beat: fine, she allowed. She looked fine.

Back at the booth, Judy poured them water. She'd called the front desk and the radiators were still on, too hot to return. They kept talking—about the retreat, toeing eventually toward the divorce.

"I say divorced because *girlfriend* just sounds trite, doesn't it? We acted like we were married," Judy said. "It felt like how everyone described it, you know? We couldn't share a bank account or legally be married, sure, but we did everything else. She bought the house, I bought the furniture. It was one of those where we loved each other, and the problems that came up— well, we thought if we just made it to marriage, we'd be fine. Neither one of us realized it was the end until we were talking about dogs and kids—the kind of last-ditch effort you make when you know it's not working any-more. And then it took another two years to acknowledge the problem was *us*, what we'd grown into."

Judy had grown up in Iowa, with a family that went to church three times each week. There was a separate closet in their house for church clothes, which her mother never allowed her to dry on the clothesline, because what if something went awry? What if the neighbors decided to steal their white blouses? College had been Judy's first time away from home, and in her second semester she had met the girl. Fireworks, flare guns in the night. The girl's parents contacted the administration, had her thrown out. Judy followed. "There wasn't another option, really, when neither of my parents would speak to me, and hers . . . God. They threatened to send her to a nunnery. To disown her."

Magda's heart shrank desperately small in her chest, and she could think of nothing to say but "Oh."

"It's okay," Judy assured her. She took a sip of the water, her fingers digging into the pliant plastic of the cup. "Really. We didn't realize what a big decision we were making; it just didn't occur to us. You spend so much time fearing God that there isn't much consideration of the other things worth worrying over, until you don't have them." Judy shrugged. "But we had each other when it mattered, so even when it went sour, we were desperate to make it work, because we'd given up everything, and we *had* made it work for so many years. I don't think we were able to see, after a certain point, how holding on would be worse. It's funny, though: now that it's legal to get married, it's easier to see how this thing I'd been wanting for so many years wasn't right for us. Have you been watching the weddings? Oh, you should. It's beautiful. Couples just streaming out of city hall, like it's the easiest thing in the world."

Judy drummed her fingers against the glass. "Anyway, I heard about the retreats, and I thought, *Well, why not?* Which I know doesn't exactly make sense—a man running this spiritual retreat for women—but it seems to be helping some people, doesn't it?"

Magda nodded, and Judy smiled. Her teeth were gapped, her smile open. "I know," Judy said. "I *do* know how it sounds. Maybe what I mean is that it's helping me, for now, until the next better thing comes along."

"The drugs are a bit much."

When Judy laughed, she tipped her head back. "I know. It's got to be a liability."

Magda reached for the water. Judy brought her glass to the lip of the pitcher, looking at Magda as she poured. "That's good," she said, and Magda, spilling on her own hand, said, "Good, that's good."

They walked the three blocks back to the motel, hands bridged over their heads, rain coursing through their fingers. The parking lot had filled since they had left, a row of pickup trucks, the beds stacked with portable bathrooms. One had tipped onto its side, a slick puddle forming on the pavement below. Judy, upon seeing it, burst out laughing. For the yurts, she explained.

"If there was ever a commentary on luck," she said, flinging a wet hand at the turquoise block, "*that* is it."

Saying good night in the dim glow of the lobby, Judy flung her arms about Magda's neck. "It was so nice to meet you," she said. "I mean, get to know you." And when she kissed Magda, it was an accident, surely, but nevertheless the kiss was square and warm on Magda's mouth. Judy giggled as she pulled herself away, swaying a bit as she went in again for Magda's cheek.

In Magda's room, heat still pruned the sheets, but the radiator had quieted, and the water in the shower felt cold. Truly cold, like the first swallow of the gin and tonic, the sliver of ice that had wedged itself between Judy's crooked teeth.

40

A DULL HEADACHE BEAT AGAINST MAGDA'S TEMPLES AS THE front desk attendant smiled apologetically. "Yeah, the handyman should get here soon. Oh, like when, exactly? Yeah, not sure. Soon, probably." Magda accepted a few crinkly plastic bottles of water, returned to her room. Too hot, still, and at nine she went to the conference room.

The women were raucous and joking, preparing for the day's festivities. Someone, she heard, had brought peyote. The chalkboard on the podium, scrawled upon in scratchy penmanship, read: *REFLECTION*. Beside it was Judy, the skin below her eyes puffy, a half-empty water bottle in her hand. A hand on someone's shoulder, an assistant at her side, whispering. Magda waved and turned quickly away, looking back a moment later. Judy had not seen her.

When they were clustered in their breakout groups, an instructor told each of the participants to write on an index card the things she found herself lacking. After five minutes, she was meant to pivot and write instead, on the opposite side, the things she found likable—lovable, even—about herself. When the timer clicked on for the first part, women scrawled with abandon. Magda looked at the cards beside her to see furtive writing: *where are the men, I hate my tits, my stomach is goddamn big, I can't afford braces, I'm so lonely I could eat my own heart.*

The instructor then told them it was time to radically overhaul those assumptions, that instead of viewing certain qualities or circumstances as deplorable, the goal was to *shift those assumptions*. The instructor, who was tall and lithe and had perfect teeth, assured the women that everyone had their own anxieties, but that it was possible to turn them on their head. That would be part three: considering what, from the first exercise, could be overhauled to amplify the characteristics of the second. She was chewing gum, its blue hue visible as she spoke. "What can you learn from the things you hate about yourself, to, like, turn them into things you love?"

"You've been awfully quiet, haven't you?" said one of the women to

Magda, tapping her playfully on the shoulder, and then looking at her sheet, which Magda had tried to obscure with one hand. Judy stood up front, biting down on the plastic shank of her pen. Magda squinted toward her page, distracted by the woman peering at her own.

"How will you overhaul your *solitary nature*, then?"

They were all much younger than she, their notebooks tipped toward the group: everything in plain sight.

"Well," Magda said. "I suppose I won't."

"Oh," said another woman. "I'm sure you can."

"Yes," chimed in the third. "There's definitely a way. Did you hear what she—"

"No," Magda said. "There probably is not."

The first woman shook her head, said that if Magda really wanted to change, she absolutely could.

"It's difficult to combat solitude," Magda said lightly, "when the person you love most is dead."

A pause, then, and one of the woman coughed, then saying into her hand, "Well, maybe . . . maybe you, like, need to meet new people?"

Magda looked down, and another woman said, "Oh yeah, definitely, there are always more people to love."

Magda wouldn't write it down, of course, but what she hated about herself, in that moment, was that slipstream of yearning, how badly she wanted for someone to shake her from her solitude. To look at her and *say* something. Wasn't it meant to be the case that she understood people, could rifle through their minds and assemble meaning? She'd spent so many years carefully reckoning with her own brain, modifying behaviors, wants. What she couldn't abide was the amorphous feeling stretched before her: a cautious, jelly-legged curiosity, the oblique feeling of wanting, always, to know more about someone than they did her. She left the index card on her chair and walked slowly from the room.

At lunch break, the sun a slow boil, Magda said goodbye to the motel. On her way out, the front desk attendant offered Magda a few more plastic bottles of water. "Least we can do. Do you need anything else?" he asked, turning back toward his computer before she could answer.

Temperatures had risen overnight—a heat wave, the news proclaimed, a *flash* heat wave—and while the radiators were finally shut off, the air-conditioning had yet to switch on. In the parking lot, the portable bathrooms radiated heat in long, shimmering waves.

Back inside, then, her heart thudding, the attendant surprised when Magda tapped on the counter, and said that, actually, she wouldn't mind borrowing a pen and paper.

She wrote down her phone number, and, above that, *If you're ever in New York*. Handing the sheet back across the counter, "Judy. She's with the big group. Thank you."

41.

JUDY CALLED AS THE AFTERNOON LIGHT BEGAN TO PINKEN, LAPSE into dusk. "It was good you left when you did," she said, static crinkling her voice. Muffled speech, then, Magda's heart sinking at the realization Judy had called, simply, to say goodbye. Over the static Judy said loudly, "She was *dehydrated*, they think, that's why she fainted, but they had to evacuate the rest of us until they could be sure, you know." Then came some murmuring, and Judy said, "Look, I have to run, but let's stay in touch? I'll text you."

Magda tried at first to adhere to the general rules of grammar, but it took too long, tapping her pointer finger resolutely over each letter. Easier to spell words correctly and simply forgo punctuation. She typed the missives while fueling the car or banked on the lip of the road, muttering the words aloud as she wrote them. *hi how are you it's me magda eklund*

Boomer and Theo were nonplussed.

"Was it our Magda who said she would never, never, *ever* start texting?" Theo asked.

"If I'm not mistaken, it was also Magda who said that overuse of cell phones dumbs down society and its base functionality."

"Wasn't it also her," Theo posited, "who said we were at risk for becoming androids?"

"'Smartphones and dumb people,' I think is the exact quote."

She cut in, "Okay, okay. But I'm finding, now, it's not so bad."

Without punctuation, everything was immediate, urgent. Judy, on the other hand, had a certain worshipfulness toward exclamation points. Everything! Was! Incredible! All! The! Time! When Magda had asked Theo first what a *lol* was, he told her it meant *lots of love*, which caused a rush of heat to envelop her whole body, but he was quick to correct himself.

"Laughing out loud," he half shouted into the speakerphone. "I looked it up."

The men, with whom she had staunchly resisted texting, now sent messages instead of calling. Theo wrote the way he spoke: informally. Long, rangy paragraphs, not often circling back to the original point, but were more amusing than if he did. He signed each missive *with love*, even photos of the troubling. *Hi Magda, All fine here, except Freud attacked Kline. Kulber-Ross moving through five stages of grief. With love, Theo*

Ha ha ah! Typo. KEEBLER ELVES. With love, Theo

Ha HA! No cookies. Kubber-Ross. With love, Theo

Well, you know what I mean. With love, Theo

Boomer's messages were brusque, cursory enough to feel evasive. *K* was the entirety of one message. Another, longer one: *Nice.* Functional, but intimating harshness. Judy, conversely, sounded over text exactly as she did in life—the same way Sara's letters had felt vaguely precious, the value inherent to the act of her penning them. Frenetic Sara intent on communicating a moment to Magda, all other tasks briefly out of mind. Text messages seemed to simultaneously obliterate and exacerbate that line of thinking. One could be doing three things at once—no reason to delay conversation. In the digital world, everything was worthy of acknowledgment and response. Everything! Deserved! Attention! Immediately!

Magda's responses to Sara had rarely felt cavalier, because of the sheer amount of time required to craft a satisfactory letter. They had to be funny, or if not funny, then witty. Magda would try sometimes to dash one off spontaneously, and as she prepared to slide the paper into its envelope, she would find some critical flaw. A misplaced comma, some daunting overstatement of excitement—worse yet, commentary on art that, upon further reflection, was juvenile. Embarrassing. She would then have to rewrite it.

Magda especially liked the moments just after receiving a text message, before it had been opened, when there was only the blinking icon of the name, and beside it, the number of unread messages. To see that offered the same jolt Magda had felt in opening her mailbox and finding a letter with Sara's name on it. How, without knowing the contents, she knew that the letter would conclude with something funny—Sara, forever the jester—or long-winded, Sara having worked herself into a fervor while writing. The lines of handwritten text became increasingly cramped until they were stacked two to a line, the biggest thoughts expressed in the smallest print.

I've never been! Can you describe it?
  lots of low buildings not like Manhattan but right outside the city limits is dessert cacti and sand as far as you can see
    desert not dessert
    Ok, you HAVE to send a picture! Lol
    Oh, wow! Wish I was there. Glad you're having a good time in the desert! Go get some dessert!!

Magda's photographs were blurry, backlit. She toiled over landscape and city, the images conveying neither beauty nor intentional composition. There were other things to photograph: people walking, in conversation, wearing unusual clothes downtown. A woman dressed as a clown, a matching red cotton ball affixed to her dog's nose. Three boys skateboarding in tandem, all dressed in the brightest of purple. *garden variety eggplants*, to which Judy responded immediately: *So good! Haha!*

The buildings came out best, largely because they couldn't move away from her. Magda found that she couldn't quite focus on the landscapes, either; more often than not, the pictures reflected the level of light visible in the sky. Everything in the forefront was hazy, shadowed. The people were glimpses, intimations, passing through the photos like gusts of wind.

I want to see pictures of you, too!

Magda tried, she did. There was a button with which to turn the camera toward oneself, but those were the images she liked least of all. She wasn't quite looking at the camera, couldn't get her smile right, and the constellation of lines mapping out from her eyelids seemed craterous. Eventually, between a bank and a grocery store, the clown reappeared, ambled toward her. The dog was panting, its cotton ball nose on the verge of slipping off. Afterward, the clown surveyed her work. "Those are good," she said, returning the phone to Magda.

There were five photos. The first, blinking. Second, third, fourth, her mouth gaping, midway through asking the woman to please tell her when.

In the fifth photo, Magda was squinting, one hand lifted to shield her face from the sun, the other arm dangling uselessly at her side. The sky behind her was a seamless, assertive blue, swept clean of clouds. But she was smiling, her upper lip pulled tight over her teeth. Waiting for the moment, unsure whether it was upon her, deciding to smile anyway.

Oh, wow. Beautiful!

Magda drove until she found a hotel that looked nice: a rounded half courtyard, milky glass doors. The valet smiling apologetically as he stubbed a cigarette on the ground before taking her keys. Her room, and its massive bay window, which overlooked the city. An overstuffed armchair was set flush to the desk, a notepad and pen laid flat on the burnished wood. Magda took a picture of the view, which was a little fuzzy, her own reflection thinly visible. She sent it to Boomer, and to Theo, and after a moment, to Judy as well.

nice view. get someone up there to wash those windows.—HB
Forget what Boomer said, it is nuce. With love, Theo
NIECE! With love, Theo
Nice! Widow fine. With love, Theo
WINDOW. With love, Theo

Just before dusk came the rain, casting down in sheets that broke waves into puddles on the sidewalk. Magda, from her window, watched people jump over them, newspapers and coats slung across their heads. Dr. Stein's voice in her ear: "Not too fast." The forecast had warned of the inclement weather streak. Climate change, as Theo had warned, the headlines announcing imminent global collapse streaked with rain and muddled into sludge, tossed into trash cans and onto welcome mats as people hurried inside.

A jolt in her pocket.

I hope you're getting better weather than we are!
    the storm is something else i just saw someone ruin their book by using it as an umbrella
    Oh no! I'm so sorry! What were they reading? I NEED a new book.

Magda had expected the messages to peter off, believing each text to be the final one, to go without response. A thrum in her heart with each incoming text, each time she was proved wrong. Still, Magda tried to ignore that old, steady impulse: five more minutes, one more message. And yet it went on, Magda's phone placidly buzzing as she showered, as she ate limp spaghetti atop the starchy hotel sheets, as she watched a cowboy movie in which the men turned into robots and then back to men again, and as she turned off the lights. *Good night!! I hope you have nice dreams!*

42.

May 2009

Dear M,

Do you remember that letter I sent you last summer? It must have been June, and maybe it was two years back, but there you have it: old age has rendered me forgetful. I said something like how there was nothing I could write that I hadn't told you, but I'm realizing that isn't true.

I'm in London, you know, and I keep seeing dogs that look just like Eugene. Three or four of them, over the course of this past week. The first one outside the Tate Modern, as we were setting up. It felt chronically unfair, for that white-spotted flank to appear on the other side of the street, or the park. Each time I felt the impulse to find you, grab your arm, only to remember that of course it isn't Eugene, nor is the person walking him ever going to be someone I know. It is just another dog, another person; neither is mine.

Even so, do you know what I thought upon seeing that first dog? I thought briefly it was some sort of a sign that you would, in fact, be flying out to see me, even though I knew in my rational mind that couldn't be the case, that of course you wouldn't cross the Atlantic with that puppy. Still! That dog seemed to be everywhere. I kept looking around, thinking you might surprise me, and then, on the last day, cresting the Heath, there he was, lunging after some tennis ball.

It will sound strange, probably, but the dog I saw reminded me of myself. The way he was focused on this dirty ball, when the hill was covered—covered!—in new ones.

I'm kidding, mostly. It's just that it's hit me, just now, how people spend these whole lifetimes without getting what they want, without thinking about it, really. Instead, we chase familiar objects. Or try to be known by those familiar to us. The truth is I always want to tell you what I'm thinking, even if sometimes I suspect you already know what I'm trying—and failing—to say, as I suspect you can see is happening now.

Yours,

S

43.

IN THE NEW MEXICO DESERT, SAND ROSE FROM DUNES. CHOLLA
bent sunward, seeking light. Hot enough that the air-conditioning stayed
on full blast, Magda's arms peppered by gooseflesh. When she gently
rolled her knuckles along the dashboard, she found it was hot there, too,
practically burning.

Sara's obsession with Georgia O'Keeffe had been grounded not just in
art, but in the mystery of Georgia's personal life, rumors swelling around
her like the tide. "Imagine driving around in a Model A," she said sometimes, shaking her head. "Imagine living so *alone*."

And yet there was a communal aspect to her art, Sara argued. She'd
made Magda visit the Whitney, where *Summer Days* and the other paintings from that collection were on display. Sara, by this point, had become
obsessed with prolonging her own longevity and, when she walked, was
prone to rattling from the sheer number of vitamins hauled along inside
her purse. "Look *for* the pain this time," Sara admonished Magda, pointing at the print of *Summer Days* that hung above her kitchen sink. Magda,
though she tried otherwise, saw only sun-bleached bones.

Sara had balked at Magda's response to the work, and insisted that one
day they would see a collection together. She would find a way to get Magda
to change her mind. One evening, before their main courses arrived, Sara
flung a paper on the table. *O'Keeffe Museum Opened in Santa Fe*, read the
headline. It had been underlined twice. Sara lifted her coffee cup, then her
eyebrows. "Soon," she said, and Magda dashed milk into her coffee, nodded
as she began to stir.

After breakfast on her second day in Albuquerque, Magda drove to the
Georgia O'Keeffe Museum. She wore the prescription sunglasses Dr. Stein
had recommended, which spun the road into shades of blue, relieving her
temporarily of a headache. Water, she reminded herself.

Driving through the desert, there were no bathrooms, and so she relieved herself on the hot sand that bordered the road. She looked around, just to confirm there was truly no one around, the heat hazy and relentless. A lizard sunning itself on a rock eyed Magda but did not move. The road, pocked by craters, seemed to stream on indefinitely. The wind made large, gulping sounds against her back, the car rocking slightly, sand kicking up from under the tires.

Just that morning, she had sat on the hotel's roof deck, drunk four glasses of water with hardly a breath between. The capacity for consumption felt unrelenting, as if in one day she could drink enough water to stay hydrated for years. The hotel room had a cactus on the bedside table, a flag with GROWN IN NEW MEXICO emerging from the soil. Outside, there was a heaviness to the light, and the way it cast yellow across the sidewalk. At some point she had begun enjoying the trip, Magda realized, wanting a way to extend this suspension of her reality. Something she had noticed in patients, a halting nostalgia for the present moment, a hyperawareness as it slipped on, as time always did.

For something she had pictured for so long, the building itself was understated, unmemorable. A taupe building, blocky with soft corners, it took residence on the corner of a quiet street. She missed it on the first pass, her phone's navigation system bleating after her to turn, keep going, no, turn left, turn back.

There was a welcome sign by the entrance, which Magda stood in front of: there it was, after all this time. On impulse, Magda pulled up Sara's number, and a new conversation opened. Blank. It was something that had not occurred to her before to try, a different experiment. Magda took a photo of the sign and sent that, along with the text: *finally we made it*. She held her breath; the message went through.

Inside, the corridors were narrow, glossy wooden floors underfoot, art lofted along the walls. Beams of long overhead lighting that cast yellowed light low and reverent. Rows and rows of paintings spread out: the sunflowers, abstractions, all of Georgia's other flowers.

After Sara, Magda had lost interest in the vagaries of artwork; without Sara to guide her through a museum, there seemed little point. To go alone required imagining what Sara might say, and bits of their actual conversations returned in startling detail—about things she hadn't considered important, like how O'Keeffe's introduction to New York begat her rendering of natural things, like leaves and flowers. Magda had found those paintings to be the most moving of all, but in seeing a reproduction of *Summer Days* up close, she went a bit faint. The canvas caught the overhead light, and it seemed, then, a palatable way of considering death: bones, swept clean of anything else, practically glowing.

The sign on the wall said no photography, but Magda, seeing no one around, went ahead anyway. *i thought you might like this it's one of my favorites*, she wrote to Judy.

Magda leaned closer to the painting, and Sara shifted in her bag, lurched forward. The flash of memory surprised her: Fred's dour expression, how he had all but bolted from the kitchen when Magda suggested that they might read Sara's letters together. When he reappeared, his glasses were askance; she repeated herself, and he, again, ignored her. What if that was what Sara would've wanted, Magda wondered, but she hadn't been able to ask? Even in the museum, the question resurfaced: What, in that moment, would Sara want?

A cough behind her, some stranger peering over his sunglasses at the painting. After that, shuffling away. Farther back, a security guard with his head craned over a phone, and Magda, heart thumping, reached into her bag, carefully unscrewing the top of the urn. She pinched not sand but silt, grains sifting through Magda's fingers as she pulled her hand to the top of the bag, let the ashes trickle to the floor.

Her heart bleated a frantic melody as she walked outside, toward the entrance, where heat whooshed up from the brick path, all along her legs and spine, and she felt abruptly, intensely faint. She felt that same brief dizziness she had experienced after the tattoo, the question hanging over her: What are you running from? It had felt right, though, leaving some of Sara in a place she would have loved.

In the parking lot, a buzz in her pocket. Judy: *Something I think YOU will like!* A photo of a red convertible streaked by dirt, where a massive dog with dripping jowls sat in the passenger seat, its neck thick and muscular.

Magda went back to the thread with Sara, and her own message blurred against her vision. Nothing.

Back to the message from Judy, which had not yet become funny. Perhaps Judy had not understood the significance of the art, or was someone for whom art did not communicate something greater about the world than a dog, panting dumbly in the sunlight. Or perhaps Magda was the one who was too dense. Magda couldn't conceive of what they were actually saying to each other—what it meant, where the center of gravity was holding.

It had been stupid, to write to Sara. Magda got into the car, thought of her own foolishness—for believing, for forgetting, for allowing herself a shred of hope. For thinking that if she scattered the ashes, if she did right by Sara, if she did all that, then maybe her friend would come back. It had been long enough that she ought to know better.

Who is this? chimed a new message.

magda is this sara

The dog. She looked at the photograph again, zoomed in on the wet, squinted eyes, the meaty head. The dog had not reacted to Judy and her phone, it had held its pose, and Magda unexpectedly found herself tearing up. As with *Summer Days*, she had misunderstood. The dog believed wholeheartedly in his owner's ability to return to him. It was a picture about faith.

Through the foothills and closer to the city. Thirsty again, her throat dry and scratchy. No new messages had come from Sara's number. By Albuquerque, Magda was thinking of how she would describe the paintings to Judy. There was a comforting quality to the afternoon sunlight, the way it rested upon one's skin like a blanket. She could say something like that, couldn't say how she kept looking at her phone, wondering if somehow Sara might call. Alive and dead, everywhere and nowhere.

The phone buzzed, and Magda looked toward the passenger seat.

A honk. Tires screeching.

Then Magda was bolted forward, and before covering her face, she reached for Sara.

You've got the wrong number.
Sorry.

44.

MAGDA WOKE DISORIENTED. SHE HEARD A FAINT BUZZING, THE hum of machines and an air conditioner's sputtering. A fogginess to her vision as she examined the IV in her arm, the bag of fluid beside her bed. She was alone in the room, though there was a doctor's coat shrugged onto a chair, as if someone had left with the intent of returning very soon.

When Magda next found herself awake, the light had changed. The side of her exposed arm nearer to the window felt prickly from the sun, and she was trying to move the blanket to cover it when two men walked in. One introduced himself as Dr. Ramirez, explained the particulars of her case: where she was, what had happened, that she was lucky. Things, he assured her, were looking up. The other man, a police officer, asked what she remembered. When she did not answer him, when she asked after the car, Dr. Ramirez shook his head. *Totaled.*

"And my friend?" she asked. He looked to the officer, then back to Magda, brows pinched together.

"What do you remember?" the officer repeated.

Then she was asleep again.

She remembered having the right of way, reaching into the passenger seat. She remembered the collision, and the jolt of initial impact. How afterward, time slowed, wrapped itself around her. There was this hummingbird heartbeat of a moment as she realized what had happened, just before the airbag deployed against her.

After that came the pain, spiky against her forehead, and the sound of something dripping—the engine, she thought. Then there was the car that had struck her, whose driver lay with his head bent to his palm. She remembered next how he'd looked at her through the windshield, the circle of his dark mouth and those darting eyes, and the creak of someone opening her door, saying they had seen the whole thing, the police were on the way. Magda remembered opening her mouth, and then the world went dark.

After that, there was a scream—hers, it had to be—and the concerned faces of several young men, who were going to escort her to the hospital.

A thick needle was inserted below her wrist, and Magda's surroundings went creamy, the world light and soundless as the ambulance whirred on. She remembered next the doctor explaining what had happened, and then asking if someone had been with her. "A witness said you were asking about someone. Was that the other driver? Was that the friend you mentioned earlier?"

Magda closed her eyes. When she next opened them, the doctor was gone, and the world outside had gone dark. A monitor pulsed steadily behind her, an IV in her right arm. Her head ached, and there was a dull throbbing in her mouth, a metallic tang on her tongue. She had bitten it, she remembered, when the airbag punched into her chest. Her neck was sore and corded, pain lingering when she tried to adjust the pillows, ricocheting into her skull unless she lay very still.

She slept lightly, dreams blank and stretching ahead until she woke, doused in sweat. She saw the green blinking lights of her machines, and, outside, streetlights hugged by dew. It was early, the fog just breaking, when the nurse arrived to bring her to radiology. In the MRI room, the technician asked whether she had a pacemaker, aneurysm clips, anything metal in her body. When Magda shook her head, he handed her a clipboard with forms asking after the medications she took. The words went blurry before her, and after some time, he took it back from her lap, and she dictated, "Multivitamins, calcium, Ripsledin, Tyrc, Proxyditin, Linthugo." He handed her a small packet of rubber earplugs, and said, "It gets very loud. And I'll need you to stay really still, okay? Just try and keep your breathing regular, nice and easy." He inhaled and exhaled dramatically, then with a sheepish smile, asked, "Any questions?" She shook her head, wincing at the pain. As he placed a soft pad around her neck, he repeated, "Nice and easy. If you need me, just shout. I'll be right outside."

Magda was slid into the machine headfirst, her nose inches from the top of the tube. It was spackled white, chips flecked away in places to reveal a darker metal. She heard the radiologist's voice, faint through a speaker, and then chirring. After that, buzzing, a rapid series of beeps. The room was stilled and gray around her, the color of metal, the aches in her body magnified, the only thing to focus on beside the paint chips. Tears slipped sideways and into the brace, and Magda tried to steady her breathing. The machine went quiet, the room brighter, and then she was being slid from the machine, the tears coming faster. The radiologist's hand slipped around hers, and he said, "Lots of people get scared in there, believe me; you're doing just fine. We'll take a few minutes' break, okay?" He handed her some tissues, removed the pad around her neck. Up close, she saw his nose was dotted with freckles.

Magda nodded, and the radiologist left. Her chest heaved, and she cried until the man returned. As he refastened the neck brace, he seemed to lose track of his movements. His eyelids were freckled also, and his hands, both of which covered hers. The warmth a relief.

Back in the machine, Magda thought of her conversation with the policeman. He had asked what she remembered, and she had forgotten to correct him on one thing, which was that she hadn't asked after the other driver.

Where's Sara?

That's what she had said to the witness before the world went dark.

It took another day for her to call Boomer, whose voice belied no concern for the vehicle. "In the middle of the day, Jesus Christ, no, of course you shouldn't worry about the car, I'll have it towed to the dump. A drunk driver," he said, his voice cracking. "Jesus Christ. All that matters is that you're okay."

Theo, who called later, said the same. She was lucky to be alive, but if he ever found that miscreant he would destroy him. "Pummel the guy, no questions asked." The monologue made her tired, the ache of familiarity after so many weeks of solitude. Someone else, handling things. Theo was still talking about what he would do as Magda fell asleep; and when she woke up, the headache was still sharp against her temples. The phone, screen now alight with voicemails, had been plugged into a charger. She turned it over, facedown.

When she woke next, Dr. Ramirez was examining her chart. He sat beside her, running through his questions before clipping the pen to the board and saying, "Your friend." His eyes dark, creased at the corners. The kind of man who had cried while proposing to his wife, would cry upon the birth of his children: a man like Dr. Stein.

What he said: "We cleaned up what we could, but there was damage."

What he did: held up Sara, showed where she was caved in. Where she was missing.

Another day passed. Magda drank apple juice out of a thick plastic cup, gripping the edge with her teeth. She let Boomer book her flight, waving away his insistence of paying, despite being tethered to a hospital cot with an IV tucked into each arm. He paid anyway. The walls did not change; they remained green, hemmed with yellow trim. She read the jokes that Theo sent to her, but a sickly feeling swelled in her stomach at the sight of anyone else's name. *another one please*, she wrote to Theo; all of the other messages, she ignored. When Dr. Ramirez visited, she pretended to be napping, and sometimes that deceit was enough to lull her into misty, forgettable sleep.

"The good news is that there appears to be no significant injury," Dr. Ramirez told her. "You were bounced around a bit. *Mezclado*," he clarified, motioning with his hands. "But there appears to be no damage to the brain."

When she slept, Magda dreamed of being at home—specifically, of being in her childhood bed, tucked under flannel sheets, moments before waking up. The sounds outside her window of the neighborhood stirring, clothes lifted by breeze and shaking on the line. The faint murmur of Hedda and her mother in the kitchen, and the gentle shuffle of her father pacing upstairs.

Dr. Ramirez called Dr. Stein, and he did not, for once, ask what she was doing for herself. He sounded older, his voice thick with relief.

The nurses culled Magda's belongings from the closet, asked that she go through them to ensure that everything was there. The bag itself was sticky with sunscreen—another casualty—and gritted by paper towel where someone had tried to wipe the oil off. Clods of paper were affixed to everything: the credit cards; reading glasses; pills to ease her pain; calcium; a plastic sheet of multivitamins, unopened; sunglasses; a melted tube of lipstick, sticky to the touch; the one necklace Hedda had sent her for Christmas, nearly thirty years prior. Yes, she nodded, everything in its place. One of them had affixed a thick line of clear tape to Sara, wrapped bands of it around the top, where she was dented.

It felt impossible to continue home, but, Boomer reminded her, the flight departed at 7:11 a.m. on Friday. Theo called to say he would meet her at the terminal; at long last, he had bought himself a car. It had been meant to be a surprise, upon her return, and yet it was strangely fortuitous. "Don't worry," he assured her. "I'll drive you home."

"I can't do it," she told him. There was a thin ringing in her ear—tinnitus, Dr. Ramirez had said, common after whiplash. The world was a dial tone.

A pause and Theo said, "It'll be easy. I'll come to you. We'll fly back together."

"No," she said. "The road trip. Sara's plan."

Such was the tenderness in his voice that Magda nearly cried as he said her name, and then, "She would understand. I promise you, she would." When she began to cry: "Oh, Mags."

Inside the suitcase, her clothes were bundled around Sara, whose lid had shifted slightly, but miraculously remained shut. Was Magda fine because her friend was there, or worse for it? She wasn't sure. Someone must have tucked Sara into the clothing, because Magda remembered the moment vividly—one hand on the wheel, the other stretched into the passenger seat.

Dr. Ramirez had called her lucky. The injuries were minor—relatively, anyway. A pinched tendon in her neck, tearing between vertebrae. The sporadic numbness in her left arm caused by the fissures between C7 and C8, the same for the dull zipping sensation that flashed all the way down to her fingers. They liked to be careful, he explained, with older patients, but there was nothing to indicate she wouldn't recover.

It didn't feel much like luck, though. Magda had been lucky in a way Sara hadn't—she'd not been felled by a heart attack at the kitchen table;

she had been lucky, too, not to have been the one to discover Sara. Yet to survive others proved a tricky balancing of reality and future potential bound to go unexercised. She could see, easily, what her life would have been were Sara to have survived; she could see the negative space meant to be occupied by Sara.

It had been different when her parents died—those losses sad, but expected. With so much time and distance between them, to grieve her parents felt like climbing into a skin long since shed. What she mourned was the distance. Her father had gone ill three years after she'd left for New York. Liver failure, the final, total rejection of those years winnowed away with beer and bourbon. He'd come home hung heavy with the sour stink of alcohol, his eyes yellowed.

Only Hedda and her mother remained, and when her father stopped being able to work, her mother spent most of her time at the nursing home, extra shifts that made her miss dinner. She stood sentry as the elderly endeavored to scrub themselves, or went to the entertainment room, where she gamely rolled dice for men who yelled that bingo night was a hoax, it was rigged.

When Hedda wrote to Magda, there was little news—*more of the same*, in her cramped scrawl. She deferred her own plans for a year, and then another, after which it seemed she wouldn't go to college at all. Magda, conversely, found reason not to leave New York. Her finals coincided with Christmas that first year; she spent Christmas Eve drinking cheap, sickly sweet port on the fire escape of one of her classmate's apartments. Dizzy and cold, she looked down at the stalled traffic, thoughts of Ohio dancing across her mind: she should have returned. If she hated herself for anything, it was that, the selfishness with which she had forged ahead in pursuit of her own ambition, how she'd carved forth her own path and left Hedda behind, without a knife.

The next year, he was worse, and neither Hedda nor her mother expected her home, which made it easier to stay away. Easier to ignore that selfishness and absorb herself in studies. When Hedda called, she talked about alternative therapies, cutting-edge treatments. If their father ate seven apples a day, if he cut out bread and alcohol, if he did all of those things, then maybe. Hedda read the studies aloud, laboriously, with idle pauses as she waited for Magda to weigh in.

It had been drinking, in the end, but it had been easier to ignore the problem and rest, for a while, in the liminal space of unknowing. People wanted answers that complied with their own desires; they did not seek answers that would ravage them. Bill's wife had, for a time, taken a pregnancy test each morning, Bill had solicited men online. To try and push against the boundaries, to force a conclusion where one didn't exist, that was human nature. A way of seeking new information, was what Bill said, when what he was doing was avoiding confirmation of something he already knew.

When her father became ill, Magda imagined a holding pattern, after which, having completed medical school, she could return. She thought of Skinner's conditioning, or electroconvulsive therapy, of everything she had learned, bundled together. She would be able to return if she could figure out how to do so as another, better person. She would stay, and next time, Hedda could go.

After college, Magda had stayed away from Ohio, because it was impossible to watch her father grow steadily worse, to try and make those amends with her mother. She had stopped writing to Hedda because she had failed her, had left Hedda to deal with the worst thing alone; decades later, hadn't forgiven herself for it. She had taken from Hedda a future and gently laid olive branches over the scar tissue, had convinced herself that was enough. Magda had been the one to leave, just as she had abandoned Sara, as she had tried to reconfigure their friendship into what she had most wanted it to be, every day resenting what it wasn't.

Each time, she had been the one to do the leaving, and for the simplest of reasons—that she couldn't face the issues at hand. All those years spent whittling through people's lives, their most private problems, and there was the truth of it: Magda couldn't accept things for what they were, just kept trying to remember them differently.

45.

THE NEXT MORNING DAWNED BRIGHT, SUN TACKY AGAINST Magda's eyes. When she opened them, there was Theo, in his turquoise seersucker pants and a daisy-print shirt. Pen in his mouth, the *New York Times* crossword splayed across his lap, the heel of his palm stained blue. "Develops hearing loss, eight letters," he prompted. She didn't realize she was crying until he said, "We all go a bit deaf, it's nothing to *sob* about."

But there was, of course, the fact of his having arrived. The reality of Magda's own body, the way she was shepherded into a neck brace and handed vials of pills, the instructions for which were delivered to Theo by Dr. Ramirez. Theo nodded assiduously, diligently tapped instructions into his phone. The ringing in Magda's ears and the tenderness of her neck were enough to keep her distracted, allow Theo and a nurse to shuffle her bags into a taxi waiting out front. When she hobbled toward the entrance, she did so with a familiar clattering: the sound of bottles of pills bumping against one another, as Sara's vitamins and supplements had done only a year prior.

It was in the car, bumping along to the airport, when Magda's stomach began to rise. The road went wavy, her pulse thready and loud in her ears. Magda reached for Theo's hand to steady herself, and found herself sobbing. Theo's brows knit together, and the driver turned around to check on them; through that, Magda kept crying.

For as much as her body hurt, that pain was undercut with something else. It was something that she wished she could tell Sara: that aging was awful, it was, but much of that stemmed from the difficulty of trying to stay alive. To age *well*, as Sara had said. The pain came from knowledge, coupled with the shame of having not sufficiently appreciated something during a time in which it was unblemished. "If I knew *then* what I know

now," Bill had said to Magda once, shaking his head. "I mean, if I'd known all this."

"Then what?" she had asked, pen on the clipboard.

"Well," he said. "I wouldn't have made that particular mistake."

She had told him that to categorize any minor decision as being essential to one's life was a compulsory practice, not a logical one. The whole endeavor, she explained, was pocked with impossibilities. Still: had she only slept in—just the once! Had she not stopped for coffee in the hotel lobby, had she taken a little longer to locate her sunglasses, had she not become so fixed on the idea of Judy. If she had done any of those things—save, perhaps, for the last—she would have continued on, oblivious but fine.

What she had not said to Bill, and hadn't considered herself, was that even if she *had* continued on her way, there might have been another car. If not a car, then a break in the water main during her evening shower—say, a pipe explosion that would knock her senseless. If not the pipe, the next morning she might have slipped in the parking lot on a left-behind plastic bag, tucked neatly into a puddle, the station wagon beside her backing up, up, up, until—

That was the point. There was no way of knowing from where the danger stemmed until the moment, the problem, was upon you. To be brave in spite of that was no small miracle.

In between the hiccups, Magda explained. He looked blankly at her, and she said, eventually: "Must be the muscle relaxers."

"Oh, sure. That explains it. Sure." He returned to his phone, the nub of his nose illuminated in its soft light.

Out the window, the road and its surrounding foliage looked soft. Magda's neck felt loose, her limbs pliable. The first time in years she could remember her body presenting to her without complaint: everything fine, no pain. It would return to her, but with her eyes squeezed shut, there seemed enough respite that she could imagine it would stay this way, just for a while.

Theo did not let go of her hand until check-in, when the agent slid their tickets across the countertop. They walked toward security, the click of his wheeled suitcase underfoot, and he said, "You know they have dogs at airports now? Yeah, to sniff out bombs. And drugs, but they're trained as bomb dogs." Her face went slack, and he hastily added, "I'm just trying to say it's safer now than it ever was; they check everything very carefully."

They shuffled forward in line, plucked free their shoes. Theo lifted their bags to the conveyor belt, where they whirred away, into the dark grotto of the X-ray machine. The agent analyzing the monitor held a pen between her teeth, pointed it toward the screen. Her colleague squinted, leaned forward. Theo went through the body scan first, and spoke across the belt to the agent while Magda waited, arms in a triangle atop her head. Shivering, her feet bare against the linoleum.

"Go on through," said the agent, motioning her to where Theo stood alongside two other agents, one of whom held Sara aloft. All of them speaking in hushed tones until Theo, shoes in hand, burst out, "Well, why *her*?"

Magda had once asked a similar question to Sara: Why do you love him? She had said it with a terrific kind of violence, the words slanting upward to an accusatory finish: *him*. As in: Of all the people you could possibly love? As in: Of all the people you could allow to love you?

She couldn't remember, really, what Sara had said in response, just that the conversation went slack between them. To an onlooker, nothing would have appeared to be amiss. Magda would have lifted a fork to her mouth, Sara would have sipped from her glass of water, wiped her fingers on a napkin. At the end of the meal, while Sara was in the bathroom and the plates were being cleared, that was when Magda would have given her card to the waiter. The apology wouldn't be readily apparent to an observer, but it was there—all of it was—if one looked close enough.

Theo, out in front, took Sara from the agent's hands. He walked back to where Magda was, and it was when he slid her foot into a shoe that she began crying again.

In the waiting area, Theo observed her at a slight distance, like she was something hot against which he might burn his hand. The muscle relaxers had worn off, leaving her irritable and sore. She was there, that was indisputable, but she ought to be elsewhere, utilizing her second chance. The attendant stood alone, intermittently clicking at her computer, and Magda said, "I can't go back right now."

Theo didn't look up from his paper. "We can take a later flight; it's not a problem. Oh, Christ, the *score*. Always an off year for the Mets. Well, we're not missing anything."

Though the prospect of boarding a plane brought the hairs on her neck to attention, Magda shook her head. "I just need to go somewhere else first."

The paper crinkled as he set it down. "Okay," he said slowly. "Where are we going?"

"You don't need to—"

He rolled his eyes. "You can't even carry your own suitcase, Mags. How are you going to travel alone?"

"Well," Magda started. A bolt of pain raced up her neck, and she winced, Theo's mouth tightening in response.

"You're wearing a neck brace, you can't lift anything, and you're frankly hopeless at navigation on the best of days."

"Well," Magda repeated.

Theo drummed his fingers against his legs. "At some point, you need to realize that you can't do everything by yourself. So I'm going to ask again, where do you need to go?"

"Ohio," she said. "I need to see my sister."

For a few moments, he sat in silence. "You know, I've never been to Ohio." And then he stood up, said, "I bet it'll be nice in the summer."

46

July 2011

Dear S,

You remember how I'd sworn otherwise, said we'd never go anywhere again? You'll be glad to know I was wrong. I imagine there wasn't any doubt in your mind about us following the plan. It would happen simply because you had willed it to, because of course that was the way things ought to go.

I always admired that about you, the confidence. It doesn't come naturally to me; what I do, am best at, is finding fault lines. What I've realized, in being away, is that those are impossible to spot until you are underwater. The first crack in the ice is often invisible, this thin, trembling thing pressed lightly into the surface.

A patient of mine said that once. I know what you would say: enough with the metaphor; say it right; just say the thing for what it is. I'd argue—am arguing—that metaphor is effective. You'd say it's not the whole of it, that metaphor is a half-hearted way to tell a story, but I think what that means is that one person cannot tell the full story. One person can't possibly know it.

What I'm saying, I suppose, is that I was wrong.

You couldn't have known this, either, but there are dozens of letters crowded under my desk, drafts I couldn't send you. I thought at the time they weren't clever or observant enough, and yours—God, they were funny. I worried awfully hard about saying the wrong thing, such that it became difficult, in the end, to decipher what the right thing would even be, how I might delight or surprise you.

I reread a number of your letters on the road—more since being in the sky, where I am right now—and I'm struck each time by how much you told me. And then I read some of my letters and thought of how scripted they feel, uptight. How perhaps I've always been a better custodian of other people's feelings than of my own.

It made me think that the whole point of doing anything is to be seen, to find someone to bear witness to joys and sadnesses alike. Which I think is what you were trying to do for me, with the road trip. Give us a second chance, try and rewrite some of the other person's story. That was the idea, wasn't it? Forgiveness of all those old wounds.

I should have guessed, because that is just like you—the need for a formal conclusion. You couldn't stand it when I trailed off midstory, or if we saw a play that was bound to end badly. By your standards, I mean. Halfway through the second act you'd ball up the bag of popcorn, dunk it into the trash, and leave. I'd exit the theater to find you annoyed and waiting in the lobby. "Took you long enough. What happened?"

You couldn't stand anything left incomplete, wanting. And so we find ourselves here.

I hope you won't mind that I added one last stop to our trip, before we go home. You, back with Fred. And me, for once trying to draw my own conclusions.

Yours,

M

47.

MAGDA HEARD BEFORE SHE SAW: THE WOMAN IN THE YARD WAS laughing. With one hand, she held a phone to her ear; the other fluttered as she spoke. Whoever was on the other end of the call, Magda thought, was someone the woman knew well, liked very much. All the while, she tended to her garden. The woman picked up a trowel, placed it down again, rubbed two fingers against a leaf of aloe. She laughed, loudly, as she stepped away from the plant and adjusted her hat.

It wasn't too late, Magda reasoned, to change her mind.

And not until seeing the woman place phone into pocket did Magda realize that the other option, leaving, wasn't possible. In her hands was a bouquet of wildflowers, plucked from the nearby park.

The woman was turning toward her house, and when Magda hurried across the street, her footsteps were sound enough for the woman to look back and see her. The woman gingerly stepped toward her, and Magda urged her own feet forward, called out.

Upon hearing her name, Hedda paused.

Magda, waving the bouquet above her head, reminded herself it was too late, now, to turn back. There she was, with an offering. Her neck ached, a muscle seizing at this movement. Too far for Hedda to grasp them, but still she lowered her arm, thrust the flowers forward: *Here.*

Hedda moved slowly, squinting toward her. Magda saw that she favored her left leg, the right just slightly out of sync. In stepping closer, Hedda seemed unsure if her own vision could be trusted, and Magda, feeling her own hand slip from the bouquet, nodded. She could, yes. She wouldn't run.

Magda held out the wildflowers, her fingers beneath stained with yellow tracks. Hedda, leaning in to sniff them, asked if it was really her. Her eyes ran over the seam of stitches knit into her forehead, the bruising

192

that butterflied out to her hairline. Hedda's chest seemed to collapse, go concave, as she noticed the litany of injuries. Those, and the years—what had unfurled since they last were together.

"Yes," Magda said. She could feel her body straining from the tension, the headache a reminder she ought to be lying down, ought to be drinking water, ought to have quit smoking many years prior. There was no shortage of things she should have done differently. She perhaps should have not come at all; Theo, waiting in the car across the street, would be worried. He'd call Boomer. They would think she had again fallen to pieces, and here she was, trying to relitigate the past, wrangle it into a better shape.

The screen door flipped open, and a child tumbled out, shouting back at someone who was just out of sight. He jumped from the porch and landed, hard, on his feet, before running to Hedda's leg. She leaned down and whispered to him, and the child ran back toward the house, the man Magda had seen appearing in the doorway. She waved, gently, at her nephew.

"Yellow," she said. "It's perfect, it's just like you wanted."

Hedda's hair was short, clipped in the back with a blue enamel pin that looked homemade. She was saying something, and Magda couldn't quite decipher what it was, not when Hedda's hand cupped the neck brace and her gaze dipped low to Magda's bag. Not even when Hedda saw the urn glinting up from the canvas and drew Magda in, tight, for a hug. No, Magda's mind didn't clear until Hedda took her hand, was bringing her toward the door, the decision already made. Only then did she think to say yes.

If people did change, she thought, it happened in moments.

III

Home, Again

48.

MAGDA FELT A DIP IN HER STOMACH AS THE CAPTAIN ANNOUNCED their descent. Beside her, a mother and child held each other, snoring, the little girl's face nestled into the crook of her mother's neck. Magda leaned over them slightly to see through the window. Early afternoon following a rainy morning, and the clouds clung together like strands of silk, separating as the plane nudged toward the ground.

Lower, and the dotted land revealed itself for what it was: siloed redbrick houses, squares of green that became lawns. Farther back, a little girl exclaimed—"The little houses!"—and her father made a hum of dissent. "Skyscrapers," he corrected. The city still small and far away, its silhouette rising to meet the clouds. The child's eyes widened. "*Big* houses," she said reverently.

The flight attendant appeared behind Magda, offering beer to the man who had pounded away at his keyboard for the entirety of the trip. The mother and child, roused from their sleep at the sound of the tab popping open, requested soda, which came in miniature, melting globs of ice clinking against plastic.

"In *English*," the mother admonished the child. *"Inglés, por favor."*

"I want a *straw*."

"You have one," the mother replied, rolling it between two fingers.

"Not *that* one," the child wailed. "It's 'sposed to *bend*."

Lower still, and the children's ears began popping. A scream, then shushing, but the noise returned, louder. Magda understood; she worried less in the sky than she did in the last moments before once again touching ground. The mistakes came when people became careless, when they stopped worrying, when the lane for taxiing seemed two feet farther than it was in fact.

Though she clenched her hands into fists, nothing of note happened: the wheels squealed onto the pavement, and the plane ground to a halt.

White knuckles relaxed into pink. The woman beside Magda began clapping, and so, then, did Magda. Across the aisle, a businessman was reaching for his bag in the overhead storage, the woman next to him turning on her phone. Someone else was taking a call. Yes, the flight had been delayed; well, he couldn't have been expected to tell her that while in the air, that was *crazy*. Magda wrote a message to Hedda: *home safe thanks for your hospitality*. Then she reread the message, found it too formal, sent a second one: *i love you*

In standing, Magda found that her right foot had fallen asleep, and so she waved the mother and child past her before the other passengers streamed by. Already, they were in a hurry, most of them fixed on their phone screens. Emails had come in, business had transpired, lives had been interrupted by an interlude in the sky. The flight attendant, following the last of the passengers, asked if she was all right, if she would require any assistance. Magda shook her head.

The urn felt lighter in Magda's bag as she exited the plane, well behind the others. There were only the flight attendants and the captain, loosening his tie, to walk by as she moved from plane to solid ground. If she was lucky—and she had the feeling she might be—her bag would have already begun its rounds on the carousel.

"It's an old saying. Really, you've never heard it?" Bill had asked Magda. "That's what people say, that you can never really go home."

Perhaps it was not that, exactly. Perhaps it was true that you could return, but not to the same place. Or it was true that you could return to the same place as a different person. Both of those things had felt true when Hedda drove Magda through town, and while her initial impulse had been to look away from the church, it had risen from the ground as a new building. "They bulldozed it a while back," Hedda explained, pointing toward the bright brick façade. "That scary basement is gone. It's nicer now."

Magda's bag was the first one out, ringing its way around the carousel, toward her. She had been home, and here she was now, going home again.

Theo waved as if the world were ending, and he were the only person who could signal it. There, at the curb: unmissable in those seersucker pants, tipped forward on his toes, one arm extending fully to his left side, and then to the right, until he was certain she had seen him. He shook his head, remarking, "I can't believe I let you fly back alone. If I hadn't had those sessions, I would've stayed. I *love* Ohio."

On the highway, Queens streaming past them, Magda remembered that Theo was a truly horrible driver. Oblivious and distractible, one moment annoyed by a swerving SUV, the next nearly cutting off a sedan. He rambled on about work, how Marty had recently shuttered her practice. "Just like her, to be first," he said, rolling his eyes. Magda, door handle in a vise grip, said, "So you talk to Marty quite a bit?"

"Yes," Theo said, edging the car into the right lane. "Well, here and there since that dating event—no, *you* watch it!"

A bleat of the horn, a Volvo driver shaking his head as he accelerated past them. Magda loosened her grip on the door handle, asked Theo to tell her more.

His newest patient was twenty-four, pregnant, and beside herself with anger. The father was a former boyfriend who balked at the idea of parenthood, and had since left to "find himself"—Theo removed his hands from the wheel to offer air quotes—at Burning Man. He'd be parsing through past lives and traumas while she sweated through the summer in their Bushwick studio, uncertain of whether or not they had broken up, and if she would be raising the child alone. She didn't know, Theo said, whether or not to leave.

"Say what you will for our generation," Theo said. "But we didn't have to find people online. It wasn't like it is now: too many options to actually *choose*. It just seemed obvious, when you met someone."

"Well, you were engaged to Joan within weeks."

"I was," he allowed. "And before, there was that other girl in medical school."

She faced him. "No, there wasn't. Nobody you told me about, anyhow."

"Remember when Boomer dragged everyone to that art show? The one with all of the butter?" When she didn't respond, he continued, "You wore a blue dress, and you had your hair up. I told you to call me."

"I did call you," she said. "A few times, actually. James didn't—?"

"James was a horrible roommate," Theo said, glancing at her. There was a significant lull in the conversation, which Magda felt increasing pressure to fill.

"And then came Joan."

"Right," he said. "And that was that."

Magda wasn't sure what to say, so she took to looking outside instead. Suddenly, she felt so hot that even with the window rolled down, she was sweating. They passed a family drinking from the same water bottle, a screech bellowing out as the youngest child tipped the contents over his head.

Talk radio chimed out from the speakers, and when Theo leaned forward to adjust the dial, Magda peeked over at him. His skin was a few shades darker, a red patch high on the forehead that had been recently scraped for cancerous cells. Dr. Stein had told him—gently, but with a degree of firmness—that he did not need to come into the office every month. Annually would be fine.

Another station wagon flashed by, and Magda remembered the flash of the young man's open mouth, the warmth trickling down her own head. Nauseous, she closed her eyes, and Theo's voice quieted, went soft around her when he noticed.

Only when they pulled up outside her apartment building did Theo speak again, and only to say he would be back in a couple of days. "You remember, that belated birthday dinner Boomer is planning," he clarified.

"Of course," she said. "Another one." She thought to say something else, but he was already out of the driver's seat and unlocking the trunk.

He waved her away, lofting the bags over his shoulders. "No, no, let me. You've had a long trip."

The apartment seemed as if it had been waiting on tiptoe for her return; it smelled headily of home, of dust and sun-baked furniture. She suspected Boomer, despite his assurances, had not been by to vacuum and to air out the rooms; a finger run along the kitchen counter revealed a thick layer of grit.

Though it was nearly ninety degrees, Magda drew a bath. When she opened the window, in piped candied cigar smoke—Mr. Tyson, surely, avoiding his daughter—and she, too, lit a cigarette, dangling her toes in the water. If not the same temperature as the air, it felt close. On impulse, she slipped into the bath fully dressed—and, on another impulse, stubbed the cigarette against the sink.

The clothes bubbled out from her skin. Layer by layer she peeled them off, draped the skirt and blouse on the rim of the tub, water dripping steadily to the floor.

Shouts warbled in through the open window. Downstairs, the daughter had caught Mr. Tyson, wondered why he had no goddamn respect for her. Magda peeled off her underwear, her socks. Surveying her body through the steam: the new little pooch of her stomach, the familiar knobby knees and hips, all of her pinkened by the water.

Magda sat awhile longer, the water and her body going cool. Just the other day she had been in New Mexico. She had thought everything was fine. Everything had, briefly, been fine. When she emerged from the water, stepped to the mirror, the bruise would still be there, blooming all the way up and along her hairline. But while she sat in the bath, there existed a world in which the suitcases were not in the living room, her phone not humming with unread messages, the urn not still patiently waiting in her purse. No, for a moment she forgot where she was in time: she was young again. Magda was for a moment in the glassy water of the arboretum by the yellow house, the surrounding world gone still, holding her breath until she heard Hedda call her name, they were going to be late for dinner, hurry hurry hurry.

Days had passed since Magda's return, and her bags remained by the front door. She had not swept the apartment or tended to the pile of laundry in the suitcase. Since the flight, her joints felt swollen, the tightness in her neck intensifying as she bent toward the bags. In Ohio, she had thought that when she got back to New York, she might get off the plane and go directly to Fred's. He would look at Magda, then at the urn dented in her hands, and she would place it on his doorstep, walk away. If Fred wasn't home, it would be Gloria into whose hands the urn would be placed, she who Magda turned away from.

This, it seemed, Magda could not manage. The urn remained in the duffel, wrapped in a sweater; Magda remained, largely, upon her couch. She was able to call Hedda, order in dinner, but leaving the apartment felt acutely difficult. It wasn't quite that she wanted to be on the road, or that she didn't want to be at home. It was that there wasn't another directive, nowhere else to go. She had not, it seemed, learned anything from the trip; she had not, in the end, come any closer to understanding Sara. Had not found a way—not a permanent one, at any rate—to miss her any less.

Boomer and Theo each called her house phone to check in on her; Boomer, Magda could tell, was taking precautions with her. When he updated her on patients, he delivered the news very slowly, as if he knew she would be writing it down. He said something else, too, but by then she had placed the pen on the countertop, was wondering where the cigarettes were. "Got it," she said, when he stopped speaking.

"Theo loved meeting your sister," he told her. "He said you trounced them both in dominos, but that she got the cooking gene."

"She did," Magda said, to which Boomer laughed.

"So your birthday dinner we'll do out, then."

"But we already—"

"Magda." Boomer laughed. "You're not going to win this one."

Outside, there were those same garbage cans brimming with excess, the familiar dips in the entryway from where previous tenants had lugged and dropped furniture. In the hallway, the body spray and smoke wafting from Mr. Tyson's apartment. Next door, baby powder mixed with something dusky, heavier. The young couple was gone, replaced by a man who made loud and cryptic phone calls about business. The specifics were unclear, but his occupation seemed to require much shouting about money. Magda wondered what had happened to the couple—whether they were together, and elsewhere, whether they had separated, whether the memory of the building would hold or become weightless, detaching itself from them, and later, from her.

She was trying, as she had on the flight home, not to think of what would happen when she returned the urn to Fred. Whether it would in fact languish in a cabinet, or tucked under a stack of books, where the only person to happen upon it would be Gloria. And how, if that were the case, only unfriendly eyes would be cast upon the urn.

All that time—all of those miles—and she had somehow thought that things were indelibly changed, that she was restarting. But perhaps it wasn't that her world needed to become any different, really, it was that she needed to learn how to be. Be forward-thinking, in the way she encouraged her patients. Still came that familiar cycle of counterfactuals: had Magda been paying closer attention, had she not reached for the phone, had she, just the once, gone to the movies, let the rest go. She'd tried explaining that to Hedda, who had simply laid a hand over hers: "*Tillräckligt*," she'd said. *Enough.*

Please stop texting me, wrote the person who wasn't Sara.

Magda moved to delete the number, stopped, let her finger linger over the screen until it went dark. What had she thought could change? Over the years, she had perhaps given too much credence to the possibility that things could simply stay the same, when the only constant seemed to be that, surely, they wouldn't.

missing you, she typed to Hedda. She pressed SEND.

In the hallway, Mr. Tyson hooted upon seeing Magda, insisted on carrying her garbage bag to the bins outside. Outside, cigar dangling between his teeth, he asked where she had been, said that he had been worrying about her. "I thought you'd *moved*," he said, aghast.

"At our age? Of course not."

He cleared his throat. "Good," he said gruffly, scrubbing his voice of relief. "I'm glad to hear that. Too many new people, as is."

"Would you move, at this stage?"

"Nah," he said. "Need to stick around for my daughter. She needed someplace to go after Davey got arrested, and this gives her something to do, ya know? Taking care of me." He laughed. "I pretend I don't smoke; she pretends I'm gonna change. One of the stories we tell each other."

"I'm quitting," Magda said, lighting her cigarette.

"Yeah," he told her, taking another drag. "Me too."

49.

SINCE MAGDA'S RETURN TO MANHATTAN, SHE AND HEDDA HAD
fallen into an early evening routine: Magda calling as she walked home
through the park or, once arrived, bustling about her kitchen, Hedda
answering from either her garden or the front porch. That night there
was the recognizable creaking of a rocking chair, Hedda explaining
that the grandchildren were playing in the yard. "They're sweet, don't
get me wrong, but they can be menaces. You have one of your own, and
in time you forget just *how* exhausting it is. They can be little assholes,
really."

Magda, surveying the contents of her refrigerator, chuckled. "Since
when do you curse?" she asked, pulling free a ream of kale and sniffing
it. Glumly, she concluded it was safe to eat.

"Oh, only when I need to make a point. They can be assholes, though,
in the same way I'd imagine your patients can be."

Magda fumbled in the cabinet for a cutting board, found it dusty.
"What, you mean childish? In your case, I suppose you're lucky, given that
they are, actually, children."

Hedda snorted. "You have to let them run themselves out, burn off the
crazy energy. Imagine if our parents had tried that with us, when we were
fighting, instead of, what—"

"Pretending it wasn't happening?" Magda chewed one of the leafy
greens, winced. "Is kale meant to be bitter, do you know?"

"You have to massage it," Hedda said. "Olive oil, salt, pepper. I'm surprised Sara never told you that."

Magda rummaged for a bowl. "In the year before she died, she was on
this smoothie kick. She'd drink, oh, a quarter of the mug, maybe, before
leaving the rest on the counter. There was this awful smell as the greens
wilted, and then she'd go to the farmers market and buy more kale. She
kept forgetting, or wanting to forget." She stood over the sink, glowering.
"I don't think I'm meant for kale."

This time, Hedda laughed. "You don't need to be. And aren't you meeting the boys for dinner, anyway? I do like that Theo. He's quite fond of you."

"I was trying to do what they call meal prep," Magda said. "But yes, I am."

She was early to the restaurant and ordered a charcuterie board, knowing both the men would've forgotten to eat lunch. The platter arrived before they did, salami bent into the shape of roses, crudité lining the edges, an elaborately wrapped Brie at the center. Magda took a picture of the cheese, its wrapping complicated and briefly funny.

She opened the thread with Sara, closed out of it. She keyed in Judy's name, the scroll of unread messages unfurling. Too many, over too many days. *I miss—* The ache in her stomach, her own foolishness. If, in the car, she hadn't reached for the phone, what then?

Boomer had explained, in the office, that there was a way of seeing all of the images sent to one particular person, as well as all of the ones from them. He had reached over her shoulder, showed Magda the button to press, and the new, smaller collection of photos swelled before her. "See?" he said. "Those are the ones between us."

The chain with Judy boasted fifty-seven photos. Shadowy images of Gardee on the podium; that panting dog, still in its car; Judy with a wide expanse of mountain behind her, laughing toward the camera so enthusiastically that her crowns were visible, blinking up from the cavern of her mouth. Then, all of those things Magda had wanted Judy to see. A grainy sunset captured through a hotel window; blurry desert interrupted by her massive, superimposed thumb; the museum. From Judy: the dog in the convertible; a filmy mug of coffee with her hand wrapped around it, from the day after the crash. Magda scrolled through the loop of photos, and it didn't matter then the quality, only that they had been transmitted, with the guise of importance: *This matters to me, and so perhaps it will to you.*

After the coffee came the final three photos from Judy: a half-eaten sandwich; the sun as a slice of peach glinting over the horizon; another one of those YEEHAW napkins, Judy's pointer finger and thumb spanning one side, holding it gently in place.

Magda put the phone down, placed one of her final antinausea pills upon her tongue. As the tacky exterior melted in her mouth, Magda thought, *This is a pill that will make you normal.* She was misconstruing things again, trying to rattle signs from the ether, shake something until it became something else—a thing that it was most definitely not. She closed her eyes, and when she opened them next, the men were on their way to the table. Boomer walking briskly, Theo shaking off his coat like a dog, one hand rising in greeting.

Over charcuterie and the first glass of wine, the men envisioned their retirement. "Before we're too old, I mean," Boomer said toward his plate, to which Theo made a joke about wintering in Florida.

"Me," Theo said. "I'll go downtown, to the Village, or even Brooklyn. Full bohemian. Some glass house with a rooftop garden. Batik-print sheets. Hemp sandals."

"I don't think you understand bohemian," Boomer hedged.

Theo laughed. "This, from a man who wants to retire to Boca Raton."

"I didn't—no, never mind." Boomer turned to Magda. "What about you, when you retire? And Sar—?"

Theo slid an elbow against his ribs. "We're talking about *me*, remember? And Magda's going to live with me. She's going to get a pair of Birkenstocks."

Magda, watching, was touched by the gesture. A warm feeling beamed through her stomach, as it did when someone tried looking after her.

The waitress returned with another bottle—Sancerre, perfection with the charcuterie. She stuttered a bit in saying so, noting the meat was gone and the only remnant of the cheese its wrapper. Boomer waved off her embarrassment. "Good either way."

"So where are you going to go?" Theo asked Boomer. "Or do, whatever you're thinking with retirement."

Boomer idled back in his chair, the candle casting shadows over his handsome features. "I'll go out to the summer house, I suppose, look after my mother. And besides that, I don't know. At this point in my life, I have everything that I need; it's more about figuring out what I want, really."

Magda settled back in her chair, slightly drunk but happy to be observing it all. She half expected Boomer to say something else, but he didn't, and then came their main dishes, and then out came a cake with one candle teetering atop it, the men singing "Happy Birthday" and the adjacent tables joining in. "Make a wish," said the waitress, clapping her hands.

There was a version of her life, Magda supposed, in which she, too, stopped working. Spent her weekends at the farmers market, or visiting Boomer at the beach house. Spent the day before Christmas rattling around on a plane, her carry-on filled with wrapped gifts for the grandchildren, who, along with Hedda, would meet her at the airport, fingerpaint-smeared signs lofted overhead. WELCOME HOME, AUNT MAGDA! Even in such fantasies, Magda parsed the farm-grown herbs alone, the neighboring seats on the plane left unoccupied.

She blew the candle out, Theo saying to Boomer, "I really thought they'd forgotten"; Boomer saying, "No, they *know* me here, they wouldn't." Theo, then, congratulating her on her seventieth birthday.

Boomer chimed in, "Yes, it starts now." His head tilting as he watched her.

"What did you wish for?" Theo asked.

Boomer batted at his hand. "It's bad luck if she says. Didn't you know that?"

Theo wrapped an arm around Magda's shoulders. "You hear that?" he whispered into her ear. "Old Boomer's gone superstitious."

50

OH, THEY WERE GLAD TO HAVE HER BACK—ALL OF THE PATIENTS said as much, tripping over greetings in the rush to update Magda on their lives. Gwen had made strides: she had gone on a girls' trip and not spoken with her husband for an entire weekend. "And," she added, "I was, like, totally fine?" She looked at Magda with her eyes wide, asked, "That's progress, right?" When Magda smiled back at Gwen, she absolutely beamed in response.

Bill said he had met someone new, a man with no interest in finance whatsoever. Henrik was cheerful and bright and generally unflappable, had moved to New York to become an actor, though for the time being he was ferrying tourists across Central Park in a bicycle cart, and bartending on odd evenings. "He might not be a *good* actor, actually," Bill said, before adding thoughtfully, "but I don't think I care."

None of that lessened the bite of Ernesto's name, though it was better, Bill assured her, than being alone at home. While Magda was away, the two of them had spent a weekend on Fire Island and, not long after, gone to the Catskills with some of Henrik's friends. "He's not looking for a relationship," Bill said, shrugging, when Magda commented on his happiness. "Which is fine for now, while I figure things out." He had acquiesced to his wife the apartment, and their little dog. He was done smoking. Mostly.

"These things don't always happen all at once," she said. "The important thing is that you're trying."

Hi!

Hi there, it's been a while! How are you?

Just wanted to check in and make sure everything is all right. I hope the weather is improving since we last talked! Did you make it back to New York?

Hello!

Hello?

On her slow jaunts homeward, Magda mentally drafted responses. Instead of sending them, she put away her phone. Too much to focus on where she was—the inevitable return of Gwen's paranoia, the tightening coil of Bill's anxiety. The old ways of being hadn't served her, had they, not with Sara. Something that felt obvious could later be proved as wrong, inadmissible evidence against one's memory. For Magda, it had seemed that if something *felt* true, then surely that indicated some inherent truth. Yet that gave no credence for the fact that, when it had most mattered, she had been wildly, abjectly wrong.

No, it was better to recalibrate her focus: she would home in on her sessions and her friendships. She and Theo would be spending more time together until September, Boomer having absconded again to the Hamptons. "I forgot his mother was out there; I always thought it was about boating," Theo said. He shook his head, and Magda pressed a palm to his shoulder. In the following days he began narrating the lives of their goldfish—with Kline deceased, Alzheimer had joined their troubling—and lingering in the doorway as she brewed coffee. The conversations stayed light as they chatted in the elevator, made plans for dinner on Tuesday.

They went to a café near the office, the low sun spangling his shirt red and orange. Sirens whooshed past, and his gaze followed an ambulance before returning, slowly, to Magda. He drummed his fingers against the tabletop, absently fiddling with the seam of his napkin as he recounted the latest in a series of awful dates.

"Not awful, exactly, but unremarkable," he amended. "It's nice to be out with you instead. It's discouraging, this dance of getting ready, then hopeful, then, inevitably, let down. And then there's the added pressure of having less *time* to find the person, and not expecting that there will be time for a do-over if this one doesn't work out. Dating online somehow only makes that worse. What Boomer said at your dinner, about having what he needed, going instead for what he wanted . . . it got me thinking."

"About what you're looking for?"

"That, yes, and whether I've been looking in the wrong places." He pulled from his glass of beer; a trail of foam swept clean above his lip. With the back of his hand, he wiped it off, looking at her, and, just as quickly, away again. "If maybe I should've been looking at what was here the whole time."

Seeing him in that moment, Magda felt keenly the friendship lay between them, a thing that, stepped any further forward, would be irretrievable. She wasn't sure what to say, and so said nothing.

He went on. "It's been on my mind since we were in Ohio. Seeing you there, with your sister, I felt this overwhelming sense of affection. And it's not like it was a random thought; I *had* considered it before, ever since that session with Sara, but I didn't want to—oh, I don't know. I didn't want to push things." He ran a hand through his hair and, seeing her expression, prompted, "The session? She didn't?"

Magda had been shaking her head, she realized. She reached for her wine.

"Right, okay. Well, I had no way of knowing—she'd booked under a pseudonym—and from the time she opened the door to the end of the session she was berating me, for the full fifty minutes, that I had never called you back after that gallery opening, way back in med school, and that somehow, five years after the divorce, I still hadn't asked you to dinner. That's what she wanted! Over and over, that's what she kept telling me."

Magda focused very hard on the glass, raising it again to her mouth.

"I told her that you didn't think of me that way anymore, if you ever had," Theo said. "And she said that if I weren't the biggest idiot in the world, that she and I could have been friends. You'd just been away, and I thought, oh—I don't know what I thought, really. Maybe I am an idiot, it's just that I've thought you were beautiful since med school, and then in Ohio . . . It got me wondering."

After seconds, or a minute, Magda said, "She never told me."

He sighed. "To be fair, neither did I, and maybe I should have. It seemed like you two had drifted apart those last few years. I thought you had talked about it, and that was why she came to me." He ran a hand over his forehead, looked toward the street. "But then you didn't say anything, and I didn't, and so . . ."

Magda drained her wine, said, "No, she and I weren't talking much toward the end." When she apologized, he looked down at his own plate, moved the vegetables around without eating any.

"I figured you might say no," he said eventually. "But I thought what's the harm, really, in trying, if you might say yes."

Her heart ricocheted a frantic beat, looking at Theo: his open face, the hopefulness of the expression. It felt, in a strange way, like seeing herself on the day she had caught a glimpse of her own reflection, in the mirror with which she was meant to be checking Sara's hair. The obviousness of desire, tucked under the pretense of friendship. "I know how it feels, wanting someone you can't have."

Theo's half-smile waned, his brows knit together. "You do?" He looked off toward the street, and dipped his head. "Oh God. Boomer? All this time?"

Without meaning to, Magda laughed. "It wasn't him . . ." She trailed off, and Theo looked down, saw the urn glinting atop her bag.

"Really?" he asked.

Magda's breath caught in her throat. "Always," she said. "It was always her."

The silence then was not the easy, companionable sort they were used to; it seemed to halve the space between them, the distance microscopic but impossible to reconcile. In walking to the curb, where a taxi was already idling, Magda looked over to find Theo's shoulders stooped, looking smaller than he used to. Softer. Magda wanted badly, in that moment, not to leave, and despite the fact that they were not friends who hugged, she wanted to put her arms around him. *Here's the thing*, she would have said, but she didn't feel capable of speaking until she had sat upon the cracked pleather seat, the cabbie asking where she wanted to go, and by then Theo was already walking in the opposite direction.

When she got home, she left him a voicemail apologizing.

He called her back later, his voice soft, muffled by drink. Kept saying he had misunderstood, but it would be fine. "That Sara," he said, and Magda could tell he was shaking his head while she blew smoke out the kitchen window. She was quitting, she thought, definitely. "I just need some time," Theo said. "A bit of space."

Magda stared down at the phone in her hand, clicked back to the chain with Sara.

i still miss you, she wrote, and the three dots burbled up, disappeared, came back. Disappeared again.

Please. Just stop.

The thing about Schrödinger's cat was that, in the end, the animal was functionally irrelevant. The cat's fate depended solely on how the subatomic particle behaved. Not that the cat would understand the machinations of quantum physics, but still—how long could a thought experiment be sustained? How long could a cat be both alive and dead?

i'm trying, she wrote, to which there was no response.

Not indefinitely, then.

51.

LATER THAT WEEK, JUDY LEFT A MESSAGE: "I'LL BE IN NEW YORK in September," she said over the static. Her voice went wobbly, uncertain. "I mean, if you want to meet?"

Magda deleted the voicemail. At a certain point, perhaps, the present just trundled along into the future. People followed paths they had carved forth—or been assigned—years prior. What she was doing, then, was dusting the leaves off of a familiar one. Allowing, once again, for that hope to balloon upon seeing someone enter a room, that momentary visceral flash of relief. She had gotten it all wrong, Magda thought; she had gotten it hopelessly wrong. Again, she had deluded herself. She couldn't allow herself to do that any longer; she had to try, at least, to accept things for what they were, rather than what she so hoped for.

August continued on, patients complaining about the weather, the price of their child's after-school football league, whether it would be possible to continue on with the new diet through the fall, after things picked back up again. A job that nearly came to fruition, but whose company wrote to blame unexpected budgetary changes. Readjustments—just how it goes in this economy. One patient, the writer, had sold his robot space saga novel to a publisher; the wedding had gone off without a hitch; his wife wanted them to buy an apartment, but he wanted to wait. Another patient had sent postcards from her vacation. *I M DOING FINE RLY.* Magda spoke with Boomer, called Hedda twice a week. The messages from Judy slowed, and Magda powered down the cell phone, tucked it away. A return to the usual way of things, as it was meant to be.

52

ON THE LAST DAY OF AUGUST, BOOMER APPEARED AT HER APART-
ment with a shiny new doorknob and keys. "It's really time we change the
locks, don't you think?"

The fact that Magda's spare keys had gone to Sara, and were never
recovered by Fred, had irked Theo tremendously. Never mind that they
were unmarked, wholly anonymous; he worried after her. Since the dinner, though, he had said nothing; he had, in fact, been dodging her in the
office. A curt nod here and there, a solicitous gesturing past himself in
the kitchenette. "Really, go ahead" was all he'd said to her in a week.

Boomer rummaged for his glasses, without which he wouldn't be able
to read the assembly instructions. Even then, he stood squinting, half in
the apartment and half in the hallway. The eggy overhead light seeped
into his hair as he repeated on occasion, "Okay. Okay, okay." Magda leaned
against the exterior wall to let Mr. Tyson's daughter by. She bent down,
plucking a miniature wrench from the carpeted floor, and handed it to
Magda before continuing on. Magda was struck by the solemnity of her
features: the heavy brow, pinched expression. "I didn't even notice it had
fallen," Boomer said. He called out after her: "Hey! Thanks." The daughter
smiled at him, and her entire face changed. Brighter, suddenly.

Examining his handiwork a few minutes later, Boomer concluded,
"Okay, this looks good."

"Great," Magda said from the kitchen. She could barely hear him over
the kettle's screeching, and laughed when he walked in, blanching at the
sound.

"You know, they have electric kettles," he said. "The kind that don't
break your eardrums. I have an extra one. I'll bring it by."

Rummaging in the cupboard for tea satchels, she shrugged. "I'll keep
using this one; I'm used to it." The heat radiated into her palms, and she
passed one mug to him before saying—casually, she hoped—"Have you
spoken with Theo?"

"Here and there," he said. "Have you?"

She shook her head, and he suggested that might be for the best. A short break, he meant. "I don't know what happened at that dinner, but both of you seem out of sorts as a result."

"I just . . ." she trailed off. "I said something, but it wasn't meant to be unkind."

"Of course not," said Boomer. "But he thinks he's in love with you, and so he's bound to take rejection the wrong way."

"How did you—"

He tilted the mug against his lips. "Ah, too hot. Look—do you remember that dinner after Sophia's funeral?"

"At the Italian place?"

"That one, yes. He got awfully drunk, and he felt sorry for me, I think, felt like he should say something. And so he leaned in and said, 'You know, you were it. For her, you were it.' Which felt at the time—I thought, *God, how insensitive. She's not here; what could* that *matter now?* But in the weeks after, that phrase kept resurfacing. It didn't feel quite as impossible then, getting up in the morning, or remembering to put the coffeepot under the machine before brewing. So I kept it to myself, and eventually I started to feel grateful for it, like he'd redeemed me. I couldn't have stopped Sophia from killing herself, do you see? And I didn't think to say anything to Theo until we were at Sara's funeral. I finally thanked him then, and he shook it off. 'That's what we all want, isn't it?' he said, and he was looking over at you."

Magda sat back in her chair, the tea heavy in her mouth. She had been listening so intently, her throat felt raw, like she herself had been speaking, muscles still tensed in anticipation. "And then?"

"Well, a drink later I told him that I had to be honest, because he'd given me that gift. And I said that you were our dearest friend," he said, adding hurriedly, "but not for him."

She startled, sputtering, "Why?"

He drew out the exhale so it came out like a sigh. "Well."

"Because I don't think—"

"Mags," he said, his eyes on hers. "Some of us noticed where you were looking."

Magda's body tensed. Breath shallow, each exhalation getting caught in her throat. She put down her mug for fear she would otherwise drop it, looking around the room until her eyes landed on Boomer, who was still looking at her.

A buzzing, and he patted the back pocket of his pants, dug into it. "Damnit," he said, "Where..." And Magda slid the phone from the sideboard and into his hand. *Thanks*, he mouthed. "Hi. Yes, I'm on my way. Okay. Yes." He nodded, and Magda went into the living room for his jacket. "Yes," he was saying when she returned. "Definitely."

"I'll walk you out," she said. "Give me a minute." She removed the trash bag from its bin, tossing in the old lock and, after a moment, the old keys. Boomer hefted the bag down the stairs, knuckles white against the railing. On the front steps, he glanced at his watch.

"You know, I could smoke," he said. "Shouldn't, but..."

At this, he shrugged, and Magda reached for her cigarettes. Tapped the bottom of the pack, offered it to him.

"So you knew," she said finally.

He tilted his head, shrugged. "I'd wondered, over the years, why we hadn't met anyone you were dating. And then the past year, seeing you grieve Sara, it wasn't what you'd expect to see, between friends."

"Did Theo know?"

"I don't think so," he said. "Theo tends to see what he'd like to."

She tried to laugh, but it came out garbled. She cleared her throat. "Not that it matters, but I never said anything to her. I never told her she was it for me, nothing like that."

"Well. If she really was it for you, don't you think something would have happened?"

A burst of a laugh, then, too abrupt to sound genuine. Quietly, she said, "I hoped so." A bloated string of traffic before them. One car honked, the driver in front of it rolling down his window to extend a middle finger. "But no, she never felt the same."

Smoke wafted into her periphery as Boomer moved down a step to sit beside her.

"It's not like you can ever know how people feel. Look at Theo, right? Or me. For months after the separation, I kept getting Sophia's mail. It became this joke, that when we met for lunch or a movie I'd bring the latest pile to her. Like we weren't going to stop being married, she just hadn't been home. And so I'd toss the junk and organize the pile, include these little notes that said *urgent* or *forget it*. And she seemed fine, she really did, until she died. After that I kept thinking how I should have known. I should have sensed it, right, because she didn't care about the mail anymore. But I didn't ask how she felt about anything, because I didn't want to know how she felt about me."

A smattering of ash tipped forward from his cigarette, landing on his leg, and he wiped it away. "We, out of everyone, should be better at this, right?" He laughed. "Better at people, I mean."

"I don't know if we're bad at people, exactly."

"Not bad," he said. "It's just that we—or I, maybe—keep getting them completely wrong."

"Boomer," Magda said. "Sophia loved you; she must have told me a hundred times."

The sun moved behind a cloud, and the air turned cool, a breeze ruffling Magda's top. She shifted, the step suddenly too hard below her. Smoke plumed before them, and a woman on the sidewalk scowled up at them as Boomer took another drag. He exhaled in her general direction.

"That's what I mean, though," he continued. "I didn't want it to be the end, so I couldn't accept that it was. But I didn't ask her, I didn't say my piece, all I did was write those little jokes on the envelopes and hope that eventually she would change her mind."

Boomer picked up his water bottle, set it down again without drinking from it. "And what does it matter now, what I wanted versus what actually happened?" He stood, swiping the back of his pants with his palms. A mild wind twisted at his hair, and he smoothed it reflexively.

"I scattered some of the ashes," she said softly as he craned his neck to examine his pants.

"What?" he asked, and she shook her head. There was a pause, the tendons of his neck pulsing as he concluded his examination, seemingly satisfied. "The thing is, it's easy to mistake caring for other people as caring for ourselves." Stubbing the toe of his loafer against the cherry of his cigarette, he went on, "Accounting for their needs, but not having to think about what you really want. Ah, damnit."

He indicated at the screen of his phone, alight with an incoming call.

Go, she motioned, *go, go*, and he said, "Give it some time. Theo will come around."

Boomer moved easily down the steps. "How is she today?" His voice growing smaller as he walked, one hand cupping the phone, the other worrying at his ear. He waved from the street corner, and Magda waved back at him, then rubbed the tips of her fingers over the four-leaf clover on her wrist.

He had known, and the discovery hadn't shifted anything between them, or in him. Not even in her, despite this private knowledge having been made public, made *obvious*. Magda had been seen and she had been fine. It might have been different, had she known Theo wanted her; she imagined a wardrobe brimming with Technicolor dresses, a calendar packed with thrice-annual doctors' appointments. Who she might have been, for wanting him. For wanting someone else.

An ache in her stomach as she ran a finger along the serrated edge of the new key. The taste of tobacco thick on her tongue, her mind foggy, thoughts jostling against one another. "Hold the door," a man called out across the street, scaling the stairs and twisting through the scant opening. In the dimming light, she could see the wrinkled underside of her wrist clearly beneath the ink, that cool steady jet of her pulse. Mostly fine, maybe.

53.

BACK INSIDE, MAGDA CALLED HEDDA, WHO WAS—AS USUAL—gardening. Magda's greeting was lost to a thin breeze whisking by, jumbling her sister's response. Annoying at first, but it had become familiar: Hedda's voice overrun by the whooshing sound, only to return a few seconds later, Magda trying to piece together what had been said. "Bit of a nightmare, really, with the deer," she was saying, to which Magda, fingers sharp with the scent of bleach, tutted. She opened the faucet, set the phone to speaker.

"Really," Hedda went on. "The owner of the flower shop suggested buying urine wholesale, dousing the plants. Ridiculous. And I had one of the grandchildren with me, and what do you know—I go outside later and the plot is covered. Not just number one, either, you know. I mean, she'd . . ." Hedda paused. "Well, you know what I mean."

Magda stifled a laugh. "Maybe she thought she was helping," she said, to which Hedda scoffed.

"I hope your day is better."

"Oh," Magda said. "It's like ever. I'm doing just fine."

Hedda chortled. "Saying that isn't the same as actually being fine."

"I am," Magda insisted. "I'm back to my regular life. Everything is exactly as I left it."

"That's my point: everything is the same," Hedda said. "But how does that make you feel, Magda Eklund?"

Magda quieted. On the other side of the phone, she heard the *clink* of pruning shears, Hedda's light panting, a grunt of frustration. Except the moment wasn't about Hedda, or how she felt, was it? It was about Magda. She glanced about the apartment with its familiar furnishings, Sara on her usual perch. "Not so fine," she admitted.

"Mags, I know," Hedda said. "And I have sympathy, I do, but at the moment I'm absolutely up to my elbows in shit. So you're not fine—okay. Now what are you going to do about it?"

54.

yes i want to see you yes

55.

THE NEXT WEEK, MAGDA TOOK THE BUS TO LAGUARDIA. DUST shrouded the windows beside her, and through those particles she watched tall buildings fade steadily from her vision. Flush against her stomach was a red satchel holding the urn, both of her arms crossed over the bag. Seeing it in her reflection, Magda recognized the posture from her own sessions, the item totemic. Something to grasp for fear that all else might spill forth.

In front of Magda was a man slightly younger than she, and bald, the patch of skin crowning his head warmed pink by sunlight. He held his fingers lightly over that spot, then dipped his hand down, over his eyebrows. Magda leaned forward to see what he was reading. *IMPROVE YOUR MEMORY IN 5 MINUTES*, promised the app. She settled back.

Magda mused that she wouldn't be opposed to an improved memory, the gaps in her own increasingly obvious. Things disappeared, others coming back with a stunning, lucid clarity. Yet that wasn't her mind's failing, exactly; it had been, for so many years, barbed against trespassers. Trying to protect her, blocking out what it could not hold. Still, it was difficult to accept the steady degradation of one's recollections, to see not the whole picture but the knife marks of tiny memories. *This is how it is*, Magda would find herself thinking, and then, a moment later: *But is it?*

Across the aisle, a young woman flipped through a book. Next to her, thick-legged children sat with their legs butterflied, laughing at something on a phone, as their mother sat quietly reading. On the other side of the bus, a man with a cigar poking out of his jacket pocket, was tapping his feet. Beside him, a couple with matching white high-top sneakers. Her socks were short-short; his were longer. Her shoes pristine, and the rubber of his soles coated lightly in dirt. Magda was struck by the sadness of that, their coordination felled by a wrong step. Did such small things make anyone else sad, she wondered, or was it just her? She was thinking that she might be the only person buzzing with worry in Manhattan, as the girl rested her head on his shoulder. The boy, still looking at his phone, tilted his head to lie atop hers. One of the children turned to his mother, pointing at the phone. "I can't say it," he complained.

"Try again," she offered, and he sputtered forth, "Apopa. Apopa . . ."

She gave him a patient smile. "Very close. Apocalypse."

In Magda's hand were flowers. Too dramatic, she worried. Dramatic and overdone and possibly desperate, if not a misread of the entire situation. The florist had wrapped the bouquet in a soft pink tissue paper, which rubbed against her wrist whenever the bus lurched forward or into a stop.

The tattoo still surprised her, that ink with her pulse humming directly beneath it. Ink, and then, millimeters from the surface, the rush of her entire little life. Hedda had noticed it and laughed. "A *tattoo*," she had said, repeating it as she ushered Magda into the guest room.

That night, unable to sleep, Magda had crept through the maze of children's toys and books lining the living room, and gone onto the porch. Upstairs, the lights were out, the hum of air-conditioning units steady overhead. The air was so clean and brisk it felt nearly painful to breathe. She lit a cigarette and a thin stream of smoke trickled over her, into the yard. Across the street, a woman with headphones on was scrubbing dishes over the kitchen sink. After finishing the cigarette, Magda loosed another handful of ashes into the grass below. They did not, as she expected, take to the breeze, instead shivering downward and then out of sight. Hedda's grandson might walk over them the next day, or perhaps they would be lifted, later, by some wind.

When they were very little still, and sharing a bedroom, Hedda had experienced terrible night frights, often squirming into Magda's bed and twisting into her sheets for fear of the dark. Even when she did fall asleep, she would often wake in the night and whisper, "*Blåsväder*," and Magda had to explain the dark sky wasn't ominous, not bad weather, it was only the sun napping. It would wake up soon, she promised. Eventually, things had to settle into one state or another.

"You know," Hedda said the next morning, pointing at Magda's wrist. "Do you remember how I used to . . ." And Magda, who remembered everything, said yes.

Magda had stayed the whole weekend there, Hedda's grandchildren running wild at her feet. They batted against her legs with wooden trains, from their mouths hanging wet bits of tomato and strawberry. The littlest one begged to see the place where his *gammelfarfar* used to teach, and Magda had walked him into town, looking every few seconds at their clasped hands: still there, still safe. The boy quickly tired of the building and tugged Magda outside, asked her to go instead to the playground. Later, Magda and Hedda sat in the kitchen, the children jostling their legs, one of them pulling at Magda's skirt to say there wasn't ketchup, and he *needed* it, and look at this ball, and come *on*, let's go outside. At the table on the lawn: eggs and mint iced tea, examining the new lines of Hedda's face, the familiar creases of her smile.

"She reminds me of you," Hedda said, then, pointing at the five-year-old, who sat hunched over a piece of paper. Magda saw how she deliberated between markers, picking one up and uncapping it before looking again, inquisitively, and choosing another marker. Before opening that one, she would close the first, holding the chosen one for another moment before slowly, cautiously making a mark.

At the airport, Magda checked the signage obsessively, two separate TSA agents making their way over to offer assistance. After the second one left, she went to the bar opposite the arrivals board and ordered a hamburger. Soft to the touch, greasy, lettuce wilting against meat. She ate medallions of pickle, counted down the minutes until it was time to meet Judy at arrivals, only to find out Judy was already at baggage claim.

Down the escalator, the metal chugging along as Magda thought through what she would say. There was an explanation owed for her gaping absence.

She had tried, with Hedda, to make those same apologies. The second night, slapping the mosquitoes bent to their arms, she had tried to explain herself. What came out was the story of liberating Sara's ashes at the museum, and Hedda was quiet before adding on, "And then came the guards, right, and you had to make a break for it, and *then* . . ." And in that way, she absolved Magda. It hadn't been so bad, had it, not like she was *arrested* or anything.

"I did crash the car," she admitted, to which Hedda shrugged.

"You can't win them all," she said. "What's the old saying? *Det är tidens tand. Liv.*"

Something their mother had said: *That's how it is, these days. Life.*

It wasn't until the drive to the airport that Magda, over Hedda's humming, said, "I should have told you about her dying. I just, I couldn't. I'm sorry I've been so awful to you."

"You have," Hedda said. "But you've been far worse to yourself."

Hedda adjusted her sunglasses, then pulled one hand from the wheel and placed it on the cupholders between them. Magda placed her own atop it, closed her eyes.

At the bottom of the escalator, there was a jolt as Magda's feet met the flat, unchanging ground. A swell in her chest at the sight of Judy waving. Magda reflexively turning around, because surely that woman wasn't waving at her. But maybe that was always the way of it—this subtle, clenching disbelief? Moving toward her, Magda thought back to the day after Boston when she and Sara had returned the car—*oh*, she thought, *no*—and then Judy's arms were around her waist, a hand in her hair. "Hi," Judy said.

She had asked, over the phone, if she might stay at Magda's apartment for a few nights, just until she settled in. Before leaving for the airport, Magda had laid the extra set of sheets on the couch. After finishing takeout from Two Wok, they watched *An Affair to Remember*. The last thing Magda remembered before nodding off was Kenneth saying, sadly, that he hoped Terry had found happiness: "And if you're ever in need of anything, like someone to love you, don't hesitate to call me."

She woke after midnight to the frozen credit reel, Judy snoring beside her. A blue pulse of static on Judy's face, the sheets still folded beneath her legs. Magda tiptoed into the bathroom to brush her own teeth, craning her head over the entryway to check once more: Judy, still there. Magda stood in the doorway until Judy tossed in her sleep, then, worried Judy might wake and see her, ducked back into the bathroom. Sat on the lip of the tub for another five minutes, listening.

Those first few days, they kept a distance from each other, oppositional and shy—as if slightly polarized. Magda would wait outside of the kitchen to allow Judy enough space to rummage in the refrigerator. She would bow back so Judy could exit the apartment first. Judy left an inch or two of space between them on the subway, in the back seats of cabs, not quite warmth but the intimation of it. She touched Magda infrequently, and then, it seemed, without thought. "Do we need this?" she said, pointing at a cardboard box of peaches at the supermarket. "They're fresh," she went on, answering her own question as she tapped Magda's wrist. Magda was reminded of the feeling of that last plane ride, tipping toward the ground.

"My friend can't host me anymore," Judy said on the third day, frowning down at her phone.

Magda's heart clenched. "You could stay for longer, if you wanted."

Judy's hair looked the same when she woke up as when she fell asleep, she was rarely without a book, she was left-handed and so she preferred to walk on the left side of people, so as not to bash them with her hands while talking. Judy was an ambitious but unaccomplished cook, asking Magda's opinion on dressings by holding a spoon in front of her mouth, then offering her own feedback. "Too much salt, isn't it? I know. I *knew* it wasn't right."

Magda was wanting, already, to hold on to these things indefinitely. The same way she could still remember—and might always—the slow uptick of Sara's bottom lip when she was amused, how she screwed up her forehead in concentration, then would complain about the lines mapping out from her eyelids. Magda thought, *I won't always remember such things*, and then, later that day, while picking up groceries, she found a box of the dandelion root tea Sara had loved. At home, it tasted as bad as she remembered, Judy grimacing theatrically after the first sip, refusing a second. "You *like* that?" she asked, and Magda saying, "Very much," after she spat her mouthful into the sink.

FREE, Judy wrote on the cardboard flap of the box, before leaving it outside of the building, then turning away from the front door to scrawl below that: BUT NOT GOOD.

As the week unfurled, Magda waited for Judy to explain her plans, and, eventually, to leave. While at work she imagined the steady thud of her own footsteps coming up the stairs, her front door swinging open to reveal

Judy gone. A low fluttering in her chest at the prospect, again as Magda imagined running into Judy, later, at some party, Judy turning away and toward someone else. Toward Janet Yengelman, who was loudly saying that she couldn't see how Judy had been with someone like that, someone who just didn't *understand*.

Magda waited and said nothing, came home from work and was glad to find Judy there. Each day she returned and felt a swell of relief: Judy on the couch; Judy with her head out the window, painting her nails on the fire escape. Judy, there. She would say something, she thought, surely, but not until the end of the second week, as they were walking to a museum, did Judy broach booking a hotel. "You've been so generous," she said.

"You don't want to stay?" Magda spoke without meaning to, her words tripping over themselves. Too sharp, anxious.

Judy squinted across the street, where the no-walk signal was flashing. "I think what I'm saying is that I don't understand what you want. And I wouldn't want to take advantage, overstay."

The light blinked green, the two stepping into the street as Magda tried to speak, found herself unable to wrap her mouth against the words. She settled for taking Judy's hand instead, pressing a damp palm against hers.

That was when Judy kissed her, as if it were par for the course, as if Magda were so used to affection that she could receive it by surprise, as if anyone should be surprised to be wanted, as if people didn't wait their whole lives to be kissed like that in the middle of a crosswalk.

56.

SURPRISING, HOW QUICKLY INTIMACY COULD BLOOM. ALREADY, a third shape, the *us*, hedged its way into their conversations. This nebulous form into which they were evolving, the state of *us* a protracted conversation. It was something Magda had never herself confronted, only tried to explain to patients: that, in each relationship, there existed two people, neither of whom could be fully understood. She had said as much to Gwen, who blinked back tears. "Right, but I *love* him. I'm trying to understand all of him. Isn't that the point?"

On most days, the relationship held its own shape. Text messages between sessions and plans after work, the shift of Judy's things from the living room to the bedroom. The strange and sometimes uncomfortable heat of another person's body pressed against hers at night, the feeling she had upon waking up of wanting to absorb Judy, wanting to look at her for as long as she could without scaring her. Fear, desire, twinned shapes.

On some days, Judy was lost to Magda, hardly texting and returning to the apartment after dark with a greasy plastic bag in each hand. "I'm just trying to work through it," she said, before recounting an update in the separation, the unyielding sadness of letting go of something one had built. "I don't want to be angry around you."

"You don't need to pretend to be something other than who you are, how you're feeling," Magda said to Judy, who fixed on her with an impassive expression.

"Neither do you," she said eventually, turning back to the stove.

"She needs space." Boomer shrugged. "Sometimes people need to work through things alone." He looked toward the shared wall of his office, the one abutting Theo's, then back to Magda. "Give it time."

That night, legs fused together on the couch, Magda said, "I'm trying to be myself; it's more that I don't know how to do that without her."

Judy looked up from her book. One of Magda's sweaters hung long on her arms, the wrists dipping down to her fingers. "It's the same for me."

"Is it?"

Judy set it down, brow pinched. "Well, of course it is. I was with my ex for decades; I'd never been alone as an adult. She was my—my North Star, really. But that's how we learn who we are, isn't it? Through wanting, or hoping, or the lens of other people's love. Losing them—to death or divorce, whatever it may be—you're stuck trying to figure it out on your own. When you lose someone, it becomes a matter of filling the space they left behind. No, what is it—someone called it *repairing* the space. I like that better: fixing something that was left a mess."

Magda leaned closer, making Judy laugh. She kissed Magda's forehead, rumpled her hair.

It was true what Boomer said: Each time she disappeared, Judy did return. Each time, it loosed a string of gratitude from a coil inside Magda. *Thank God it's you.*

That anyone could expect love—consider it their due, even—remained confounding to Magda, as did the idea that when love arrived it would be in a neatly wrapped package. And yet, after hours apart, when there came again a knock at the apartment door, the surety that coursed through her did so like the flapping wings of some wild bird.

There was a desperate quality to the desire to know Judy; Magda found herself wanting to understand everything that had been necessary to bring Judy there, to New York, sitting opposite Magda on a couch, the subway, at a movie theater. As if that information could offer a measure of security. As if it were a skein of yarn that she could unravel until the two ends could be identified: the beginning, an end. As if by knowing the whole story she could prevent its ending.

The reciprocity required, that, too, proved a challenge. Not because Magda didn't want to unburden herself to Judy—she did, but the act of doing so felt strange. She had to remind herself at which points in conversations she was meant to interject, offer a story from her own life. When

Judy told Magda a fact about herself, it sometimes took Magda a while to truly understand what she herself had gotten wrong. The fact that it was Judy who'd left her ex, when for so long Magda had imagined it to be the other way around. That Judy had a brother with whom she was in somewhat regular contact, that after the ex she had dated other women, two of whom lived in New York and with whom she wanted them to be friends. That while her voice was high and sweet, in middle school she had been an alto, but had to sing with the boys' tenor section because there were so few of them. "Is *that* what did this to you?" her mother would ask, later. In the telling, Judy laughed when recounting this, but the sound was raw.

There were times that Magda still worried Judy would leave. She left for work one morning—Judy sprawled on her side, snoring gently—and by the time Magda reached the park was thinking, *What would happen if Mr. Tyson's cigar fell to the carpet? Would Judy smell the smoke? Would she be able to get out in time?*

"I met someone," she told Hedda during their weekly call. She squared her shoulders, steeling herself for response, which came quickly: "Oh, that's wonderful." The chop of pruning shears cut over Hedda's voice as she added, "What's her name?"

Magda, mouth hanging open, hurriedly changed the subject. She asked if Hedda remembered what the two of them listened to in the car with their parents. "It was Handel, I'm sure of it," she said, and Hedda paused, said, "I remember it differently."

That was just it, though: everyone would.

What it came down to was choices. To, say, go to a party, approach some woman with dark, curly hair. To say the normal things, like *hello* and *how are you* and *goodbye*, for years, for most of a lifetime, to say *I love you* and *I miss you* until what was left were just the imprints of those conversations and the shadows of what those words had intimated. To remember, despite wondering what might have been, that those little moments, those damned constituent parts, comprised the whole. The gravity of one's happiness was formed by those choices, even if it wasn't a choice so much as a surrender.

I loved it, Magda wanted to say. *I loved it all.* But sometimes, recently, she wondered if that was true so much as that she had made it impossible to love someone else.

How she tried: Judy's suitcase moving into the closet, Magda rescheduling evening sessions in favor of dinners, leisurely walks in the park. She introduced Hedda to Judy over the phone, left for the bathroom to find them laughing uproariously when she came back, Judy saying she would absolutely try that.

Magda and Hedda spoke of Handel awhile more, before Magda cut her sister off. "Her name's Judy," she said. "And I think she's moving in."

Hedda repeated it, rolling the word in her mouth. "I like it," she said. "Strong name."

"You'll like her," Magda said.

"Oh, I'm sure. Look, the grandkids are back, but we'll talk later? And you know, Mags, *det är aldrig för sent.*"

Magda rolled her eyes, but fondly. It was something she would've said to one of her patients, but that didn't make it less true: that it wasn't—for any of them—too late.

Hedda, as if she'd overheard Magda's thoughts, interjected. "The overthinking? You need to stop; you're only ever being an asshole to yourself."

"The cursing." Magda chuckled, and at the same time they said, "Only to make a point."

That night, Magda and Judy went for drinks with Boomer and Theo, who brought along a date, a pediatric oncologist. She beamed up at him throughout the evening, white-blond hair framing her face, and when she and Judy excused themselves to use the bathroom, Boomer said, "Too smart for you, but we like her." Theo then turned to Magda, who nodded.

"We do indeed," she said, at which his whole face split into a smile.

By October, Judy had copies of the new keys.

"You seem different," Bill said, upon entering the office.

57

FALL VANQUISHED THE MUGGY DAYS, SPUN THEM INTO CRISP, lucid ones. The sheen of dew slicking the windowsills lifted by sunrise, Magda padding into the kitchen to find Judy with one long hand out the window, testing the wind against her pointer finger. Coffee steaming on the counter, the whir of the fan kicking up corners of the paper. Dog-eared already. "I marked the good stuff," Judy would say.

Fred still hadn't returned her calls, Boomer saying that he had taken a longer vacation than planned. "And now he's catching up on work, I suppose. Why he called *me*, I don't know, but he's back. Been home, apparently, but busy. He said he'll meet you next Tuesday for the usual breakfast. Said you'd know the spot?"

Magda had hoped that the urn would be back with Fred before Judy saw it, but it had been uncovered by Judy nosing through the cabinet in search of spaghetti. A crestfallen expression on her face as Magda rushed to speak. A favor, temporary measures—it was a long story.

"I'd like to hear it," offered Judy, and so Magda told her.

After that, the urn took residence on the bedside table, and then on the mantel, where it observed their nighttime conversations on the still-old couch. Magda waited for discomfort to cloud Judy's features, to look over and find her grimacing as moonlight winked off the urn. She worried over what would happen, but Judy only continued to say, "Tell me about her." Magda, trying to explain what she and Sara had been, found herself fixing on Eugene, take-out dinners at her apartment. Those moments did not encapsulate the whole, but she was saying what she could, learning how to get to the rest.

What she described was the wet of Eugene's nose, the dutiful current of his breathing. What was there to like about Eugene, besides these things—his reliability, loyalty? There was an immutability to dogs that allowed them to love deeply, and with utter forgiveness. So Sara came home late sometimes, so what—hadn't she, in the end, returned? The bowl brimming with food had eventually been placed upon the floor, the leash shaken from its hook. "Come on," Sara had said, in her usual tender way, and both Eugene and Magda stood.

"It doesn't bother me, if that's what you're wondering."

"What?" Magda startled, Judy pointing toward the bookshelf, where the urn was tucked sideways between two novels. Practically out of view.

"You keep taking her to the office, hiding her away. I'm just saying, you don't need to do that."

Don't I? Magda wondered. She'd imagined herself returning home to find Judy, bags packed, on her way out the door. "I thought you'd moved on," she'd say, and Magda, stutteringly, would respond, "Can't you see I'm trying?" It seemed impossible that Judy could remain calm, unfettered, about what had happened between Magda and Sara, that she could not be threatened by the ambiguity left in Sara's wake.

Judy raised her palms skyward, turned toward the coffeepot. "Look, do whatever you want. I'm just saying, we all have pasts. It isn't an issue for me."

For the time being: Magda brought the urn to her office, where it sat hidden in one of her desk drawers. Its presence was best on the days when her feelings were whorled, and even opening the drawer to see the glint of light against silver seemed to sturdy her against unwanted thoughts. What would happen if it wasn't Mr. Tyson's cigar but Judy deciding that Magda wasn't for her, what if she left unceremoniously, what if she changed her phone number, or what if they grew apart with the yawning discontent between Bill and his wife, one person knowing with certainty what they wanted, and the other, wilting. What would happen, with only one hundred and thirteen shared photos between them—what then?

Judy said her ex's animosity was dimming, a shifting tide. "You can only ever solve your side of it, anyway," she said with a shrug. "There might not be any more answers."

How one stopped seeking them, though—that wasn't easy. Not that it had been what Magda wanted, but in recounting the summer she felt that Sara had tried—in her way—to give Magda happiness. Had hoped she would find it. Magda thought of her, after Boston, going into Theo's office agitated and blameful. Taking her own anger out on Theo, explaining to him how things ought to be; Theo, with his good nature, considering the possibility. Had Sara known, always, that she couldn't give Magda what she wanted? Was there a part of her that had thought maybe she could?

Magda found herself thinking of that in sessions, needing to sip from her glass of water or shake the tension from her ankles. That was the moment she found herself most resenting, that Sara had considered someone else to be a substitute. That she thought people could be loved in the same way. "Anger means you're moving forward," said Judy. "That's what my therapist says, that it means you're processing."

Though it was possible, also, that the way Magda remembered this dynamic was incorrect, not what Sara had intended. That it was another star in this constellation of misunderstandings, intimacy as a toehold for something else. What it came down to could be that brains were wired differently. Look at Gwen, flinging herself forward with closed eyes, Bill huddling in place. Magda, whose brain barbed itself in anticipation of the next inevitable slight. It wasn't that anyone got better, necessarily, so much as they found better ways of interacting with the world, learning how to be in it.

On her next call with Hedda, she asked, "Do you remember what happened to Lucy, from church?"

Hedda hummed, said, "Honestly, Mags, I don't even remember her."

At the grocery store one day, Magda turned to Judy with a box in hand. "Do you remember this?"

"That was foul," Judy said, surveying the dandelion tea, and not until much later, when Magda thought of it again, did she realize that she now associated the tea with a memory about Judy instead of Sara, surmising that she might not always remember the same things; that others, maybe, could hold that space instead.

"It's been a bad few years, after Mom, but I've been thinking," Gwen said. Then, correcting herself, "*We've* been thinking. About kids."

"You'll be a wonderful mother," Magda said, which made Gwen blush.

"I want a daughter," she said, looking down at her shoes, and Magda smiled, because not until then had she realized that despite everything, she, too, was hoping.

Judy hated chamomile and cardio exercise and smoking.

"I used to smoke sometimes, but I don't anymore," Magda explained to Dr. Stein.

Things that were better:

A hand to hold at the movies.

Someone sitting opposite her at breakfast, lunch, dinner.

Two empty suitcases, pressed together in the hall closet. Toothbrushes, bowed like flamingos in their cup beside the sink.

Remembering something that needed urgently to be imparted to the other person, and reaching across the table, to the opposite shore of the bed.

58

MAGDA HAD ONLY JUST ARRIVED AT THE RESTAURANT WHEN HER phone dinged. *Hi! Still on for museum at 2?!*

yes of course. She pressed SEND as Fred slid onto the bench opposite her, already apologizing. He had meant to call back, things were just busier than ever, they had hardly been home at all. He cleared his throat, shook out his napkin. "You look great," he told her. "It's been too long."

He had filled out in the chest and face, the weight softening his severe features—the narrow nose, those creases below his eyes. His polo was periwinkle, bright enough to offset his tan. "Nice shirt," she said. "You look good."

With a chuckle, he said that Gloria had bought it in Venice. "Too expensive."

"Like the orange sweater?"

Sara had commissioned that one herself, a sturdy wool piece with their initials embroidered across the front in a puffy yarn. He had worn it exactly once, on one of their vacations to New Hampshire, and only because they were staying in a cabin with no neighbors in sight. He cringed performatively. "I'll never forget that thing; it was pilling before I finished unwrapping it."

"Where is it now?" she asked.

The waitress arrived with their coffees, and he waited until she left before saying, "Oh, it'd be with you, wouldn't it? Somewhere in that box of clothing, I bet."

They had been in Italy for most of the summer, Fred told her, in a little villa owned by one of Gloria's friends. "So quiet," he said. "We spent most of the summer reading in the yard, occasionally walking into town. I hadn't been to Tuscany in God—"

"About twenty years."

He ran a fork through his salad as Magda sipped her coffee, considering him.

"Here's the thing," he said. Reaching for his own mug, he pursed his lips, and it wasn't until the ring glinted silver in the light that Magda realized.

"Oh," she breathed. She moved her foot slightly to press against the side of the urn. "Congratulations."

Fred explained it had become more complicated than he had originally believed, Gloria's feelings unchangeable, Sara's return now rendered impossible. "I wanted to make it work, somehow, but I can't . . ." he said, trailing off. "I just can't make the wrong call here."

Below the table, she pinched her own leg. "Right."

"I like to think I handle things better now," he said lightly, tracing the edge of his napkin with his thumb. "Not that I don't still make mistakes, but not"—at this, he waved aimlessly—"not of that caliber."

"Why did you do it?" Magda asked. Her thigh ached where she had grabbed it. A silence until the waitress returned with their food, at which point Magda had somewhere else to focus her attention, pushing the eggs around before looking up. When she did, Fred was gazing into middle distance.

"I was lonely," he said. His eyes tended downward, and then he looked at her, his mouth approximating a smile. "I wish there were a better reason, but that was it. And then along came someone who said the right things, who *was* available, and I just, I gave in. I hated myself for years, more so, honestly, for knowing that you hated me as well."

Fred pulled a hand back through his hair, and with the other, rotated the pad of his thumb against a pointer finger. "It was a long time ago," she said.

"I was so jealous of you," he said quietly. "Your access to her. It was like you were inside of her head, and I was just beside her. It felt, sometimes, like I was watching my life go by."

They sat without speaking as the noises of the restaurant swelled around them. Silverware clattered to the ground, a beat of laughter bursting out. "Just send it back," a woman was saying at the table beside them. "If you don't like it, Dave, just send it back."

The pulse rose in Magda's throat, her hand moving, reflexively, to her chest. She placed her right palm just above her heart, the fine bones of her fingers grazing collarbone. She pressed it there, lightly at first, and then harder, holding steady until her nerves suppressed.

"Bathroom," Fred said, standing up. His eyes met hers then, and he looked down, head tilting right. His mouth opened slightly, and he seemed to startle, clearing his throat. When he was gone, she looked up again, and in the reflection it became obvious. A gesture she had seen hundreds of times: Sara's palm pressed firm over Fred's heart as she leaned in to kiss him, moving the hand up his neck and, finally, to rest on his jaw. Magda had turned away from watching over the years—it was too intimate, she felt, for a witness.

The same gesture as that night in Boston, Sara's hand at the neck of her nightgown before pushing it away so that her fingers rested on Magda's breastbone. An accident, Magda had thought, as her breathing quickened, as she moved closer to Sara. Their lips met, Eugene began barking, and Sara's hand bent to the shape of Magda's jaw. How long that moment stretched on, the two of them with their mouths pressed together, Magda afraid to breathe, to draw Sara closer. To be pushed away.

When he returned to the table, Fred wouldn't look at her. He started to say something, stopped himself, his eyes roving.

"Look," Magda said, as she had all those times before. He looked at her, and she thought, *Here it is; it's time*, but what came out of her mouth was, "I can hold on to her. If that's easier. And when you're ready to have her back, just call me. I'll bring her home."

Fred nodded, and Magda again said, "Look," realizing afterward from his expression that he was expecting her to say something else. "You were it for her," she said. "The whole thing."

He pursed his lips. "Thank you," he said, thumb beginning its rotation on the napkin.

"Fred," Magda said, and he shook his head, placed a hand over his eyes.

From the adjacent table, the woman hedged, "Is he okay?"

Magda said, "We're all fine here, thanks."

Dave's friend tossed his hands up, Fred's gaze returning to Magda.

"She'd say things like, 'Magda would never,' 'Magda and I always.' What she and I were doing, it didn't, it never . . ." He cleared his throat. "It was our life. You have to understand that; it was our life—hers and mine."

He glanced out the window, startling when Magda spoke. "No," she said, with a confidence that surprised them both. "You're wrong. It was my life just as much as it was yours."

On the street, a mother brayed at her children to get into the car. "Get *in*," she kept saying, the littlest boy looking up at her with a vexed expression. The clouds overhead were a filmy white, motionless. On the other side of the street was a couple wearing baseball caps—one Yankees and one Mets, the man gesturing so broadly each move threatened to upset her coffee. Magda leaned against a newspaper stand as Fred fumbled around in his jacket pocket. "Ah!" he said, triumphantly brandishing a pair of sunglasses. Magda watched the couple across the street. The woman stepped neatly to the side to avoid her companion's flailing arms. Another man, walking past Magda, brushed her shoulder with his own. "We're coming up on the holidays; they're getting anxious," he said, as Fred told Magda that Gloria was meeting him outside. She'd be there in a minute, if Magda would like to meet her. Again.

"Another time," she said. She turned away, and he was hunched over, swiping at his phone. "Fred," she said, and then again, louder, at which he noticed her. "Congratulations again," she told him, waving. He smiled before looking back down, his mouth set in a tight line.

It had grown hot during their lunch, the humidity unexpected and overbearing as Magda made her way laboriously down the street. At the end of the block, she looked back. Emerging from a cab: Gloria. Her sleek gray bob was shot through with white, and she wore a dress which matched Fred's sweater.

Gloria stood, the door yawning out behind her. Fred kissed her cheek, and she cupped his chin. His hand clasped the small of her back. A redundant move, one Magda knew from the thousand times she had seen Fred helping Sara into a chair, getting her attention at the gallery, the signal when they had been at a party too long and Sara clearly had no intention of leaving.

There could be, Magda thought, people with the innate ability to love, and she herself might be someone who could not love so easily, or casually, or again. Watching the way Fred had cemented himself to Gloria just then—always, a hand somewhere; if not her shoulder, her back, or her lower arm—the tenuousness of love felt evident, as if when one looked away the other person could disappear entirely.

Magda suspected there wouldn't be another time. She had meant it, hoped she had spoken with warmth—but she did feel that she and Fred had exhausted themselves to one another. They could ostensibly continue exchanging what was left of Sara—her belongings, their memories of her, the urn itself—but to what end? They had nothing left to offer each other.

Gloria raised a finger to Fred—*one minute!*—before disappearing into the back seat. She emerged with Eugene, and Fred paused from scanning his phone, began to laugh. There he was, Eugene, wearing Fred's same sweater in miniature. Gloria inclined her head to kiss his graying brow, and handed Eugene to Fred. They slipped into the car, Magda's breath hitching in her throat, and then, like that, they were gone.

Magda walked slowly on. The weather had proved surprising to Manhattan, the people outside rejoicing in the strangeness of the season: cool enough for a sweater, hot enough to be bare-legged. She walked by families with squealing, Popsicle-smeared children. Dogs panting lightly alongside their owners. Couples—men with other men, women with other women—holding hands. She remembered the psychiatric ward on which she and Theo had worked, so many years ago, and the intake of patients whose disorder was marked as "homosexuality." She watched a woman lean toward and kiss another woman, and the people who saw this display gave no indication of distress, disgust. They hardly acknowledged it. People continued streaming by these women as they held each other close, and Magda, finally, remembered that she, too, had somewhere to be.

Inside the museum: a damp coolness to the air, hushed footsteps. Magda shuffled through the atrium. Rapid changes in temperature triggered her arthritis, and Magda was glad, on that day, to have arrived first, to be allowed this bit of privacy. Moving through the galleries, she eased herself onto one of the benches opposite a Rembrandt. *i'm here where are you*

She had been sitting for a while when Judy came around the corner, neck craned. She wore one of the baseball caps Theo had found in the building's lost and found, SUMMER FOREVER leering above the nest of curls. "I love this one," he had told her at their last dinner, Judy with a hand set over her eyes, squinting into the sun. "Take it."

A hefty man sat on the opposite side of the bench, blocking Magda from Judy's sight line. She thought to stand and move toward Judy, but found herself enjoying this quiet watching, as Judy leaned her head in the opposite direction. Judy was walking toward the wrong room—the Rodins, Magda thought, as she slowly rose to her feet.

Already well behind Judy, Magda remembering the way Fred had caught her mimicking that old gesture of Sara's. How his expression had warped, hardened. She could call him later, if she wanted. *Listen*, she might say, *it wasn't anything; you misunderstood.*

Oh, but she thought, he hadn't—it was she who had gotten it wrong, this whole time. It was just her name that Sara had said that day, on the way back from Boston, Eugene howling at some unseen and unknowable beast behind them. Sara, whose skirt was stained with the dog's urine, and she had said it again—*Magda*—who had pretended it meant something else. Like, hand over a wad of napkins, stay focused on the road ahead. "Not now," Magda had said, flustered, grip tightening on the wheel.

But suppose she had veered to the shoulder of the road and, as the gravel popped loose from the tires, waited for Sara to speak. Suppose she had leaned in right there, or suppose she had waited for the cool of the garage, the engine rumbling into quiet, as she said it. *Sara.* If not her name, then the impossible thing: *I would be preposterously happy if I were with you.* If not the impossible thing, even if she knew Sara would say no, suppose she had leaned in anyway.

In the Rodin gallery, people moved between casts of cool, creamy marble. Judy was bent over a statue, circling it with a program bent to her lips. Magda watched as Judy crouched before the ghost of Eurydice, who lingered just behind Orpheus. His hand was pressed to his eyes, her arms encircling him. Judy leaned in, her eyes fixed on the barely perceptible space between the lovers.

Closing the distance between them, then, Magda wove around a small woman tapping at her phone. A man with his ear inclined to his audio guide. They were walking through centuries, Magda thought, entire lifetimes. Something her mother had once said floated to the top of her memory: *I en bra bok står det bästa mellan raderna.* In a good book, the best is between the lines. "All Orpheus had to do," Magda's father had told her as a child, "all he had to do was keep his eyes ahead until he saw sunlight. If he did that, if he didn't look toward the underworld, the gods would have allowed him to have her back."

Sara, too, had adored that piece—ironic, as she had never been one for ambiguity. While she had left midway through plays, that had been of her own accord; she had, on multiple occasions, been forcibly ushered from a movie theater for too loudly rebuking a film's plot. When Magda, emerging at the doors with their coats and bags, would explain the movie's evolution—how a climax wasn't an *ending*, per se—Sara waved her away. "It's clear the way that one is going," she'd say. "Honestly, I don't even need to see the rest. You don't even need to tell me what happened."

Later, reliably, she would call Magda and have her describe in detail what had transpired after she was escorted outside. If Magda veered from the plot, Sara would grow impatient, badgering, "And then?"

"Just admit it," Magda would tease. "You're desperate for a happy ending."

Even through the phone, she knew Sara's mouth to be lilting upward, her next words muffled by the palm clapped over her smile: "And *then*? Go on. Just tell me, what happened next?"

And then Magda was beside Judy. Around them swelled the din of conversation, of other people's lives: someone was tired, another person grumpy, another one looking for someone who had gotten lost. The urn bumped against her hip as Magda set a hand to Judy's shoulder, and Judy turned, already smiling, lips rising over those crooked teeth.

"Finally," Magda said. "I found you."

Acknowledgments

The first part of a book that I read are the acknowledgments; to write my own feels surreal.

Thanks to my agent, Mollie Glick, and her team at CAA. Mollie is an incredible advocate, perplexingly unflappable, and basically always right, demonstrated early on when she proclaimed: "Well, this is a Helen Atsma book."

Which brings me to my editor, Helen Atsma, who is as brilliant and as wonderful to work with as a writer could hope for. (Also perplexingly unflappable.) Thanks to the whole team at Ecco: Miriam Parker, Sonya Cheuse, Rachel Sargent, Meghan Deans, Vivian Rowe, Allison Saltzman, Nina Leopold, Jin Soo Chun, Lydia Weaver, and Janet Rosenberg. Immensely lucky—and grateful—to be in their good care.

At John Marshall Media, thanks to Ng Jun Yang for engineering the audiobook production. Thanks to Suzanne Mitchell, who directed and produced the audiobook with such care and vision—and thanks to the incredible Cynthia Nixon, who voiced and brought the characters to life.

During the course of writing and revising this novel, three people who were incredibly dear to me died—my grandparents, M&Z, and my friend, Dorothy DeVoti. M&Z were the first ones to read this novel, and thanks are due to the three of them, many times over, for their love and support. Special thanks to Bill Devoti, in whose home I finished writing the book.

To my writing group—Amber Oliver, Imani Gary, and Vedika Khanna—for our years of collaboration; I love building new worlds with you. Thanks also to my early readers—Isabel Mader, Sam Gordon, Peter Kispert, Desireé Dallagiacomo, and Jillian Buckley—for their judicious feedback. To Laura Asnes Becker, Alex Pei-hsia Britt, Marya Spence, Jamie Carr, Matt Harper, Michael Fynan, Patrick Ryan, Michelle Zeng, Dorian Randall, and Ferd Beurfel.

Thanks to SAGE for fostering intergenerational queer community, and most especially for bringing Lena Harris into my life. To the next generation, and the next.

To my parents, Storm and Deb. To my sister, Willa. Thank you, thank you, thank you.

And because nothing is made in a vacuum, thanks to some of the things that inspired and sustained me throughout this process: Patricia Highsmith's *The Price of Salt*, Elisabeth Kübler-Ross's *On Death and Dying*, the left-behind glove in *Carol*, Taneum Bambrick's *Oven Street*, Félix González-Torres's *Untitled (Portrait of Ross in L.A.)*, Erwin Schrödinger, Joan Didion's *The Year of Magical Thinking*, *The American Journal of Psychiatry*, Carter Burwell's "Opening," Madeleine Cravens' *Object Permanence*, Richard Siken's *Scheherazade*, the banner hung aloft in Bill Devoti's house that reads GOOD MORNING, DOROTHY, I LOVE YOU, and Auguste Rodin's *The Cathedral*, for the reminder of how closeness and space are, often, between two people, entwined.

And, last, thanks to my therapist. Plenty to talk about in our next session.